## DATE DUE

| | |
|---|---|
| JUN 25 2012 | OCT 10 2017 |
| JUL 02 2012 | MAR 05 2018 |
| JUL 26 2012 | OCT 22 2018 |
| AUG 21 2012 | NOV 24 2018 |
| SEP 27 2012 | JAN 11 2019 |
| APR 06 2013 | MAR 15 2019 |
| | MAY 03 2019 |
| JAN 25 2014 | MAY 11 2019 |
| JAN 30 2014 | JUL 18 2019 |
| APR 25 2014 | NOV 18 2019 |
| JUN 11 2014 | DEC 09 2019 |
| JUN 09 2015 | SEP 10 2021 |
| OCT 12 2015 | AUG 09 2022 |
| MAY 12 2016 | NOV 14 2023 |
| NOV 26 2016 | |
| MAR 06 2017 | |

# THE
# FALSE
# PRINCE

# THE ASCENDANCE TRILOGY
## BOOK ONE

# THE FALSE PRINCE

## JENNIFER A. NIELSEN

SCHOLASTIC PRESS · NEW YORK

Copyright © 2012 by Jennifer A. Nielsen
Map by Kayley LeFaiver
All rights reserved. Published by Scholastic Press, an imprint of Scholastic Inc.,
*Publishers since 1920*. SCHOLASTIC, SCHOLASTIC PRESS, and associated logos are
trademarks and/or registered trademarks of Scholastic Inc.

Library of Congress Cataloging-in-Publication Data
Nielsen, Jennifer A.
The false prince / by Jennifer A. Nielsen.
p. cm. — (The ascendance trilogy ; bk. 1)
Summary: In the country of Carthya, a devious nobleman engages four
orphans in a brutal competition to be selected to impersonate the
king's long-missing son in an effort to avoid a civil war.
ISBN 978-0-545-28413-4
[1. Impersonation — Fiction. 2. Princes — Fiction. 3. Orphans — Fiction.
4. Courts and courtiers — Fiction. 5. Secrets — Fiction.] I. Title.
PZ7.N5672Fal 2012
[Fic] — dc22
2011006692

10 9 8 7 6 5 4 3 2 1                    12 13 14 15 16

Printed in the U.S.A.                    23

First edition, April 2012
Book design by Christopher Stengel

*For Mom,*

*Every great thing I ever learned from*
*you was taught by example.*

# · ONE ·

If I had to do it all over again, I would not have chosen this life. Then again, I'm not sure I ever had a choice.

These were my thoughts as I raced away from the market, with a stolen roast tucked under my arm.

I'd never attempted roast thievery before, and I was already regretting it. It happens to be very difficult to hold a chunk of raw meat while running. More slippery than I'd anticipated. If the butcher didn't catch me with his cleaver first, and literally cut off my future plans, I vowed to remember to get the meat wrapped next time. Then steal it.

He was only a few paces behind now, chasing me at a better speed than I'd have expected for a man of his girth. He yelled very loudly in his native language, one I didn't recognize. He was originally from one of the far western countries. Undoubtedly a country where killing a meat thief was allowed.

It was this sort of thought that encouraged me to run faster. I rounded a corner just as the cleaver suddenly cut into a wood post behind me. Even though he was aiming for me, I couldn't help but admire his throwing accuracy. If I hadn't turned when I did, the cleaver would've found its target.

But I was only a block from Mrs. Turbeldy's Orphanage for Disadvantaged Boys. I knew how to disappear there.

And I might have made it, if not for the bald man sitting outside the tavern, who stretched out his foot in time to trip me. Luckily, I managed to keep hold of the roast, although it did no favors to my right shoulder as I fell onto the hard dirt road.

The butcher leaned over me and laughed. "'Bout time you get what's comin' to you, filthy beggar."

As a point of fact, I hadn't begged for anything. It was beneath me.

His laughter was quickly followed up with a kick to my back that chased my breath away. I curled into a ball, prepared for a beating I wasn't sure I'd live to regret. The butcher landed a second kick and had reared back for a third, when another man shouted, "Stop!"

The butcher turned. "You stay out of this. He stole a roast."

"An entire roast? Really? And what is the cost?"

"Thirty garlins."

My well-trained ears heard the sound of coins in a bag, then the man said, "I'll pay you fifty garlins if you turn that boy over to me now."

"Fifty? One moment." The butcher gave me a final kick in the side, then leaned low toward me. "If you ever come into my shop again, I'll cut you up and sell you as meat at the market. Got it?"

The message was straightforward. I nodded.

The man paid the butcher, who stomped away. I wanted to look up at whoever had saved me further beating, but I was hunched in the only position that didn't send me gasping in pain, and I was in no hurry to change that.

The pity I felt for myself wasn't shared by the man with the coins. He grabbed my shirt and yanked me to my feet.

Our eyes locked as he lifted me. His were dark brown and more tightly focused than I'd ever seen before. He smiled slightly as he studied me, his thin mouth barely visible behind a neatly trimmed brown beard. He looked to be somewhere in his forties and dressed in the fine clothes of the upper class, but based on the way he'd lifted me, he was much stronger than I expected of a nobleman.

"I'll have a word with you, boy," he said. "You'll walk with me to the orphanage or I'll have you carried there."

The entire right side of my body throbbed, but the left side was okay, so I favored it as I started to walk.

"Stand up straight," the man ordered.

I ignored him. He was probably some rich country gentleman who wanted to purchase an indentured servant for his lands. Although I was eager to leave behind the tough streets of Carchar, servitude wasn't in my future plans, which meant I could walk as crookedly as I wanted. Besides, my right leg really hurt.

Mrs. Turbeldy's Orphanage for Disadvantaged Boys was the only place for orphaned boys in the northern end of Carthya. Nineteen of us lived there, ranging in age from three to fifteen. I was almost fifteen, and any day now, Mrs. Turbeldy would send me away. But I didn't want to leave yet, and certainly not as this stranger's servant boy.

Mrs. Turbeldy was waiting in her office when I walked in, with the man close behind me. She was too fat to credibly claim she starved along with the rest of us, but strong enough to beat anyone who complained about that fact. In recent months, she and I had settled into a routine of barely tolerating each other. Mrs. Turbeldy must have seen what happened outside, because she shook her head and said, "A roast? What were you thinking?"

"That we had a lot of hungry boys," I said. "You can't feed us bean bread every day and not have a revolt."

"You'll give me that roast, then," she said, holding out her plump hands.

Business first. I clutched the roast more tightly to myself and nodded at the man. "Who's he?"

The man stepped forward. "My name is Bevin Conner. Tell me yours."

I stared at him without answering, which earned me a whack on the back of the head from Mrs. Turbeldy's broom. "His name is Sage," she told Conner. "And as I told you before, you'd be better off with a rabid badger than this one."

4

Conner raised an eyebrow and stared at me as if that amused him, which was annoying because I had no interest in providing him with any entertainment. So I tossed my hair out of my eyes and said, "She's right. So can I go now?"

Conner frowned and shook his head. The moment of amusement had passed. "What can you do, boy?"

"If you bothered to ask my name, you might use it."

He continued as if he hadn't heard me. Also annoying. "What's your training?"

"He don't have any," Mrs. Turbeldy said. "None a gentleman like yourself would need, anyhow."

"What did your father do?" Conner asked me.

"He was best as a musician, but still a terrible one," I said. "If he made a single coin from playing, my family never saw it."

"He was probably a drunk." Mrs. Turbeldy rapped my ear with her knuckles. "So this one's made his way through theft and lies."

"What sort of lies?"

I wasn't sure if the question was directed to me or Mrs. Turbeldy. But he was looking at Mrs. Turbeldy, so I let her speak.

She took Conner by the arm and pulled him into a corner, which was an entirely useless gesture because not only was I standing right there and perfectly able to hear every word, but the story was also about me, so it was hardly a secret. Conner obliged her, though I noticed he faced himself toward me as she spoke.

"First time the boy came in here, he had a shiny silver coin in his hand. Said he was a runaway, the son of a dead duke from somewhere in Avenia, only he didn't want to be a duke. So if I took him in and gave him preferential care and a place to hide, he'd pay me a coin a week. Kept it up for two weeks, all the time laughin' it up on extra servings at dinner and with extra blankets on his bed."

Conner glanced at me, and I rolled my eyes. He'd be less impressed when she finished the story.

"Then one night, he took with a fever. Got all delirious late in the night, hitting at everyone and yelling and such. I was there when he confessed it all. He's no son of anyone important. The coins belonged to a duke all right, but he'd stolen them to trick me into caring for him. I dumped his body into the cellar to get better or not, I didn't care. Next time I checked on him, he'd got over the fever on his own and was a good deal more humble."

Conner looked at me again. "He doesn't look so humble now."

"I got over that too," I said.

"So why'd you let him stay?" Conner asked Mrs. Turbeldy.

Mrs. Turbeldy hesitated. She didn't want to tell him it was because I picked up goodies for her now and then, ribbon for her hats or chocolates from the cake shop. Because of that, Mrs.

Turbeldy didn't hate me nearly as much as she pretended to. Or maybe she did. I stole from her too.

Conner walked back to me. "A thief and a liar, eh? Can you manage a sword?"

"Sure, if my opponent doesn't have one."

He grinned. "Do you farm?"

"No." I took that as an insult.

"Hunt?"

"No."

"Can you read?"

I stared up at him through the parts of my hair. "What are you wanting me for, Conner?"

"You'll address me as Sir or Master Conner."

"What are you wanting me for, Sir Master Conner?"

"That's a conversation for another time. Gather your things. I'll wait for you here."

I shook my head. "Sorry, but when I leave the comfort of Mrs. Turbeldy's fine establishment, I go on my own."

"You're going with him," Mrs. Turbeldy said. "You've been bought and paid for by Master Conner, and I can't wait to be rid of you."

"You'll earn your freedom by doing whatever I ask of you and doing it well," Conner added. "Or serve me poorly and serve me for life."

"I wouldn't serve anyone for an hour until freedom," I said. Conner took a step toward me, hands out. I threw the roast I'd been holding at him and he flinched to avoid it. Using that moment, I pushed past Mrs. Turbeldy and darted into the street. It would've been helpful to know that he'd left a couple of vigils at the door. One grabbed my arms while the other clubbed me over the head from behind. I barely had time to curse their mothers' graves before I crumpled to the ground.

# · TWO ·

I awoke with my hands tied behind my back, and lying in the bed of a wagon. A throbbing headache pulsed inside me, worsened by the jostling of the wagon as we rode. The least Conner could have done was give me something soft to lie on.

I resisted the temptation to open my eyes until my situation became clearer. My wrists were tied behind my back with a coarse rope, one that might be used to lead a horse. If it was, then I wondered if the rope was a last-minute idea. Maybe Conner hadn't expected to be taking me by force.

Conner should have come more prepared. This thick rope worked to my advantage. It was easier to loosen the knots.

Someone coughed near me. Didn't sound like Conner. Maybe it was one of his thug vigils.

As slowly as possible, I inched one eye open. The cool spring day had become a bit overcast but wasn't yet threatening rain. Too bad. I could've used a bath.

One of Conner's vigils was at the far end of the wagon,

looking at the view behind us. That probably meant Conner and the other vigil were on the seat at the front of the wagon.

Another cough, to my left. I let my head bounce with the next jolt of the wagon to see where it had come from.

Two boys sat there. The shorter one closest to me seemed to be doing the coughing. Both were near my age. The coughing boy looked sickly and pale, while the other was larger and tanned. They each had light brown hair, though the coughing boy's hair was nearer to blond. He had rounder features as well. I suspected wherever he came from, he'd spent more time sick in bed than at work. And just the opposite for the other boy.

I judged myself to be a blend of the two. Nothing about me was remarkable. I was only of medium height, one of many ways I disappointed my father, who had felt that it would hinder my success (I disagreed — tall people fit in fewer hiding places). My hair was badly in need of cutting, tangled, and dark blond but getting lighter with each passing month. And I had a forgettable face, which, again, worked in my favor.

The boy coughed again and I opened both eyes to determine if he was sick or had something to say and was clearing his throat to get our attention.

Only he caught me looking at him. Our eyes focused so solidly on each other that it was pointless to pretend I was still asleep, at least to him. Would he give up my secret? I hoped not. I needed time to think, and time for some unfortunately placed bruises to heal.

Time was not on my side.

"He's awake!" That was the larger boy, who got the attention of Conner's backseat vigil.

The vigil crawled across the wagon to slap my cheek, which wasn't necessary because my eyes were mostly open. I swore at him, then winced as he yanked me into a sitting position.

"Not too rough," Conner called from his seat. "He's a guest, Cregan."

The vigil now known as Cregan glared at me. I didn't say anything else, figuring the phrase I'd just used to curse at him had satisfactorily explained my wishes for the cause of his death.

"You've met Cregan," Conner said, then added, "Mott is our driver."

Mott glanced back to nod a hello at me. He and Cregan couldn't have been designed to look more different from each other. Mott was tall, dark-skinned, and nearly bald. What little hair he did have was black and shaved to his scalp. He was the one by the tavern who'd tripped me when I was trying to escape the butcher. In contrast, Cregan was short — not much taller than I was, and shorter than the tanned boy near me. He was surprisingly pale for a man who likely spent much of his day outdoors, and he had a thick crop of blond hair that he tied back at the nape of his neck. Mott was lean and muscular while Cregan looked softer than I knew him to be, judging by the way he'd clubbed me at the orphanage.

How strange that there could be two people so different from each other and yet my dislike for them was equally fierce.

Conner motioned to the boys in the wagon with me. "That's Latamer and Roden."

Latamer was the cougher. Roden had ratted me out for being awake. They nodded at me, then Latamer shrugged, as if to say he had no more of an idea why we were here than I did.

"I'm hungry," I said. "I'd planned on having roast for dinner, so whatever you've got had better be good."

Conner laughed and tossed an apple onto my lap, which sat there because my hands were still tied behind me.

Roden reached over, snatched the apple, and took a big bite of it. "One of the rewards for not having fought coming along. I'm not tied up like a prisoner."

"That was mine," I said.

"The apple was for anyone willing to take it," Conner said.

There was silence for another moment, except for the sound of Roden eating. I stared icily at him, though I knew it'd do no good. If he came from an orphanage as I did, he knew the rules of survival. Rule number one said you took food whenever it was available, as much as you could get.

"Neither of you fought Conner?" I asked Latamer and Roden.

Latamer shook his head and coughed. He probably didn't have the strength to fight. Roden leaned forward and wrapped his arms around his legs. "I saw the orphanage you came from. It was ten times the place I lived in. Then Conner comes and says if I cooperate, I could get a big reward. So no, I didn't fight."

"You might have given me that nice speech instead of having me hit over the head," I told Conner. "What's the reward?"

Conner didn't turn around to answer. "Cooperate first, then we'll talk reward."

Roden tossed his apple core from the cart. He didn't even have the decency to eat all of it.

"You can untie me now," I said. It probably wasn't going to be that easy, but there was no harm in asking.

Conner answered. "Mrs. Turbeldy warned me that you have a history of running away. Where do you go?"

"To church, of course. To confess my sins."

Roden snorted a laugh, but Conner didn't seem to find the same humor. "I can starve that blasphemy out of you, boy."

I leaned my head back and closed my eyes, hoping to end any conversation involving me. For the most part, it worked. Roden said something about his devotion to the church, but I let it go. None of it mattered. I didn't plan on being here much longer.

About an hour later, the wagon stopped in a small town I'd been to once before. It was named Gelvins, although as small as it was, I'm not sure it deserved any name. Gelvins was more like an outpost than a town, with only a few shops on the street and a dozen pathetic excuses for homes. Carthyan homes were normally well built and sturdy, but Gelvins was poor and its farms dry. A sturdy home was a luxury few here could dream of, much less afford to build. Most of these thin wooden structures looked like they would be finished in a stiff windstorm. Our wagon had stopped in front of a shack with a small sign over the doorway identifying it as the Gelvins Charity Orphanage. I knew this place. I'd stayed here several months ago after Mrs. Turbeldy temporarily kicked me out.

Conner took Mott with him and left Cregan to guard us. As soon as Conner left, Cregan jumped out of the wagon and said he was going to get a quick drink in the tavern and that he'd personally kill any boy who tried to escape.

"Another orphan?" Roden asked. "Conner's probably been to every orphanage in the country. What could he possibly want with all of us?"

"You don't know?" I asked.

Latamer shrugged, but Roden said, "He's looking for one particular boy, but I don't know why."

"He won't want me." Latamer's voice was so quiet, the snorting of our horses nearly drowned him out. "I'm sick."

"Maybe he will," I said. "We don't know what he wants."

"I plan on being whatever he wants," Roden said. "I'm not going back to any orphanage, and I've got no future on the streets."

"Who is Bevin Conner?" I asked. "Do either of you know anything about him?"

"I overheard him speaking to Master Grippings, who runs the orphanage where Roden and I lived," Latamer mumbled. "He said he was a friend of the king's court."

"King Eckbert?" I shook my head. "Conner's lying, then. Everyone knows the king has no friends."

Latamer shrugged. "Friend or enemy, he convinced Master Grippings that he was here as a service to the king."

"But what does that have to do with us?" I asked. "A handful of orphaned boys?"

"He just wants one boy," Roden reminded us. "The rest of us will be cast away as soon as we become useless to Conner. He said as much to Master Grippings."

"Let me make it easier on you," I said to Roden. "Untie me and I'll be on my way. That's one less boy to contend with."

"I'll do no such thing," Roden said. "Do you think I want to be punished for your escape?"

"Fine. But the knots are really tight. Could you just loosen them?"

Roden shook his head. "If they're tight, it's because you irritated Conner's vigils, and you probably deserve it."

"Conner wouldn't want him to be hurt." Latamer crept toward me and said, "Turn around."

"I can't maneuver with my arms behind me. Just reach back there."

Latamer stretched an arm across my back, which I caught with my hand and twisted behind him. Roden jumped up to one knee, startled, but with my other hand I slipped a noose over Latamer's neck and pulled it so that it was nearly tightened. Roden froze, waiting to see what I'd do next.

Getting the rope off my wrists had been an easy matter. Knotting it into a noose was a bit trickier, although now was not the time to admire my handiwork. Roden didn't look impressed with my behind-the-back knot tying. Clearly, he'd never attempted something like that before, or he would have been. Or maybe he just didn't want me to strangle Latamer in front of him.

"Not an inch closer to me," I warned Roden. "Or else I'll dump him over the side of the cart and you can describe to Conner the sound of his snapping neck."

"Please don't do that," Latamer breathed.

Roden sat back down. "I don't care if you kill him and I don't care if you run away. Leave if you want, and pray Conner's vigils don't find you."

I stood, apologized to Latamer for threatening to kill him, then gave a ceremonial bow to Roden. The bow might've been a mistake. Midway through standing up straight, Cregan whacked me in the back with the flat end of his sword. I fell forward, all air knocked from my lungs.

"You know what'd happen to me if I let you get away, boy?" Cregan snarled.

I knew, and I wasn't entirely opposed to it.

"You said you'd kill anyone who tried to escape," Roden reminded him.

"And so I will," Cregan said, baring his teeth when I turned to look at him. He'd replaced his sword with a knife and leapt into the wagon in two steps. I rolled over to make a run for it, but he grabbed my shirt, shoved me back down, and pressed the knife to my throat. "Master Conner doesn't need all of you. And I think he needs you least of all."

Suddenly, I had a motivation to be needed by Master Conner. "Okay," I grumbled. "You win. I'll cooperate."

"You're lying," Cregan said.

"I often lie. But not about this. I'll cooperate."

Cregan smiled, pleased to have humiliated me. He replaced his knife in the sheath at his waist, then yanked me up by my collar and tossed me into the corner of the wagon. "We'll see."

A minute later, Conner returned to the wagon with Mott and a boy walking beside him. I squinted, certain I recognized him. He was tall and unusually thin. His hair was darker than both mine and Roden's, but his was stringy and straight and more in need of a trim than mine, if that was possible.

The boy climbed dutifully into the back of the wagon. Conner glanced at my untied hands and then at the thin vein of blood trickling down my neck. He eyed Cregan. "Any trouble?"

"None, sir," Cregan responded. "Only I believe you'll find Sage to be more cooperative now."

Conner smiled as if that was all he needed to know of the matter. "I'm glad to hear it. Boys, meet Tobias. He'll be joining us in our quest."

"What quest?" I asked.

Conner shook his head. "Patience, Sage. Patience is the mark of a ruler."

And that was my first clue about why Conner had taken us. We were all in terrible danger.

# · THREE ·

I knew Tobias. He might not have known me because I'd come and gone from Gelvins Charity Orphanage so quickly. But in my short stay, Tobias had stood out amongst the others. He was no ordinary orphan. He'd been educated as a child and continued to read anything he could get his hands on. He was given special privileges at the orphanage because it was felt he was one of the few with any hopes of one day making a success of his life.

Tobias glanced my way. "You're bleeding."

I brushed at the cut mark on my neck. "It's mostly stopped."

That was as much concern as he wished to invest. "Do I know you?"

"I stayed here about six months ago."

"Yeah, I remember. Locked the headmaster out of the orphanage for an entire night, didn't you?"

The grin on my face became my confession. "You have to admit, we ate well that night. For once."

"It's not funny," Tobias scolded. "Maybe we don't eat well most of the time, but it's because there's not a lot of food to go around. You gave out a week's worth of food that night. It was a very long, very hungry week after you left."

My grin faded. I hadn't known that.

We rode for over an hour through a lonely plain covered in gorse and nettle. Tobias remarked that he found it beautiful in a desolate sort of way. I saw the desolation, but the beauty escaped me. Eventually, it became dark enough that Mott suggested we find a place to stop for the night. The closest town was still Gelvins behind us rather than anything yet ahead, so I didn't think it should matter too much where we camped. But Mott still took us a ways farther until the vegetation changed and he found a small clearing surrounded by tall willow trees and thick bushes.

"They're hiding us," I muttered to the other boys.

Roden shook his head back at me and said, "It's safer here than out in the open. They're protecting us."

Mott jumped off the wagon and began shouting orders at each of us for what to unload from the wagon and where to put it, mostly blankets and, I hoped, food. I was assigned to remain in the wagon and hand things to the others on the ground.

"Afraid I'll run away?" I asked.

"Any trust you get here will have to be earned," Mott said. "And I'd say you have a great deal more to earn than the others." He nodded at a sack near my foot. "Hand me that."

Although Conner was the master of our group, Mott was

clearly the one keeping our show running. He was no ordinary, useless vigil. At least, I noticed that he didn't need to ask Conner's permission for everything, and when Mott issued orders to Cregan, Cregan did as he was told. While we worked, Conner stationed himself on a fallen log to peruse a tattered leather-bound book. Every now and then he'd glance up, studying each of us with more than a casual examination, then return to his book.

Cregan got a fire going, and afterward, Mott instructed us to gather around so that Conner could talk to us.

"*Talk* to us?" I said. "When do we eat?"

"We eat after the talk," Conner said, closing his book and standing. "Come, boys, sit."

I jumped out of the wagon and squeezed onto the edge of a log Roden and Tobias had dragged near the fire. They weren't too pleased to have me there but didn't complain either. Latamer squatted on the ground. I considered offering him my seat, since he was still coughing, but I guessed he wouldn't take it anyway.

Conner coughed too, although his was the kind meant to get our attention. The cough wasn't necessary. We were already watching him.

"I haven't said much as to why I've collected you boys," Conner began. "I'm sure in your heads you've created every sort of speculation, from the likely and plausible to the wild and impossible. What I have in mind is closer to the latter of those."

Tobias sat up straighter. I already disliked him as much as Roden, even though there had been far more time for me to learn to dislike Roden.

"I can't deny there's danger with my plan," Conner said. "If we fail, there will be terrible consequences. But if we succeed, the rewards are beyond your imagination."

I wasn't sure about that. I could imagine some fairly big rewards.

"In the end, only one of you can be chosen. I need the boy who proves himself to be the closest fit with my plan. And my plan is very demanding and very specific."

Tobias raised his hand. A sign that he'd been educated. At the orphanage I came from, a person only raised a hand if he was about to hit someone with it. "Sir, what is your plan?"

"Excellent question, Tobias, but it's also a very secret plan. So what I'd like to do first is offer any of you the chance to leave now. You may leave with no feelings of regret or cowardice. I've been very up-front about both the danger and the rewards. If you don't feel that this is for you, then this is your opportunity to leave."

Roden looked at me. I arched my eyebrows in response. He wanted me to leave, that was clear. And I would have stood right then, except for a nagging voice in my head that told me something was wrong. So I kept still.

Latamer raised his hand. Not because he'd been trained to, but because it had worked for Tobias. "Sir, I think I'd like to leave. I'm not fit to compete with these other boys, and frankly,

I'm not one to face danger, even for great rewards." Apparently, the nagging voice hadn't visited Latamer's head.

"Certainly you may leave." Conner politely raised a hand toward the wagon. "Why don't you get back in there and I'll have Cregan drive you to the nearest town."

"Tonight?"

"The rest of us have more to discuss tonight, so yes, go right now."

Latamer gave an apologetic smile to us and thanked Conner for understanding. I nodded a good-bye to him, and wondered, like I'm sure Roden and Tobias did, if it'd be smart to make the same choice. Conner hadn't said what would happen to the boys he didn't pick for his plan. Nor just how dangerous things might get.

Then I realized what my instincts had been trying to tell me. Mott was ahead of us, motioning Latamer toward the wagon. Where was Cregan?

I stood and yelled, "Latamer, stop!" But my warning only gave Latamer time to turn from climbing into the wagon. His eyes widened as he saw what I had sensed. An arrow whooshed past me and pierced his chest. Latamer yelped like a wounded dog and fell backward on the ground, dead.

With a furious cry, I leapt toward Cregan, who was still partially hidden in the shadows behind us, and tackled him to the ground. Cregan went for the knife at his waist, but one hand still held the bow he'd used to kill Latamer, so I got the knife first. With my body crossways over Cregan's, I started to crawl off him, but Mott lunged at me from behind and I collapsed facedown into the dirt. Cregan took a deep breath, then sat up and easily wrested the knife from my hand. That was probably a good thing. I don't know what I would've done with it if Mott hadn't stopped me.

"You killed him," I growled, getting a taste of dirt into my mouth.

Conner knelt beside me and lowered himself so that I could see his face. His voice was eerily calm. "Latamer was sick, Sage. He wasn't going to get better, and I think he proved a good lesson for the rest of you. Now you can get up and rejoin the other boys, or you can take a wagon ride with Latamer. It's your choice."

I thrust my jaw forward and glared at Conner, then finally said, "I suppose Latamer won't be much company now. I'll stay here."

"Excellent decision." Conner clapped a hand on my back as if we were old friends. He nodded at Mott, who let me go, then added, "I'm sure Latamer's death is a shock to you, but it was important for you three to understand the seriousness of what we are doing."

When I sat up, Cregan's leg brushed roughly past me as he went to help lift Latamer's body into the wagon. Normally, I'd have kicked him in return, but for the moment I was too stunned to think.

"Bury him deep," Conner said.

Still on the log, Tobias was pale and perfectly still. Roden looked as if he was having trouble breathing. My breathing wasn't working any better. It didn't help that Mott had rudely pressed his knee into my back for the last couple of minutes.

Conner's smile was a thin line on his face. "Sage, I believe your question earlier was why we had the meeting before we ate. This is why. So we wouldn't waste our food." His eyes passed over to Roden and Tobias. "How about it, then? Does anybody else want to leave?"

# · FOUR ·

Mott laid out a sack of fresh fruit and salted meat, but other than him and Conner, none of us touched it.

"It's your last chance until breakfast," Conner said. "You'll want to keep your strength up."

Roden shook his head at Conner. He didn't look like he could stomach a bite of food anyway. Tobias had been nearly frozen since Latamer was killed. He'd barely even blinked. I'd gone numb. Literally. I felt nothing.

Conner and Mott ate their meal while the rest of us sat. Slowly, the shock wore off and we began to accept that as long as we did what we were told, we'd live to see another morning. Conner offered the food to us again.

"We have more traveling ahead of us, so you'll only hurt yourselves if you don't eat."

Roden reached for the food first. He handed it to me and then Tobias. The piece of meat I took was unbearably salty and forced me into taking an apple, even though I had no appetite for it. I don't think Tobias or Roden enjoyed their food much either. A wave of nausea threatened me every time I looked in the direction where Latamer had fallen.

At the orphanage, we'd all seen our share of violence and brutality. I once saw an older boy start kicking a younger one just for rolling over onto his mattress. It took five of us to stop him. But Conner had told Latamer it would be safe to leave. He baited Latamer, to teach us a lesson about leaving. The knowledge that Latamer had been brought along only for that purpose consumed my thoughts.

If I'd figured out what was happening even a few seconds earlier, could I have stopped it? Were any of the rest of us here as no more than a lesson to the others?

"Now that you've eaten, we can continue our conversation." Conner nodded at Tobias. "Stand up. I wish to get a general understanding of who each of you is."

Tobias stood stiffly. His knees were rigid and he looked like he was about to be sick.

"Tobias, you and an opponent are engaged in a sword battle. It's meant to be a battle to the death, but it's also clear that he's better than you are. Do you fight on, knowing you'll likely die, or stop the battle and beg for your opponent's mercy?"

"I beg mercy," Tobias said. "If it's clear I won't win, then nothing is accomplished through my death. I'd hope to live and make myself stronger for the next battle."

Conner nodded at Roden. "What about you?"

Roden stood. "Fight to the death, even if it's my own. I'm a good fighter, sir, and I will not live as a coward."

Tobias flinched at that, but he said nothing. A slight smile crossed Roden's face; he knew he'd taken an edge with his answer.

"Have you been trained with a sword?" Conner asked.

Roden shrugged. "An old Carthyan soldier lives near my orphanage. He used to have me do rounds with him, to keep up his skills."

"Did you ever win?"

"No, but —"

"Then you haven't been trained." Conner turned to me. "Sage?"

"Beg mercy."

Roden snorted.

I continued. "Then when my opponent lowers his guard, certain of his victory, I'd finish the battle."

Conner laughed.

"A violation of all sportsmanship in swordplay," Tobias said.

"What do I care about sportsmanship?" I said. "If I'm about to get killed, it's not play anymore. I won't check the rules to see if my survival fits with someone's codebook of fair play."

"You'd never win that way," Roden said. "Any master swordsman won't lower his guard until you're disarmed."

"Conner didn't say he was a master swordsman," I said. "Only that he was better than me. And yes, I would win."

Conner walked closer to me. "Stand when I address you."

I obeyed. Conner was taller than me by several inches and

stood closer than I liked. But I refused to step back. It occurred to me that he was testing to see whether I would.

"Are you standing straight?" Conner asked. "You slouch so much, I might mistake you for a hunchback. And with all that hair in your face, you might be a criminal too."

I straightened but made no attempt to push the hair out of my eyes. I could see him just fine, which was all I cared about.

Conner asked, "Who do you look like? Your mother or father?"

"That's hard to say, sir. It's been a long time since I've seen myself in a mirror."

"You have a clever tongue and an arrogant tilt to your head. I'm surprised Mrs. Turbeldy hasn't beaten it out of you."

"You mustn't blame her. She beat me the best she could."

"You're a trick to figure out, Sage. Would you ever be on my side, even if I chose you above the other boys?"

"I'm only on my side. Your *trick* will be convincing me that helping you helps me."

"What if I did?" Conner asked. "How far would you go to win?"

"The better question, sir, is how far *you* will go to win." I looked him steadily in the eyes as I spoke, although his back was to the fire and his eyes were set in shadow. "You killed Latamer. So we know you're willing to murder to win."

"I am." Conner backed up, speaking to all of us again. "And I'm willing to lie, to cheat, and to steal. I'm willing to commend my soul to the devils if necessary because I believe there is exoneration in my cause. I need one of you to conduct the greatest fraud ever perpetrated within the country of Carthya. This is a lifetime commitment. It will never be safe to back down from my plan and tell the truth. To do so would destroy not only you but the entire country. And you will do it to save Carthya."

"To save Carthya?" Tobias asked. "How?"

"Later, later," Conner said. "Until then, boys, Mott has laid out a blanket for each of you by the fire. Tonight we sleep, and sleep well, because tomorrow our work will begin."

I chose the blanket closest to me. Roden lay near me and wrapped his blanket tightly around him.

"Remember when I said I never won rounds against that old soldier?" he asked. Without waiting for an answer, Roden added, "It's because I knew he'd stop if I won. I'm good with a sword."

"Maybe you can use some of those skills to get us out of here," I mumbled.

"You saw what he did to Latamer." Roden was silent for several minutes, then whispered, "They just killed him. Told him he was safe to go, then they killed him. What is Conner planning that would make him willing to kill?"

"He's planning a revolution," I whispered back. "Conner is going to use one of us to overthrow the kingdom."

## · FIVE ·

Sometime during the night, I tried to roll over in my blanket. A tug on my ankle awoke me and I sat up to find myself chained to Mott, who was sleeping beside me. I grabbed a pebble and flung it at Mott's face. His eyes flew open and he sat up, glaring at me.

"What?" he snarled.

"You chained me up?" I said. "Not the others, only me?"

"The others won't run. You might." Mott lay back down. "Go to sleep, or I'll knock you out cold."

"I've got to go."

"Go where?"

"To *go*. I'd have just taken care of it myself, but it looks like you want to come along."

Mott cursed. "Wait for morning."

"Wish I could. I've been cursed with my mother's pea-size bladder."

Mott sat up again, fumbled on the ground for the keys to the chain, then unlocked himself. He grabbed his sword and directed me to stand, then escorted me over the cold ground to some bushes a little ways from camp.

"Go here."

I did my business, then we walked back to camp. Mott grabbed the collar of my shirt and shoved me back onto my blanket. "You ever wake me in the night again and I'll hurt you."

"As long as you have me chained, prepare for waking up a lot in the night," I said. "I'm not a quiet sleeper."

He replaced the chain, tightening it, I noticed, from what it had been before. I stretched and yawned and rolled over, pulling my chained leg as far forward as I could. Mott yanked it back. Even though I knew I'd pay for it the next day, I couldn't help but grin as I pulled my leg forward again.

---

Surprisingly, that morning Mott made no mention of the previous night. I got a kick awake, but so did Roden. Tobias was up walking around, so he must have been awake already, and smirked a little to see Roden and me groan in our blankets.

Roden seemed to have recovered from the shock of Latamer's murder last night, or at least, he was back to his old self, assuring Tobias and me as we cleaned up that he intended to be the boy Conner chose. Tobias and I glanced at each other. Tobias's expression was clear — he intended to win too, only he clearly planned on pursuing that goal more quietly than Roden.

"I have bread for breakfast," Conner announced. "A

mouthful for any boy who correctly answers my questions." He broke off a piece of bread and asked, "Who are the current king and queen of Carthya?"

"Eckbert and Corinne," I said quickly.

Tobias laughed. "King Eckbert is correct, but the queen is Erin."

Conner tossed the bread to Tobias, which I thought was unfair. I'd already given him half the answer, yet he got the entire bite. Conner broke off another piece, then asked, "How many regents sit in King Eckbert's court?"

Tobias guessed ten, but Conner said that was incorrect. Neither Roden nor I answered.

"The correct answer is twenty," Conner said. "No matter how many nobles of wealth or stature exist in the land, there are always twenty regents given a seat in the court. They advise the king, although Eckbert too often ignores his regents." He popped the bread in his mouth, then took another piece while he chewed. After swallowing, he asked, "How many sons does King Eckbert have?"

"Two," I answered.

"Wrong again," Tobias said. "There is one, the crown prince Darius. There were two until four years ago, when the younger son, Prince Jaron, was lost during a sea voyage."

Conner tossed the bread to Tobias, and then said to me, "Your accent is Avenian, so you're not originally from Carthya. What brought you from Avenia to Carthya?"

"That orphanage was the farthest away I could get from my family," I said.

"Are your parents still alive?" he asked.

"I have not sought out any information on them for some time," I said. "As far as I know, I'm completely alone in this world."

"Avenia is a violent country," Conner said. "If disease doesn't strike, bandits will. Few live to old age in Avenia."

"Consider me an orphan," I said. "An orphan of family and of country. Is loyalty to Carthya a requirement for you?"

Conner nodded. "It's a must. It will take you more effort to learn facts about this country, which Roden and Tobias have grown up knowing. Are you up to learning?"

I shrugged. "Tell me about the regents."

Conner rewarded my question with a chunk of bread, and then said, "I am one of the twenty regents, albeit a minor one. My father was a man of great influence in the court, so upon his recent death, I inherited my position in the court. Thirteen of the regents inherited their positions, the other seven earned them through great acts of service to the king. Three of the regents are women; two are old men whose sons can't wait for them to die to take their places. For every regent in the court, there are five nobles in Carthya who would love to see them fall from grace so that another Carthyan can be brought into council with the king. All of the regents claim loyalty to the king, but few actually practice it. The secret none of them keep very well is that they wish to have the throne for themselves."

"Does that include you?" Roden's question was not rewarded with bread.

Conner pressed his lips together, and then said, "As I told you, my status in the court is minor. It's useless for me to aspire to the throne. It would be taken over a hundred times before I attained enough power to acquire it."

"He didn't ask whether you'd get the throne," I said. "He asked whether you wanted it."

Conner smiled. "Is there anyone who bows to the throne and does not wish that he was the one who sat on it? Tell me, Sage, have you ever lain on the hard floor of the orphanage, staring at the stars through cracks in the ceiling, and wondered what it would be like to be king?"

I couldn't deny that. Beside me, Roden and Tobias were nodding their heads. In the few moments at night before sleep came upon us, when all orphans do their best dreaming, we'd all thought about it.

Conner continued his lesson. "Second in power to the king is the high chamberlain, Lord Kerwyn. But Kerwyn is a servant to the king and could not become king himself. The most powerful of the regents is the prime regent, a man named Santhias Veldergrath. He's ruthless in his ambitions. He's climbed the ladder of power by destroying those with influence greater than his. I suspect there are more than a dozen nobles either dead or in the king's prison because of Veldergrath. He wants the crown and works the king's armies to his favor. If anything were ever to happen to the royal family, Veldergrath would be first to reach for the throne. The other regents would either bow to his will or send Carthya into civil war in pursuit of their own ambitions."

"I know of Veldergrath," Tobias said. "He owned the land my grandmother lived on. One day a messenger came 'round and told her the rent would be doubled. She hated him to the end of her life."

"He has his enemies, yes, but he also has powerful friends. Veldergrath has no compassion for the people and will suck every good thing from Carthya to himself until it's swallowed up."

"So which do you prefer?" Tobias asked. "A reign of Veldergrath or civil war?"

"Neither. That is why you are here." Conner tossed the remaining bread to the ground for us to divide amongst ourselves, then brushed his hands together and said to Mott and Cregan, "Wipe away any trace of our being here as best you can. I wish to leave within the hour."

Roden and Tobias dove for the bread, but I stayed where I was, watching Conner walk back to the cart. The hints he left for us about his plan were not subtle. It was clear what he wanted. But there was obviously some crucial information he was still leaving out. I didn't dare wonder what that might be.

Conner met my gaze as he passed by, and stopped walking. He gave me an appraising look as we stood there, then slowly nodded his head before walking on.

I closed my eyes, horrified that my suspicions might be true. Conner was holding us on the brink of treason.

# · SIX ·

Conner lectured us about Carthya for nearly the entire ride to wherever we were going that morning. He faced backward in the wagon seat while Mott drove and Cregan did vigil duty from the rear.

He pointed out the various towns all over Carthya, gesturing their direction from us and describing in detail the qualities of the different large cities.

"Drylliad is that way," he said, pointing to the south. "The capital of Carthya and home of the royal family. Have any of you ever been there?"

Tobias spoke up. "My father brought me there when I was very young, but I don't remember it."

"I've been there too, but it was some time ago," I added. "Tried to steal a pigeon from the king's dovecote. It didn't work out so well."

They laughed, which was odd since I hadn't meant it as a joke. I'd been hungry at the time and barely escaped without being detected. Sprained my ankle in a fall as I ran that didn't heal for a week.

I'd been to many of the towns he spoke of. It was clear that I was better traveled than either Roden or Tobias. Roden said he'd been born somewhere in southern Carthya and left on the steps of the orphanage in Benton. He had no idea who his parents were or anything about them. He'd never left Benton until Conner came for him.

Tobias said that he had been born in a town near Gelvins, but his mother died at birth and his father died of disease a few years later. His grandmother had taken over his care afterward, but after she died two years ago, he'd been sent to the orphanage.

"Who educated you?" Conner asked him.

"My grandmother. She worked for a man who had a vast library and let her borrow a different book each week to read to me. I miss the books almost as much as I miss her."

"Do you read?" Conner asked Roden, who shook his head.

"I've always wanted to, though," Roden said. "I'm good on my feet and thought maybe I'd join the king's army. But to rise in rank, I'd be expected to read."

"So you're a patriot," Conner said admiringly. "Then we shall have to teach you to read. What about you, Sage? Can you read?"

I shrugged. "Didn't you already ask me that?"

"You chose to insult me last time rather than answer," Conner said. "I don't expect you've had much education."

"My father said a person can be educated and still be stupid, and a wise man can have no education at all."

"Your father was a worthless musician," Conner said. "It

sounds to me like he was both stupid and without education. And Mrs. Turbeldy told me your mother was a barmaid. I hate to think of the education she might have given you."

I stared at my hands resting on my knees. "If you can give me anything worth reading, I'll make my way through it."

"Who amongst you rides a horse? In a gentleman's style?"

Again, none of us answered. I'd ridden a horse several times before, but in all my recent experience, it was usually stolen and always in an attempt to escape the horse's owner. That probably wasn't a gentleman's style.

"I hardly dare ask whether any of you have been taught your manners and other social graces."

"I have, a little," Tobias said.

Roden actually laughed at Conner's question, though he quickly corrected himself. "Master Conner, make me into a gentleman. I'll learn."

"You will all learn," Conner said. "And at the end of the next two weeks, I intend to make each of you into a gentleman, so flawless in your learning, you could pass as a noble before the king himself."

"We're going to see the king?" I asked.

Conner shook his head. "I didn't say that. Only that you could stand in front of him and make him believe you are a noble."

Roden looked over at me and smiled. I didn't share his enthusiasm.

"Two weeks?" I asked. "What's the hurry?"

Conner locked eyes with me. "Because that's when the boy I choose will be tested."

Tobias cleared his throat, and then asked, "What happens to the other two boys, sir? The two boys who you don't choose?"

Conner looked at each one of us before answering. When he spoke, he only said, "Two weeks, boys. Pray you are the one I choose."

Then he turned his back to us and we continued riding.

Tobias, Roden, and I looked at one another. Cregan read the unspoken conversation and chuckled. Roden seemed a little more pale again. Tobias lost any expression on his face whatsoever, as if he'd turned to stone. Undoubtedly, we were all remembering how casually Conner had ordered Latamer's death, and then had quickly justified it based on the higher moral status of his plan.

He would choose his winner in two weeks, and most likely the other two boys would follow Latamer's fate at the same time.

# · SEVEN ·

It was late afternoon when our wagon pulled up to a large estate several miles outside the town of Tithio. An engraved wooden sign at the entrance identified this as Conner's home. It rose two stories above the ground with a partial third floor arching over the center of the house. The roof was nearly flat and bordered by a low parapet. I wondered if any stairways led up to the rooftop for what was certain to be an impressive view of Conner's extensive grounds. The building was made of thick tan bricks and cut stone. This alone was impressive, since it didn't look like there were any quarries in this region of Carthya, meaning the rocks would have had to come from some distance away. Veins of a thin ledge ran between the first and second floor. I counted nearly twenty windows just in the front of the house. The orphanage in Carchar didn't have a single window.

Conner stood and gestured toward the estate. "Welcome to my home, boys. I call it Farthenwood. It was my father's home and the home of my childhood. I know its every secret and dearly love to come here whenever I can get away from the king's business in Drylliad. This will be your home as well for the next two weeks. I have arranged everything in advance of our arrival. I'm sure you have many questions, but we have other business first."

A line of servants had assembled in front of the wagon. A few quickly took control of the horses and one helped Conner out of the wagon, bowing to him afterward as if *he* were a royal.

Cregan gestured to us to leave the wagon, and when we did, Conner presented us each with a servant. "Follow your man to a warm bath and a change of clean clothes." He cast an eye on me. "Some of you require more scrubbing than usual, so stay in the bath as long as you must. Once you are presentable, you may join me for a hot supper that I suspect will be the finest meal any of you have ever eaten."

Roden and Tobias followed their servants into the estate. I followed mine behind them as we entered Farthenwood. The entry was massive and well lit by windows and a large chandelier directly above us. The plaster walls were decorated with beautiful murals of countryside scenes. A tapestry hanging near me depicted dozens of names and faces. Probably Conner's family tree.

"What's your name?" I asked the servant.

He hesitated at first as if he wasn't sure whether he should answer, and then said, "Errol, sir." Errol looked like the kind of young man who might never grow enough facial hair to actually require a shave. He had boyish features and a bit of curl in his light blond hair. I suspected that if the fables about the existence of elves were true, Errol would turn out to be one of them.

"I'm Sage. My companions on this trip will assure you I am

no 'sir.' Conner seems to think he owns me too, which makes me a servant much like you. So let's keep everything on a first-name basis."

"Forgive me, but I've been instructed to call you 'sir,'" Errol said. "So you should get used to hearing it."

I tugged on the rag that served as my shirt. My entire fist could easily have fit through a tear in the fabric near my hip. "With me dressed this way? How can you call me that without laughing?"

Errol glanced sideways at me and smiled crookedly. "It isn't easy . . . sir."

When I asked, Errol told me that the rooms off to the left were for a few of the choice servants, such as Mott and Cregan. They also housed a kitchen and other work areas. To the right were rooms for other servants, which several of them shared. I figured Errol's was one of those rooms. A grand staircase rose up from the center of the entry. It was lined with tall beeswax candles and was carpeted in a weave so fine I bent down and ran my fingers over it.

Ahead of me, I heard Roden's servant tell Roden that with my dirty hands, he'd have to scrub that area of carpet now. Out of spite, I made sure I left a mark there.

The second floor consisted of rooms on alternating sides of a long hallway.

"I think several of my orphanages could fit in here," Roden said.

"Conner's a rich man, that's for sure," Tobias added.

"Why does he need so many rooms?" I asked.

Errol smiled. "If he had fewer rooms, there wouldn't be enough cleaning for all of us to do."

I laughed loudly, which earned a glare from the other two servants. In a quieter voice, Errol continued, "Master Conner often has guests. He wishes to impress his wealth upon them, and usually does."

"He said he's a regent in the court. Has the king ever been here?"

"The king has not, but the queen came once when traveling with her courtiers."

"I've heard she's not very pretty," I said.

Errol looked at me like I'd slapped him. "Whoever told you that was lying," he said, as if personally offended. "Queen Erin is a strikingly beautiful woman. Master Conner himself has often commented on that."

"Is Conner married?"

"No, sir. He loved a woman once, but that didn't work out."

"Do you know why we've been brought here?" I asked. "Conner said he has a plan."

"If I knew, it wouldn't be my place to say it." Errol's eyes darted around as he spoke.

"You don't have to tell me," I said quickly. The last thing I wanted was to make Errol afraid to talk to me. "I was just curious."

"All we hear as servants are rumors and bits of the whole story," Errol said. "You couldn't trust the little I know anyway."

"No," I agreed, then changed the subject. "How long have you served Conner?"

"I came here when I was ten, sir, half my life ago."

So he wasn't much older than me. And yet he addressed me as sir.

"Are you working off a debt to him?"

"My family's debts. Perhaps another ten years, then I'll be free to go."

"Do you like it here?"

Errol nodded. "If you do what Conner wants, he's a good master."

"What if you don't do what he wants?"

"Conner sent a messenger ahead. I heard about you." Errol smiled and added, "I fear you may find out the answer to that question for yourself."

That made me smile as well. "He won't get any more trouble from me. It's becoming very clear what happens to those who cross him."

"Yes, sir." Errol stopped at a door. "You'll share a bedroom with the other boys, but your bath will be in here." He opened the door to reveal a nice-size room that looked as if it had been converted for use in bathing. The decorations here were soft and feminine, but it didn't appear to be anyone's current living quarters, so I assumed this was a guest room. I was tempted to throw myself down on the bed near a far wall for a nap, but given how dirty I was, they'd probably have to burn the bed afterward.

Errol tugged at my shirt to prompt me to undress for the bath, but I jumped away from him and said, "I bathe in private."

Errol smiled again. "If you will pardon the observation, sir, it doesn't appear that you bathe at all."

I laughed. "Well, I won't start by having my bath with company."

"My instructions are to bring you to supper as clean as a nobleman's son. I'll wait outside if you wish, but when you come out, if you are not that clean, we'll return to that bath again. I obey the master's wishes, not yours." This time, Errol was not smiling as he closed the door.

"You can relax out there," I called to him. "I'll be a while."

I looked for a way to lock the door but found none. So I dragged a heavy chair to the door and braced it beneath the door handle.

The room had a window balcony at the back of the house. I tiptoed out onto it and looked around. A gardener was working below me, but his head was bent down to the flowers. Probably not a great risk of him looking up. The exterior of Conner's home was built from rock, with a thin ledge marking each floor. It was a long fall to the ground, but there were a lot of ways to make sure I didn't fall.

I swung my body onto the balustrade, balancing myself against the outside wall. Bracing my foot against the angled curve of a rock, I dug my fingers into the crevice of another rock and climbed.

## · EIGHT ·

Errol was calling my name when I returned to the room, sweaty and tired. I hadn't been gone long, just enough to have a look over Conner's grounds for myself. Still, I wondered how long he'd been calling for me.

"Must have fallen asleep," I called back to him, splashing some water with my hand. "What do you need?"

"Your water must be cold by now," he said. "May I come refill it?"

The water was cold. But it was also perfectly clean, and I was filthier than when he'd left me.

"The water is fine," I said, undressing as quickly and quietly as I could. "I won't be too much longer."

"The other boys left their baths long ago."

"Yes, but they were probably cleaning themselves while I was sleeping. Give me a few moments."

I dove into the water and scrubbed everything that would show outside my clothes. A thick stack of new clothes from Errol waited for me beside the tub. They were a gentleman's clothes and probably cost Conner a fair amount of silver to purchase for all three of us. Mine had a linen shirt that laced up the front somehow, a soft leather half-sleeved vest with carved bone buttons, long linen pants, and a pair of calf-high boots. I didn't think much of my skin would show.

That was only my first bath, because after I emerged from the room, Errol inspected my arms above the sleeves and observed that I still smelled like an orphanage. He insisted on scrubbing me the second time.

"The water is freezing," he said. "You like your bath this way?"

"It's colder now," I said grumpily. "And I never said I preferred it, only that it was fine."

Errol's gentle manners were not reflected in his bathing assistance. It surprised me how much dirt came off the second time. While he busied himself with a brush on the bottom of my feet, I looked at my fingernails. "I don't remember them ever being this color," I said, then yanked my foot away. "That tickles. Are you finished yet? I don't like having a man help me with my bath."

Errol grinned. "Shall I have a woman sent in?"

I laughed and told Errol I wouldn't need anyone's help for my future baths. "Obviously, Master Conner has a different standard of clean than the orphanage did. Now that I know you want the entire body washed, I'll make the necessary adjustments."

After we finished, I sent Errol out while I re-dressed. I had to admit that he'd done a good job. It was possible I'd never been so clean.

"Where are my old clothes?" I asked Errol after I'd finished dressing.

"Off to be burnt, I'd guess. They're not fit for much else."

"Get them," I said firmly, and then added, "Just as they were before, Errol. Exactly as they were."

Errol considered that for a moment, then said, "I can get them back, I suppose."

"If you do, I'll see that you get a silver coin for the service."

Errol tilted his head. "Where would you get it?"

"That's a small detail and my concern, not yours. But it would buy months off your debt to Conner." I widened my arms. "These clothes aren't mine and they're not me. I suspect I'll want those other clothes back in two weeks."

Errol shrugged. "I'll see what I can do. Now come. The master is expecting you at supper."

Conner had bathed and shaved as well. He cleaned up nicely, now looking more like a noble and less like a road-weary traveler. Roden and Tobias were already seated when I walked in. This small dining room appeared to be reserved for everyday meals and more intimate affairs. It was clearly designed to impress whoever ate here with an idea of Conner's wealth. I couldn't help but do the math on how much a clever thief might earn from stealing a polished silver fork or a gold-rimmed goblet, or a single crystal hanging in beads from the sconces on the wall.

"Sit, please," Conner said, motioning to the plate at his left.

Tobias was at his right, and Roden was beside Tobias. Roden was clearly distressed that I had been seated closer to Conner than him.

As soon as I sat, servants began bringing in the food. They started with cheese as soft as butter and fruit in the prime of ripeness. At the orphanage, we got the leftovers from the kitchens of the wealthy after they were too wilted or brown to be served at their tables, usually within minutes of the scraps turning to mold. Conner was served first, but he waited for the rest of us to be served before he began. Although I was served second, I assumed I had to follow the same guideline. It was a horrible temptation to ignore Conner's example and begin eating.

My senses were overwhelmed by glorious smells on my plate and others coming from the kitchen. "Do you eat like this all the time?" I asked enthusiastically.

"All the time," Conner said. "Would you like a life of this luxury?"

"This exceeds any expectation I might have had for my life," I answered.

"It's a humble meal compared to a king's feast," Conner said.

"But who'd need a king's feast if they had all this?" Roden asked as his plate was served. Then he looked at Conner, knowing he'd made a mistake but not sure exactly what it was. He searched for the words to correct himself, and failed.

Tobias took his opening. "I'd need a king's feast."

A girl reached over my shoulder and set a bowl of burnt orange—colored soup in front of me. She had dark brown hair pulled into a single braid down her back. She wasn't necessarily beautiful, but something about her was definitely interesting. Her eyes fascinated me the most, warm and brown, but haunted, maybe afraid. She frowned when she caught me looking at her, and returned to serving the others.

"Thank you," I said, getting her attention again. "What kind of soup is it?"

I waited for her answer to my question, but none came. Maybe in Conner's home, the servants were not permitted to speak at his table. I turned away quickly, hoping I hadn't gotten her into trouble.

Conner prattled on, telling us what we could expect to eat for dinner that evening: crisp bread still steaming from the oven, glazed roasted duck with meat so tender it could be cut with a spoon, fruit pudding chilled from an underground cooler. I heard him, but continued to watch the girl as she refilled drinks for each of us. When she leaned to refill Tobias's cup, another servant bumped her with his shoulder, and a little water splashed onto Tobias's lap. Conner glared at her, irritated. I opened my mouth to defend her, but she handed him another napkin and hurried from the room before anything could be said.

When we were all dished up, Conner picked up the spoon at the top of his plate and said, "This is your soup spoon. It is for the soup and only for the soup."

Following his direction, I grabbed my spoon, trying to hold it the same way he did. It was an awkward, uncomfortable position. Maybe gentlemen had to feed themselves this way. Poverty-stricken orphans didn't. I was used to holding my spoon the same way I might grip an ax.

"You eat with your left hand?" Conner asked me. "That's unacceptable. Can you do it with your right?"

"Can you do it with your left?" I countered.

Conner sounded offended. "No."

"Yet you ask me to switch to my right."

"Just do it."

I switched hands, but made no attempt to imitate Conner's delicate grip with this hand. Instead, with my ax grip, I went straight for the soup.

"No, Sage," Conner said. "Scoop the soup into your spoon by pushing the liquid away from you, like this." He demonstrated, and added, "That way, if you spill, it will go onto the table, not onto your lap."

The last bowl of soup I'd eaten had been consumed by my holding both sides of the bowl and drinking it as from a cup. My right hand was sloppy, and as soon as Conner looked away, I switched back to my left. He noticed but said nothing.

Conner corrected Roden on how to hold his spoon: "It's not a hammer, boy." He lectured Tobias on leaning over his bowl: "Bring the food to your mouth, not the mouth to your food." But he said nothing else to me about manners. I suspected he'd given up.

Following the soup, we had some bread and more cheese.

Conner demonstrated the use of the cheese slicer and bread knives. I thought both of those were obvious, so I didn't pay much attention. Roden and Tobias seemed captivated.

The girl who had caught my attention before returned to clear our soup bowls and the bread and cheese while other servants brought us the main course. She frowned at me again, which bothered me because I didn't see what I possibly could have done so soon to irritate her this much.

"I'm already full," Tobias said.

"It's considered rude to say that," Conner said. "A host plans to serve his guests throughout the entire meal and does not want to think that he is forcing half his meal down their throats."

Tobias apologized and said his dinner smelled good, which Conner also seemed to think was a little rude. I didn't think Tobias meant to be rude. It's just that the way he said certain things made him sound haughty.

I was plenty hungry, even after the first two courses. It had been nearly two days since I'd eaten anything substantial, and months since I'd ever eaten enough to consider myself full.

Food is considered a luxury in Carthyan orphanages. They operate on whatever money an orphan inherited upon the deaths of his parents, which inevitably is little more than the shirt on his back after debts were settled. Private donations come in from time to time by wealthy citizens hoping to buy forgiveness for their favorite sins. And, like what had just happened to the three of us, an orphan was sometimes purchased from the orphanage by a wealthy family to be a servant until his debt was worked off.

Since there was so little to eat, we learned to eat fast and to eat selfishly. Which was why I hadn't understood Mrs. Turbeldy's anger about my stealing that roast yesterday. It was meant for all of us.

The final course was dessert, a cherry tart with cinnamon and sugar sprinkled on it. The same girl returned who had served me before, but this time I gave her no extra notice. Even if she had difficulties here, I had plenty of my own to worry about. I needed to focus on Conner, who had yet to reveal the worst of his intentions for us.

"Leave the room now," Conner ordered all his servants. "I won't need you again until we've finished our supper."

When the last of the servants closed the doors, Conner set his knife and fork down and clasped his hands together.

"We've come to it at last," he said, looking over each of us carefully. "I am ready to tell you my plan."

## · NINE ·

An hour seemed to pass before Conner continued. When he finally did, it was in hushed tones, as if he expected the servants' ears were pressed against the doors of our room.

"Some of you may believe you've already guessed my plan," he began. "But I assure you it is not treason. Indeed, in a roundabout way, it may prevent treason in King Eckbert's court. Carthya is on the brink of civil war and very few citizens are aware of it. A major change is coming to this country."

"What is it?" Tobias asked. We all had that same question, but Conner's glare reflected his irritation at being interrupted.

"I will come to that in a moment," he said. "Do you remember what I told you about Veldergrath? He has long planned for this day and even now has begun to amass those loyal to him so that he can force the rest of us to give him the king's crown. But other regents are also aspiring to the crown. They are quietly gathering their supporters. In two weeks, war will erupt in Carthya. It will split the country along lines of loyalty or alliances and may pit families against each other, friends against friends, and town against town. Thousands will inevitably die in that war. Avenia, the country of your origin, Sage, is watching closely, waiting for an opportunity to strike. They are hungry for our rich farmlands and the minerals our mountains provide. When Carthya is weakest and most divided, Avenia will strike, and swallow up Carthya with the force of a tidal wave. Avenia is a cesspool at best. In a generation we'll be no better." Conner tilted his head at me. "Don't pretend to look horrified at my words, Sage. You know my description of Avenia is true."

"It is," I quietly agreed.

"Then you hope to prevent the civil war," Tobias said. "But you said yourself that you could never hope to become king."

"Do you remember this morning when I asked how many heirs King Eckbert has?" Conner said. "What was your answer, Sage?"

"Two. But as Tobias pointed out, I was wrong. There is only the crown prince Darius still alive. Eckbert's younger son was lost at sea."

"The younger son was named Jaron. Since coming to court, I've been told many stories about him, some of which could not possibly be true with the castle still standing in one piece."

"I heard he set fire to the throne room as a child," Tobias said.

"And he challenged the king of Mendenwal to a duel of honor when he was ten years old," Roden added. "He lost of course, but not by much, so the story goes."

"We've all heard the stories," I snapped. "What's the point?"

"Let me finish," Conner said. "Four years ago, when he was nearly eleven years of age, Jaron was to be sent north to the country of Bymar, always a friend to Carthya. He was sent there not only to be educated abroad but, frankly, to stop embarrassing the king and queen. However, on the way, his ship was attacked by pirates. There were no survivors. Pieces of the boat washed ashore for months, but Jaron's body was never found."

"I did hear about this once," I said. "Avenia was accused of hiring the pirates. If King Eckbert had any proof, he would have gone to war."

"At least you know about your own country," Conner said. "It probably was Avenia; piracy is certainly their style. Some say the pirates have more power there than the Avenian king. But Eckbert couldn't rule out the possibility that as a border country to Avenia, Gelyn had hired them. Both countries have easy access to the waters where Jaron's ship went down."

"My father followed that news carefully," I said. "He didn't want war, no matter what else was sacrificed."

"If he was still alive, my father would have been honored to fight on behalf of Carthya," Tobias said. "I'm not the son of a coward."

It would have felt good to defend my father's honor by punching Tobias in the face. But although my father was not a coward, he would have avoided being in a war at any cost. That fact was one of the last things he and I ever fought about.

"Three regents have made the trip to Isel, the seaport town from which Prince Jaron's ship launched. They seek any proof of his death. Or his life."

"His life?" Roden sat forward in his chair. "Is it possible Jaron's alive?"

"A body has never been found, Roden. But if Prince Jaron were alive, then he would be next in line for the throne. Not Veldergrath or any other noble could claim it, and Carthya would be saved from civil war. Then Avenia would not attack."

"But it's irrelevant," Tobias said. "Eckbert and Erin rule now. Eventually, Crown Prince Darius will take the throne."

Conner leaned in closer to us. "And this is the greatest secret of your lives thus far. They are dead, all three of the royal family. The few of us who know the truth have said the royal family is on a diplomatic mission to Gelyn. Meanwhile, their bodies secretly lie far beneath the castle."

We sat there, beyond shock and too horrified to breathe. The news that not just one but all three royals were dead was impossible to bear. My stomach grew queasy at the thought of it, but I pushed those feelings down.

"How did they die?" I whispered.

"Murder. We believe they were administered some sort of poison at supper. They never awoke."

"Any suspects?" Roden asked.

Conner dismissed his question with the wave of his hand. "Don't be naïve. Eckbert had many enemies, and frankly I wouldn't trust most of his friends. I believe all three family members were intended victims, clearing the path for a noble to become king."

"So was it Veldergrath?" I asked.

"A lot of regents suspect him, but there's no evidence of it," Conner said. "We shall see who puts themselves forward to be king, and then judge."

"And you hope to find Prince Jaron and stop the nobles from fighting over the throne," Tobias said.

"Not exactly," Conner said. "Prince Jaron is long dead and I can prove it."

"How?" I asked.

Conner smiled. "I'm afraid for now I must ask you to trust me on that. It's my secret and mine alone. However, since the regents are unaware of my proof, their trip to Isel is only to end any official doubt before another king is chosen. That is where you come in. Because you see, many Carthyans have small hopes that Jaron is alive. Nobody has seen him for nearly four years. He would be fourteen today, about the same age as you boys. Surely the three of you have noticed certain physical similarities between one another." He paused a moment and his smile widened. "You also have similarities in appearance to Prince Jaron as he might look today. My plan is simple, really. I intend to convince the court that Prince Jaron is one of you."

## · TEN ·

A long silence followed Conner's announcement. This was worse than my darkest suspicions of why Conner might have taken us, and I was at a complete loss for what to do next. At best, the plan was lunacy, and at least, it was treason, no matter how forcibly Conner denied it. No sane person could hope to turn an orphan into a prince in two weeks. And a person would have to be even crazier to think that this orphan could then convince an entire court he was a long-lost prince.

Tobias politely voiced these same concerns, but was waved off by Conner, who asked, "Do you always think small, boy?"

Tobias swallowed. "No, sir."

"Do you think this is too ambitious?"

"I just —" Tobias found his courage. "It seems like what you want would be impossible."

"Nothing's impossible. I haven't come to this plan lightly or without a great deal of thought. But to succeed, I must have a boy who believes this can happen."

"I believe it," Roden said.

I snorted. Conner turned to me. "You don't believe it's possible?"

"Just because it's possible doesn't mean it's wise."

With arched eyebrows, Conner said, "And you claim to have this wisdom?"

"I claim to have nothing, sir."

"That is a good starting place. Now, Tobias, stand up." Tobias stood, looking as nervous as if he were about to be asked the one most important question in the world, and he had no answer. As it turned out, Conner planned on doing all the talking.

Conner said, "You have the right shade of hair. The face is a little narrower than I would have expected for the prince, but the resemblance has potential. Your height is acceptable and build is trim, like the queen's. I like that you have education, but you are not as quick a thinker as I would want. If someone were to question you with an answer you did not know, I fear you might hesitate and spoil the plan."

Tobias reacted to Conner's assessment like he'd been punched. I couldn't understand why it bothered him so much. None of what Conner said were things Tobias had any control over. And it wasn't like Conner would find anyone he considered a perfect candidate.

Next, Conner ordered Roden to stand. "Less of a resemblance to the prince when he was last seen, but a strong resemblance to the queen's family, so we may convince people of your identity. Your ambition and determination is admirable, though you often lack confidence when necessary. You are completely uneducated, which may also prove a problem. However, you're physically strong, which will give you an advantage with the sword and on horseback."

Conner told him he could sit, but Roden remained standing and said, "Sir, now that I know what it is you're seeking, I can make myself into this prince."

"Sit," Conner repeated, unimpressed by Roden's pleas. He nodded his head at me and I stood. "You have the entirely wrong color of hair, though we might color it over with the proper dyes. You show a preference for the left hand when it absolutely must be the right. Nor are you as tall or strong as one might expect from the son of King Eckbert. You look the youngest of the three boys, though any of you will have to lie about your exact age. How are you at learning accents?"

"You ask if I can learn a Carthyan accent in two weeks?" I asked.

"You cannot claim the throne of Carthya while sounding like an Avenian."

"It doesn't matter," I said. "I don't want the throne. Choose Roden or Tobias, and I'll leave and go where you'll never see me again."

Conner's face twisted in anger. "Do you think I care a devil's inch what you want? You are here because, despite a few physical setbacks, you have seeds of the personality I might expect for Prince Jaron. If we can weed out your bad manners and defiant nature, I suspect you could convince the nobles that you are him."

"If you weed those out, then there's nothing left of me," I said. "You'd strip those away and find I'm as boring as Tobias or predictable as Roden. Why don't you take their physical similarities to the prince and give them a personality?"

It was a rhetorical question. I didn't actually think either of them could adopt a personality.

"Prince Jaron was a fighter," Conner said. "You've done nothing but fight since we met."

"And if you try to use me for this fraud, then I'll continue fighting," I said. "You don't want a prince, you want a puppet. You've taken on this plan in secret. Why? Maybe you can't sit on the throne, but you plan to rule from behind it. Put Roden on the throne. He'll happily let you guide his arms and feed him with the words he should say next. I won't!"

"Lower your voice," Conner said. "I have no intention of ruling. Of course, at the end of two weeks, none of you will know enough about ruling to take that on alone. I will be there, to guide you as an adviser, to protect you, and to guard our secret. When you are ready to rule alone, I will serve in any capacity you choose for me." Conner held out a hand to me. "I'm offering to make you the sun of Carthya, brighter than the moon and stars combined. And you will take the throne, knowing that you have pulled your country back from the brink of war. How can you refuse this opportunity, Sage?"

"Carthya's not my country," I said, reaching for the doors to leave. "Frankly, I hope Avenia destroys it."

# · ELEVEN ·

Mott was waiting alone on the other side of the doors. Obviously, he knew what would be discussed in there and had chased the other servants away.

I stopped when I saw him, cringing a bit as I waited for him to clunk me over the head or commit some other act to force me back into Conner's dining room. There was no cowardice in my nervousness. His hits came without mercy.

But he only nodded at me. "You clean up well, for an orphan."

"I had help."

"Where were you going?"

I scratched an itch on my face. "Didn't really think that through yet. Somewhere I can be alone."

Mott apparently had no inclinations to leave me alone. He put an arm on my shoulder and steered me down the hallway. "Come with me."

We walked outside to a courtyard in the rear of Farthenwood lined with torches that flickered in the breeze.

On one wall were several swords. Each was different. One had a longer blade, another was thinner, another was jagged on one side. The tangs varied, from swords with a simple metal grip to ones wrapped in leather or crowned in jewels. One might appeal to a lifelong warrior, another to a mercenary. I suspected that one of these was supposed to appeal to a prince.

"Choose one," he said.

"How do I know the one that's right for me?"

"It's the one that calls to you," Mott said.

I reached for one with a medium-size blade with a wide fuller grooved down the length. The hilt was wrapped in dark brown leather, and a circle of deep red rubies was set into the pommel. Almost as soon as I grabbed it, the sword fell from my grasp and landed on the ground.

Mott darted forward and retrieved it, like I'd committed some sort of sin by dropping the sword.

"This is obviously too heavy for you," he said. "Choose another one."

"It was heavier than it looked, but it's fine now," I said, lifting it with both hands. "I chose it because it called to me."

"Why?"

I smiled. "It has rubies on it. I could sell those for a lot of money."

"Try it and I'll use this same sword to run you through as punishment. Have you ever held a sword before?"

"Sure." I'd once held the sword of the Archduke of Montegrist after sneaking into a room where he was staying. I'd taken it, just to admire of course, while he was asleep one night, but I hadn't held it for long before I was caught. My punishment was thorough, but it had been worth it just for a few minutes of holding a sword as fine as his.

"What's your training with a sword?" Mott asked.

"I suspect not enough to make a fair match between you and me."

Mott smiled. "I heard what Conner said to you in the dining room. Despite what he describes as your limitations, you do have a chance to take the role of the prince. But you must learn and train and give yourself every advantage you can. Now raise your sword." He demonstrated, holding his sword upright, nearly parallel to his body, and tilted outward. "Like this. This is first position."

I followed him and moved my sword as he did. "Like this?"

"Get used to the feel of it in your hand. Swing it back and forth. Learn to control it, to balance it."

I obeyed. Despite its weight, I liked the feel of the sword. I liked *me* with this sword in my hand. It stirred up memories of how I used to be, before the day-to-day survival that comes with living in an orphanage.

Still in first position, Mott said, "This is where you begin any basic attack."

"So I should avoid it, then," I said.

Mott raised an eyebrow. "Why is that?"

"If it's that basic, then it's the first move everyone learns, which means everyone knows how to defend against that one."

Mott shook his head. "It doesn't work that way. Sword fighting isn't a chess game where you make one move, then so does your opponent."

I sighed. "Obviously."

Mott pulled a wooden sword off the wall, comparable to mine in length. "Let's test you, then. See how you do for a beginner."

"Should I use a wooden sword too?"

That made Mott smile. "Even with a wooden sword, I can still do more damage to you than you'll do to me with that real one."

As soon as he finished speaking, he cut a line through the air past my sword and hit my shoulder.

"Would you at least try to stop me?" he asked.

I made a face and thrust my sword at him, but he parried it. "Not bad," Mott said. "But be bolder. Prince Jaron was known for that."

"Sounds like he's dead. So whatever his boldness was with a sword, it obviously didn't save him."

"Nobody could have survived so many pirates," Mott said. "Nobody on that ship did survive."

"And they probably all had swords," I said, swiping at empty air when Mott took a step backward. "So training me with one is useless."

"Relax your body," Mott said. "You're too tense."

"Why me?" I asked, lowering my sword. "Why am I here?"

"Why shouldn't you be?"

"Tobias is smarter than me, and Roden is stronger. Apparently, I have only slight resemblance to what he feels the prince would look like today."

Mott lowered his sword as well. "Tobias may be more educated than you, but I have no doubt you're cleverer. Roden is stronger, but a strong heart will always overcome a strong body." He smiled. "And as for the physical resemblance, it would help if you cut your hair and stood up straighter. I can't see your face half the time you're speaking. Now raise your sword. Your problem is that you're trying to hit my sword. Hit me."

"I'd hurt you."

"This is a sword fight, Sage. That's the idea."

I raised my sword and lunged at him. He stepped toward me and slid his sword up the inside of my blade, then rotated and pushed it down. My sword fell from my hand and clattered to the ground.

"Pick it up," Mott said.

After glaring at him for a moment, I picked it up, but I held it blade down, making it clear that I was finished with this lesson.

He frowned at me. "I had you figured wrong. I thought you'd be more of a fighter."

"Fighting for what? The privilege of getting myself killed one day like Eckbert's family? Even if I did what Conner wants, I'd never feel like a prince. I'd only be playing the part, nothing more than an actor for the rest of my life."

"And what are you now?" Mott lowered his own sword. "You put on a façade of toughness, but I've seen you look frightened. You pretend to care for nobody, but I didn't miss your reaction when Latamer fell. And you pretend that you could run from your family in Avenia without looking back, but I hear the tone of your voice when you speak of them. I don't think you hate everyone half so much as you claim to. You're an actor now, Sage. All Conner wants is for you to act on behalf of Carthya, rather than for yourself."

Mott had hit closer to the truth than he realized. I didn't want to think about my fears, or about Latamer, or especially about my family. I handed him the sword and said, "Thanks for the lesson, but I'll never be a prince."

"Interesting that you chose this sword, then," Mott said. "It's a replica of the one Prince Jaron once owned. If Conner can look at you and see a prince, then it's about time you did the same."

## · TWELVE ·

Mott escorted me back inside Farthenwood. It was clear that his orders were to see I was never left alone. He described to me in detail how the copy of Jaron's sword had been forged only off a drawing Conner's father once made from memory, since Jaron's sword had been lost when his ship was attacked. I cared nothing about the story and didn't even pretend to listen.

"I should probably go back to the dining room," I mumbled.

"You're sweaty now. A gentleman would never enter a dining room smelling as you and I do."

"Then where?"

"Back to your room. Roden and Tobias will join you before too long."

"There's nothing to do in my room."

"Get some sleep. Tomorrow begins your training for Conner's plan, and I assure you it will be exhausting."

"Are you going to chain yourself to me again?"

He smiled. "Of course not. But your room will be guarded.

If you try to escape, the vigil will catch you and then notify me. Please believe me when I say you don't want to disturb my sleep for a second night in a row."

"Are you one of Conner's servants too?" I asked Mott. "Does he own you?"

"I serve him, but he doesn't own me. My father worked for his father, so it was natural I should work for the son. I believe in him, Sage. I hope in time you'll believe in him too."

"He killed Latamer. After telling him he was free to go, he killed him."

"To be technical, Cregan killed Latamer, although it was on Conner's orders." Mott was silent for a moment, then said, "Master Conner is not aspiring to be a priest and asks for no hero worship. But he is a patriot, Sage, doing what he believes is best for Carthya. Latamer never should've been chosen to come with us. It was better that he die than fail in the challenges over these next two weeks."

"I think Conner wanted us to see him kill Latamer. Then we'd know how serious he is about this plan."

"Perhaps," Mott said. "And if that was his idea, then it certainly worked."

I stopped walking for a moment, forcing Mott to stop and look at me. In a soft voice, I said, "The two boys who don't get chosen for his plan — is he going to kill them too?"

Mott put his hand on my shoulder and pressed me forward again. "He has to protect the secrecy of his plan. See that you get chosen, Sage."

Errol was waiting on a bench near my room when we arrived. Mott asked him to take me into my room and assist me with dressing for bed.

"I don't need help dressing," I said to them both. "I solved the mystery of how to button a shirt long ago."

"Help him," Mott repeated.

Errol looked at me, silently pleading with me to accept the order so he wouldn't have to face Mott. I sighed loudly enough for Mott to take notice of my annoyance, and then nodded my head at Errol. "Fine. Let's get this over with."

Mott waited outside. Errol shut the door and began rummaging through the drawers of my wardrobe while I explored the room. Mrs. Turbeldy could have crammed every boy at the orphanage into a room of this size, and it seemed like a waste of space to have only three beds in here. In sharp contrast to anything I ever experienced at the orphanage, the mattresses on these beds were deep and the blankets thick. Each bed had a small wardrobe beside it, and a desk was near the center of the room, facing a fireplace. The thought that I might never again have to live like I had at the orphanage filled my mind. If only that new life wouldn't come at such a high price.

"Which is my bed?" I asked.

Errol pointed to one at the far end of the room. "That one."

"I want this one, near the window."

"That was meant for Master Roden."

"*Master* Roden?"

Errol missed the sarcasm. "Yes, sir."

"Well, *Master* Roden can have my bed. I'm taking this one next to the window."

"Master Roden has already been informed that this is his bed."

I pulled the covers apart and then spit on the pillow. "Tell him what I've done. If he still wants it, he'll be sleeping with my spit."

Errol smiled. "Yes, sir. Are you ready to dress?"

I held out my arms and let Errol do the work. He worked quickly and quietly, which only made me feel more ridiculous.

"Errol, while we ate, there was a server girl. About my age, dark hair, dark eyes."

"Her name is Imogen, sir. She came to us a year ago."

"How?"

"Conner raised the rent on her family's home. They fell further and further into debt. Conner made an offer for Imogen to come work the debt off, though with the high rates on her family's home, she never will."

"Why her?"

"Most of us think it's revenge. Imogen's mother is widowed. Conner proposed marriage to her years ago, but she refused. Some believe he wanted Imogen here so he could marry her instead when she became of age, but he quickly lost interest and assigned her to the kitchen."

"Why?"

"She's a mute, sir. Not particularly bright, either. She

performs her duties but will never be anything more than a kitchen servant. There, you're dressed."

I laughed as I looked down at my nightclothes. Maybe I was too accustomed to sleeping in my clothes, but I felt overdressed.

"What's this?" I asked, tugging at the outer garment.

"A robe. You'll remove this before actually getting into the bed."

"But I'm right here. I'm three steps from my bed."

Errol smiled again. Something about me frequently amused him. "Would you like me to remove the robe for you?"

"No. I'll do it myself."

"Can I do anything else for you tonight?"

"Where are my clothes I came here with?"

"I saved them for you, sir. They're being washed."

"They didn't need to be washed."

Errol coughed. "I assure you they did, but I'll keep them just as they were otherwise." He busied himself with folding my clothes from the afternoon. "When they're returned to your drawer, will I have anything in return?"

If he was hoping for a reward now, he'd be disappointed. I nodded curtly at him. "When they're in my drawer, you will. You can go now, Errol. Tell the others to come in quietly because I'll be asleep."

Errol closed the doors of my wardrobe. I saw Mott peek in at me while the doors were opened, but when they closed I was finally alone.

I opened the window, intending to climb out, but stopped as the cool evening breeze brushed against my face. Now the emotions washed over me like a tide. Conner's plan was worse than I'd anticipated, and no matter what Mott had said, I knew I wasn't up to the challenge. I looked out into the dark night and wondered how long it would take me to run the length of Conner's property. Beyond that was a river that would mask my escape. I could walk all night and for as long as it took until I got to Avenia, to freedom.

But I couldn't do it. Now that I knew his secret, Conner would never stop hunting me down. I was trapped here. And my choice was clear. Become the prince, or he'd kill me.

# · THIRTEEN ·

The next morning, my eyes opened before the servants came to wake us. The soft pastel light of morning seeped through the window at a low angle, so it must have been very early. I lay in bed for several seconds, orienting myself to the unfamiliar feelings of warmth and comfort. Then I remembered where I was and the strange game I was caught up in. The reality was stark and cold. I sat up in bed to have a better look outside.

"You awake too?" Roden asked quietly.

"Couldn't sleep any longer."

"I hardly slept at all." There was silence for a moment, then Roden asked, "What do you think happens to those boys Conner doesn't choose?"

Neither of us lingered too long on the convenience of speaking of "those boys," as if they were strangers. After a slow exhale, I said, "You know the answer."

Roden sighed as if he had hoped I'd have something better to offer. "The saddest thing is there won't be anyone to miss us when we're gone. No family, no friends, no one waiting at home."

"It's better that way," I said. "It'll be easier for me, knowing my death doesn't add to anyone's pain."

"If you can't give anyone pain, then you can't give them joy either." Roden clasped his hands behind his head and stared up at the plaster ceiling. "We're nobodies, Sage. I should've left the orphanage months ago, but I couldn't do it. With no education or skills, there was nothing for me on the outside. How would I have earned my keep?"

"Tobias would be fine on his own," I said. "He could work in a trade or open a shop. He'd probably have been pretty successful."

"What were your plans?" Roden asked.

I shrugged. "Everything for me was just staying alive for another week." The irony struck me as funny. "Now I just have to live out the next two weeks."

"Conner has to choose me," Roden said. "It's not about becoming king or anything — we all know it's Conner who'll have the power. But for me, it might be my only chance in life. I know that sounds harsh because of what it means for you and Tobias, but that's just how I feel. You know the other day when you nearly got away from us in the wagon?"

"Yeah."

"I wish you'd have made it. And if you have the chance to run sometime in the next two weeks, I think you should take it."

"Good to know, Roden." He'd like things to be that easy.

"Why don't you two talk a little louder and maybe you can wake the entire estate?" Tobias said with a groan.

"Hush," I said. "Soon as they know we're awake, we'll get people in here."

Tobias sat up on one arm. "You and Roden have been chatting like old friends all this time and now you tell me to hush?"

"Hush," Roden said.

Tobias lay back down. "I wonder what Conner has planned for us today."

"We have two weeks to learn everything Prince Jaron would know," Roden said. "I think this might be the last moment of quiet we'll have until then."

"It's really not a bad plan," Tobias said. "Conner's right. This might be the only way to save Carthya."

"It's an insult to the real prince," I said. "When this is discovered — and we all know that one day it will be — what we are doing here will be worse than treason. For a nobody orphan to pretend to be a prince? Who do we think we are?"

"Calm down," Tobias said. "Who says it will be discovered one day? Conner will be there at every step to guide us. He has to, because he'll hang, too, if we're found out."

"None of us is a perfect fit to what the prince should look like now," I continued. "Not to mention that two weeks isn't nearly enough time to learn everything he would know, whether Conner's there or not. If we three stick together, he can't force us to do this."

"But I want to do it." Tobias sat up and swung his feet out of bed. "You two can lie around if you want, but I intend to start learning what I need to as soon as possible."

He surprised the servants in the hallway, who insisted they had been waiting for us, though their sleepy eyes said otherwise. Errol dug into the drawers of my wardrobe, stifling a yawn.

"You can go back to bed if you want," I told him. "I'm fine here."

"You don't give the orders," Errol reminded me. "Conner does. Your clothes will be more casual today, to allow for the afternoon activities."

Reluctantly, I rolled out of bed so I could get dressed and Errol could get lost. I made Errol stand there while I dressed myself, although he insisted on inspecting me when it was finished. "Not to offend you," he said as I fumbled with a buckle, "but it's obvious you've never dressed in clothes such as these."

I smiled. "If I have my way, I won't have to dress in them much longer."

Mott was waiting for us as we left the bedroom. He informed Tobias that he'd be working with a tutor in the library while Roden and I were trained in the basics of reading and writing upstairs in a room that had long ago been converted from a nursery. Tobias smirked at us as his servant escorted him away. He probably figured that being more educated gave him an advantage with Conner, and he was probably right. Roden whispered to me that he wouldn't want to study with Tobias anyway. I agreed.

Our tutor was a man who instructed us to call him Master Graves, an appropriate name since he looked more like a grave-digger than a teacher. He was tall and thin as a shovel with pale skin and limp black hair that he combed in a way to make it appear as though he had more hair than he really did. I imme-diately decided to dislike him. Roden, however, seemed to be keeping an open mind about whether he was in fact a member of the walking dead. At least, when I whispered this possibility to Roden, he smothered a grin and quickly told me to hush.

Master Graves directed Roden and me to sit in chairs that were clearly intended for small children and faced a chalkboard. He began to write the alphabet, and then said to me, "I told you to sit down and we'll get started."

Roden looked up. He was already seated with his knees halfway up his chest.

I folded my arms resolutely. "I'm not sitting in a chair meant for a five-year-old. Get me a real chair."

Master Graves arched his head so that he could better look down on me. "You are Sage, obviously. I was warned about you. Young man, do not mistake me for one of Conner's servants. I am a gentleman and a scholar, and I will have your respect. You will sit in the chair I have available."

Since he was clearly still around to keep me from running away, I called for Mott to come in. When he ducked his head in the room, I said, "Master Graves thinks he's not one of Conner's servants. But you are. I need a chair."

"You have one," he said, nodding to the one beside Roden.

"It's too small. I can't learn that way."

"Too bad. Sit down."

"Okay, but when Roden and I don't learn our letters, you can explain to Conner why."

Mott sighed and left the room. He returned several minutes later with a larger chair in each hand. Master Graves was incensed and said, as punishment for my disruption, I would have to write my letters an extra ten times that day.

"Ten times the better I'll know them, then," I said. "How strange that you should punish me by ensuring I come out more educated than Roden, who has tried to obey you."

Graves's knuckles were nearly as white as the chalk when he began instructing us on the sounds of the letters. Roden actually seemed interested and tried hard to keep up with Graves. I fell asleep around the letter *M*.

Graves was gone when Mott shook me awake some time later. "He called you incorrigible," Mott said. "Honestly, Sage, are you trying to fail?"

"I already told you I could read a little. This morning was a waste of my time."

"I thought it was great." Roden sounded happier than I'd ever heard him. "I never expected to be able to read, and Master Graves said he'll have me in a children's reader by tomorrow."

"Great. Let me know what the children's reader has to say about impersonating a prince."

Earlier that morning, servants had brought us a small breakfast of hard-boiled eggs and milk to eat while we studied.

With such a paltry beginning, it was no surprise that both Roden and I were already hungry again.

"You'll eat after your next lessons," Mott said.

"What lessons?" I asked.

"History of Carthya. Then a lunch. Then you'll do sword fighting, horseback riding, dinner and etiquette with the master, and tonight you will study in preparation for your lessons tomorrow."

Roden slapped me on the shoulder. "He'll make gentlemen of us yet!"

I nodded but stayed silent. The thought of what Conner was making us into deserved no celebration.

# · FOURTEEN ·

All three of us shared the afternoon history lessons, which was a waste of Tobias's time because he already knew the answer to every question. He spoke so quickly, there was no point in Roden and I even attempting to speak, even if we had known the answers.

Our history tutor was Mistress Havala, who Tobias said had taught him other lessons earlier that day. She was past the age of marriage, which was curious because she seemed like a pleasant enough person. She had a round face with curly black hair that bounced a lot, and made a great effort to avoid any discussion of the real reasons why Conner had brought us here, even though it was clear she knew. There was a nervousness about her, yet her easy smile and gentle nature were a welcome respite from the serious demeanor everyone else on this estate seemed to have. I wondered what would happen to her at the end of these two weeks.

When she stepped out to ask for a drink of water, I told Tobias and Roden of my concerns. Tobias shrugged it off.

"She'll be fine. She told me that Conner asked her never to talk about teaching us."

"Threatened her, more likely," I muttered.

Defensively, Tobias arched his head. "If she doesn't talk, then it won't matter what Conner did."

"It always matters." I looked to Roden to agree with me, but his head was buried in the book in front of him as he tried to figure out the word at his fingertip.

We all fell into silence as Mistress Havala returned. Tobias lapsed into a sort of daydream until Roden and I failed to answer her next question, which he then answered without hesitation.

Mistress Havala was an excellent tutor, and by the end of the class session, we could all name the major Carthyan cities and describe their contributions to the country. Fortunately for us, few cities in Carthya can be considered major, so it was easy to learn them. Unfortunately for Carthya, their contributions to the country are equally unimpressive. The new prince would need to work hard to build up production of our natural resources. Predictably, Tobias announced he was up to the challenge. Mistress Havala raised an eyebrow at his words but said nothing.

There was a knock at the door, and two servants entered, carrying what I guessed was our lunch. I didn't know the first girl who entered, but the second servant was Imogen. She looked at me, gave her usual frown, then lowered her eyes. They set the trays down and left.

Mistress Havala placed the book she'd been teaching us from on her desk, then handed us each a meat pie wrapped in a thick pastry. I ate mine in four bites and turned to Tobias, who was only halfway through his. "Can I have the rest of yours?"

Tobias laughed, but I hadn't been joking. He finished the rest of his pie without answering me while Mistress Havala continued on.

After our history lessons, Mott returned and escorted us to Conner's stables. Cregan was waiting for us there. His arms were folded so tightly as we approached, I briefly wondered if they were knotted. "That's right," he said grumpily. "I'll be teaching you to ride." After Mott was gone, he pointed to a saddle balanced on the top of a fence. "Let's start here. This is what you sit on to ride a horse."

"You can't be serious," I said. "Are you really going to treat us like it's the first time we've seen a horse? We can all ride."

"I don't know what your skills are —" Cregan said.

"My skills are better than yours," I said. "I can outride you with my eyes closed. Probably so can Tobias and Roden."

Cregan's eyes narrowed. "Better than my skills? I'm not just a rider. I'm a trainer. I break wild horses and I can break you."

I ignored that last part and said, "I can ride anything you can ride."

Cregan smiled. "You won't bait me so easily, boy."

"Why not?" Tobias said. "If he says he can ride, why not test his skills?"

Cregan stared at Tobias, then me, then said, "All right. Wait here." And walked back into the stalls.

"Thanks," I said to Tobias.

Tobias glanced sideways at me. "I'm not on your side, Sage. Hopefully, this will teach you a lesson."

Our attention was diverted by a crashing sound in the stables. Slowly, I shook my head and mumbled to Tobias, "You don't think he has an untrained horse in there, do you?"

"Sounds like it," Tobias said.

"Can you ride?" Roden asked me.

"I've ridden before. Is that the same thing?"

"No," Tobias said flatly. "*I* can ride, but I'm not stupid enough to challenge Cregan to a wild horse."

"Just apologize and tell Cregan you want lessons," Roden said.

"And let everyone hold that over my head?" I asked. "I'll just ride the horse in a circle or two. It'll be fine."

Cregan was practically laughing aloud as he escorted a horse outside the stables. It was already trying to buck, and it was work for him to hold on to the reins. Cregan grinned wickedly. "So you can outride me?"

I backed up two steps. My father had warned me about my quick tongue countless times. Perhaps he should have warned me more often. "It doesn't matter whether I could beat you or not. You're the tutor here."

That seemed to offend Cregan. His voice rose in pitch as he said, "And as your tutor, I'm ordering you onto this horse."

I shook my head. "I'm not riding that horse. Get me a tamer one and I'll do it. You just know you'll lose if you play fair."

Cregan walked so close that I could feel his breath on me. "Scared?"

"Yeah." I was. It was a fierce horse.

"Then it's a good time to teach you some humility. Get on the horse or face the consequences."

"Leave him alone. Sage was just talking big," Roden said.

Cregan pointed a finger at Roden. "Sage won't help you in the end, boy. Don't you help him." Then he looked at me. "If you don't ride this horse now, then you won't ride again during the next two weeks. I'll tell Conner you failed here."

After a very long moment, I reached for the reins. "Fine. But I need help getting up."

Cregan laughed. "Can't even mount a horse by yourself?"

"It's a riding contest, not a mounting one. Where's your horse?"

Cregan's laugh widened. "You'll fall off so quickly, I wouldn't even have time to get into a saddle." He steadied the horse while I climbed on.

The horse bucked and I had to grip tightly to stay in the saddle. "He doesn't like me," I said.

"You should be used to that," Cregan said. "And Windstorm is a she." With a laugh, he slapped the horse on the backside.

Windstorm took off with a fury at her feet, throwing me hard against the curve of the saddle. She bucked twice, and I managed to hold on only because it entertained the devils to help me do it. Behind me, Cregan was laughing boisterously. Maybe Roden and Tobias were too; it was hard to tell with the world jostling around me. I yelped and held on as she pulled free of Cregan's control and we sprinted away.

Windstorm headed directly for a tree, as if she knew the low-hanging limb could knock me off. I ducked in time to avoid the worst of it, though some of the smaller branches scraped my shoulders as we passed beneath them.

Somewhere behind us, Cregan yelled for me to come back, but Windstorm was on a full gallop to freedom. Cregan was left with the reality that by the time he got a horse to follow me, I'd be long gone. And I was on a horse running so fast that if I fell off, I was facing more than a few broken bones. Or worse.

# · FIFTEEN ·

It was nearly dark before I heard them calling for me. I didn't answer the first few times. They weren't close enough to hear me, so there was no point in using up what little energy I had left.

Finally, Mott passed close enough that I could see him through the trees. He was on horseback and carried a lantern.

"The devils have you, Sage, answer me! Where are you?"

"Over here," I called. I had hoped it would be Mott who found me. If it had been Cregan, he'd have likely beaten the last of my strength from me as punishment. But Mott seemed to hate me less. I might have a chance with him.

He found me lying on the bank of the river, legs half submerged in the water. The water was cold and my legs had gone numb long ago, but numb was preferable to the ache I'd felt before.

Mott cantered over and slid off his horse. "There you are," he said, sounding more relieved than angry. "How'd you get so far away?"

Most of it was a blur in my mind, so I didn't bother answering.

Mott crouched beside me. "I told Conner he's a fool to consider using you as his prince."

"Princes ride in carriages, not on horseback," I said.

"As it so happens, a prince will often ride on horseback."

"Not with *that* horse."

Mott grinned. "No, not that horse. Where is she?"

"Long gone. I can't even tell you which direction."

"Conner will be furious. He was going to have her broken soon. Are you hurt?"

"I think bruises are the worst of it. She stopped to get a drink of water and I fell off."

Mott chuckled. "You stayed on through the ride and fell off when she stopped? Cregan's going to laugh all night about that."

I rolled the rest of the way out of the stream and pulled my legs up close to me. "Just tell him I stayed on through the ride. Or he'll make lessons just as bad tomorrow."

"Sorry, but at some point, you will have to learn that you can't say whatever you want to whomever you want. There are consequences for your sharp tongue, and this is one of them. I hope it will prove to be your most valuable lesson today."

*Valuable lessons* were code words for pain that no one apologized for. I'd had enough of them for a lifetime. "I'm cold. Can we go back?"

"You've got a cut on your cheek."

I brushed a finger over it, though in the darkness of the woods and with my dirty hand, it was hard to tell if there was any blood on it. It didn't feel wet. "I think it's stopped bleeding."

"Conner won't like that. He doesn't want to present a prince at court who's got cuts and bruises all over him."

"It'll heal by then." Mott extended an arm to help me onto the back of his horse. I stared at the ground for a moment, and then looked up at him. "I need your help, Mott. Conner's never going to choose me just as I am."

Mott took my hand and lifted me up. "Not as you are right now. Let's get you back and cleaned up."

"Did I miss sword fighting?"

"We canceled it to look for you."

"What about dinner?"

"They're eating right now."

"I can only imagine how Roden and Tobias will talk about me to Conner." It'd be a miracle if they didn't talk him into hanging me at his earliest convenience.

Mott began riding us back to the stables. The springtime night had cooled, and I shivered in my wet clothes. Mott must have felt sorry for me because he spent most of the ride instructing me on how to manage a wild horse. Unfortunately, I had other things on my mind, so I missed most of the lecture. Too bad, because what I did hear actually sounded interesting.

Then Mott asked, "What's your interest in Imogen?"

I shrugged. "Nothing. Why?"

"She passed me a note earlier today asking me to stop you from looking at her. So I'll ask again, what's your interest?"

"There's nothing," I insisted. "It's just that she seems so anxious all the time. Is she safe here?"

Mott hesitated a moment, then said, "When the servants feel one of them has been singled out or favored, they tend to get jealous. That can become dangerous."

I pondered that. "So you're saying when I look at Imogen, it makes things worse for her?"

"It could, yes."

Which left a horrible feeling inside me. I'd only looked at her to understand the cause of her fear, when in fact the cause of her fear was me looking at her.

As we neared the stables several minutes later, Mott said, "We were in a debate over whether you really can ride."

"Oh?"

"Conner said he thought you could. He figured you had goaded Cregan into letting you have a horse so you could ride to your freedom. We weren't sure we'd see you again after tonight."

I chuckled lightly. "Yeah, that would've been a good plan."

"So can you ride?" Mott asked. "Or are you really so stupid as to have gotten on a horse that was bucking like that?"

My soft laughter widened, then I grabbed my chest. "It hurts to laugh. I must've bruised a rib. If you want me to tell you I'm that stupid, I will. The evidence is there."

Mott shook his head. "You don't have to say it, Sage. But you do have to get yourself under control. These two weeks are going to pass fast, and you're far behind the others."

## · SIXTEEN ·

The aromas of spiced meat and fresh-baked bread were inescapable as Mott and I entered Farthenwood through a back entrance. The kitchen wasn't far away.

"I'm getting dinner, right?" I asked.

"Someone will bring it to your room — after your bath."

"Tell me, Mott, is it true that the wealthy smell worse than the poor?"

Mott arched an eyebrow. "Why do you say that?"

"It seems since joining Conner's household that I've needed to bathe much more often. My fleas have all but abandoned me."

"Let's hope so," Mott said with a chuckle. Then he handed me off to Errol for another scrubbing in a bath that had been set up in a corner of our bedroom.

My bath was so quick, Errol said he doubted I could have gotten entirely clean. I told him it was good enough considering I'd only get dirty tomorrow and not to push the matter. He didn't.

"Where's my dinner?" I growled. "Conner nearly starved us today."

"Someone should have it here shortly," Errol said. "You should hurry and dress."

"Then get out and wait for it. Knock when it gets here."

Errol nodded and left the room while I fumbled with my nightclothes. I checked the drawer again for my old clothes, but they still weren't there. I'd speak with Errol if they weren't back tomorrow.

A knock came to the door and I yelled at Errol to enter while I pulled the robe around myself.

Someone sniffed and I turned. Imogen stood in the doorway, holding a tray of dinner. She clearly wished someone else had been ordered to bring the food. For that matter, so did I.

"I thought you were Errol," I said. As if that would make any difference.

Imogen glanced at the door as if to indicate he was still in the hallway. Then she held up the tray and shrugged.

"Oh, right." I pointed to a table near Tobias's bed. He had a few papers laid out that were full of notes. He was studying material more advanced than Roden and I would ever get to before the two weeks ended.

Imogen set the tray down and started to leave, but I said, "Wait!"

It hadn't really occurred to me what to say at this point, nor could she respond to anything I might come up with. Finally, I mumbled, "I'm sorry. If I caused you any trouble, then I'm sorry for that."

She nodded what I hoped was an acceptance of my apology, and even offered something close to a smile.

"I'm Sage," I finally said. "Strange, I know, but who gets to choose their name?"

She pointed to herself and I said, "Yes, I know. You're Imogen."

She started to leave again, but I added, "Could you help me with something? I need a thread and needle. I ripped one of my shirts out on that horse ride and I've got to sew it up."

Imogen held out her hands, indicating she would sew it for me. But I shook my head. "I'd rather do it myself. If Conner finds out I've torn his new clothes, I'll get in trouble. Can you get me the needle?"

She nodded, and pointed at the cut on my face.

"It's okay. I get hurt a lot. I'm used to it."

Tiny wrinkles formed between her brows. She opened her mouth as if there were something she wanted to say, then closed it and lowered her hand.

"You are too familiar, Imogen." Tobias's servant marched into the room. He picked up a book from a shelf near the door and hurled it at her, hitting her in the back. "You were supposed to give him the food, then get out!"

In an instant, I got Imogen behind me, then pulled out a knife that had been under my pillow and held it out to the servant. "How dare you?" I yelled, so angry the words sputtered from my mouth.

"She's just a kitchen girl." The servant stiffened, alarmed by my reaction but clearly confused too.

I swiped the knife through the air, forcing him to back up. He gave a cry for help, and looked around like he wanted to run, but I had him cornered.

Hearing the commotion, Mott ran in. "Lower the knife, Sage." His eyes widened. "That's mine!" He lifted the leg of his trousers, where the knife had been sheathed. "When did you — oh, the horse ride back."

"I needed a knife to cut the meat. They didn't give me one."

Mott inched toward me and held out his hand. "Give it back, Sage. Now."

I reversed the blade and gave the knife to him by the handle. "Did you see what he did to her?"

Mott gently put a hand on Imogen's shoulder. "You may go, girl."

Imogen didn't look at me as she left the room. And I didn't stop glaring at Tobias's servant.

"He's not welcome in this room anymore," I said to Mott. "He shouldn't work for Conner another minute after what I just saw."

"You may go as well," Mott told the servant, who tripped over his own feet in his hurry to leave the room. Mott stared at his knife a moment, then wiped the blade with his shirt as if I'd dirtied it. "Your mother was kitchen staff, I believe."

"Barmaid."

"Same thing. Obviously, you have some sympathy for Imogen."

"It has nothing to do with that. She didn't do anything wrong and he threw a book at her!"

"And do you think you helped her just now? Do you think that made anything better for her?"

I kicked at the floor, angry with myself, and angry with Mott too, though for no clear reason. Maybe because I hated it when he was right.

"She's well treated here," Mott continued. "Tobias's servant will be disciplined, and you should be on your knees thanking me for not reporting this to Conner. What I want to know is why you took my knife."

"I told you, I can't cut the meat without one."

"Do you feel you're in danger here?"

"From Roden and Tobias?" I shook my head. "No."

"From me? Conner?"

"You work for Conner. If there's any danger from him, there's danger from you."

Mott didn't disagree. He couldn't. He replaced his knife in the sheath strapped to his ankle, then pointed at the dinner. "Eat up and get a good night's sleep. Tomorrow will be harder than today."

"There's nothing to do up here but stare at Tobias's stack of books."

"Try to read one. It could only help you."

"I'd rather join the others. It's not fair that I'm kept up here while Roden and Tobias get to show off to Conner."

"Conner is furious with you for losing a prize mare. Trust me when I say it's better that you stay up here tonight."

"It'd take a miracle for Conner to choose me as prince." Despite the truth of my words, I couldn't help but smile.

"Yes," Mott agreed, and then added, "Though I doubt even a miracle could save you now."

# · SEVENTEEN ·

I was already in bed when Tobias and Roden came in. If they realized that I might be asleep, they spoke to me anyway.

"We heard about the trick you pulled with Mott's knife," Roden said. "Conner wanted to give you a few lashes, but Mott said he handled it with you already."

"Who's my dressing servant now?" Tobias asked.

"Dress yourself," I muttered. "You've managed for your entire life until now."

"Conner's made us into gentlemen," he said. "A gentleman would never stoop to dress himself."

"If he put us in dresses, we wouldn't suddenly become women," I said. "You're an orphan in a costume, Tobias. Nothing more."

Roden's servant was in the room, gathering Roden's night-clothes. Tobias looked at him and said, "Build us a fire."

Roden and I both groaned. "It's already warm enough," Roden said. "Do you want to cook us in our beds tonight?"

Tobias began gathering the papers on the desk near his bed. "I want to burn these."

"Why?" I asked, propping myself up by my elbows. "What's on them?"

"Notes I've made in studying to be the prince. I don't want you or Roden to read them and gain from my efforts."

"Neither of us can read," Roden said. "It's chicken scratch on those pages as far as I'm concerned."

"Sage can read a little," Tobias said.

I yawned. "True, but you're an imbecile. If I wanted to learn about something important, you're the last person I'd come to for information."

Tobias slammed a book closed. "I hope you continue in your ways. It makes Conner's decision that much simpler."

"Conner's decision is made," I said.

"Oh?" Tobias asked. "Who is it?"

"You." Now I sat up entirely. "You're the most willing to do anything he wants, the most pliable. He knows I'd be difficult to manage, and he can't be sure about Roden. But you, you're a puppet master's dream."

Tobias's mouth opened wide, then closed. Finally, he said, "Conner may think what he likes. I'm also the smartest of the three of us, and if I become the prince, then I will rule, no one else."

"If Conner puts you in, then he can take you out," Roden said. "How do you know it won't be the way Sage says?"

Tobias shook his head. "Don't you two worry about me. Worry about your own necks instead."

Lessons the next day were much the same as the day before. Master Graves rapped my knuckles several times for staring off into space when he thought I should stare at his chalkboard instead. Mistress Havala educated us on the names of everyone connected with King Eckbert's family.

"Very few members of Eckbert's family remain alive, and most of them are distant relations, so there is little chance of meeting anyone who knew the prince well enough to identify him," she said. "But everyone will expect you to know these names."

Tobias took steady notes. I ate most of his lunch and he never noticed.

Mistress Havala spent the remainder of our time after lunch describing Prince Jaron's older brother, Darius.

"He was everything a future king ought to be," she said. "Educated, compassionate, wise."

"That's what Carthya will expect from whichever of us is chosen, then," Tobias said. "We have to do better than just imitate Jaron. We have to exceed the people's expectations for Darius."

"Leave it to you and by the end of the week, the chosen prince will have to raise the dead too," I scoffed. "None of us is going to exceed Darius."

"You won't," Roden said.

I had no comeback for him. My whole life was a testament to the truth of that fact.

There's an old saying in Avenia that goes, "Just because it's calmer than a hailstorm doesn't mean it's calm." Several times during our horseback lessons later that day, that thought ran through my mind. The tension in the air was thick and tangible. Cregan and I quickly settled into a truce of not speaking.

Or rather, I wasn't speaking to him. He had plenty to say to me.

"Conner blamed me for you losing Windstorm," he said. "You get to say whatever you want to me, challenge my authority here, and I take the blame? You think you're a fine gentleman now, so you can look down on me? Well, you're still that pathetic orphan, Sage. You smelled like a pig when you came in here, and no matter what scents they add to your bathwater, you always will."

I gritted my teeth and reminded myself that in all fairness, I probably had smelled pretty bad before.

"I'll have to pay for that horse, the master says," Cregan continued. "Paying it off will take so many years of service, I can't count them. But I won't be his servant much longer. I have plans of my own."

He wanted me to ask what his plans were so he would have the satisfaction of telling me it was none of my business. I didn't care an inch about his plans. So I stared at him steadily, which infuriated him further.

"From now on, any horse you ride will be tethered to mine. And you will get the calmest, least excitable horse in the stables. You won't be able to get it to do anything I don't want it to do."

"Wait!" Tobias said. "If he gets the easiest horse, then it will appear to Conner that he's the best rider."

I smiled at Tobias, whose eyes narrowed.

"That was your plan all along," Roden whispered.

"I don't have Tobias's brains or your strength," I said to them. "Give me this one area to compete with you two."

Cregan stared at us for a moment, clearly trying to decide whether to give me the easiest horse or not. He didn't want to help me, nor did he want to risk getting himself in trouble again with a horse out of my league.

"I'm not even best with horses," he said. "I'm a swordsman, but Mott ordered me here so he could teach swords."

"Teach us both," Roden said. "I'll learn."

Tobias rolled his eyes. "So far, you've taught us neither horses nor swords. Our lesson time is passing fast, sir."

"The devils are punishing me for everything I've ever done wrong in my life," he said, marching to the stables to get the horses. "They've sent me you three."

In the end, we all had easy horses, and our ride on Conner's grounds was so boring I thought I'd go insane. I wasn't the only one.

"You have to teach us more than riding like schoolgirls on a Sabbath afternoon," Tobias said. "The prince will be expected to show off masterful riding skills."

"Thank Sage for this lesson," Cregan said. "I can't risk any of you getting hurt like yesterday."

On either side of me, Roden and Tobias shot out glares

again. "I think you planned this," Roden said to me. "I think you deliberately spoiled it for all of us so that now Tobias and I won't have the chance to get any better."

I chuckled softly. That idea had never occurred to me, although if it were true, it would've been clever.

After a wasted hour on horseback, Mott collected us for a sword-fighting lesson. "Because Sage went missing yesterday, we'll have to make up that lesson now," he said, leading us toward the small courtyard where he and I had practiced two nights earlier. He gestured to the wall where the various swords were hung. "By the end of these two weeks, we'll have you dueling with these swords, but for now you get wooden ones."

I folded my arms. "Where's the prince's sword?"

Mott turned to look. Sure enough, Jaron's sword was missing.

"The prince's sword was here?" Tobias asked.

"Just a copy of it," I said. Mott glared at me as if personally insulted by my words, but he shouldn't have. I had been perfectly accurate.

"How did you know about the sword?" Roden asked me.

"Mott and I practiced here the other night."

Roden and Tobias reacted with open mouths and narrowed eyes, exactly as I knew they would. But they didn't have much time to protest.

"Conner will want to know of this," Mott said, ignoring their whines. "Follow me."

We found Conner in his office, poring over a thick and dusty book. Mott spoke to him privately for a moment, then had us all come into the room and stand in front of Conner's desk.

Conner's office was lined with shelves full of books and the occasional bust or trinket. Near the back of the room, he had a massive desk that faced the door and two comfortable chairs that faced the desk. It made me wonder if he had a business through which he earned his own money, or whether his was the kind of wealth passed from father to son through the generations. I suspected the latter was true.

Conner sat with his hands folded together. "This was no ordinary sword, boys. It was nearly an exact replica of Prince Jaron's sword before he was lost. It was last seen around his waist at supper the night before he boarded the ship that ultimately carried him to his doom. Now, you may think by stealing it you have given yourself an advantage. Perhaps you believe you can use the sword to shore up your claims of being the prince when you are presented at court. But that is futile because, as I said, it's not an exact replica. Anyone with a practiced eye will easily know it's a copy. Perhaps you have stolen it to give yourself an advantage in sword-fighting. Again, this is futile. Any of you may practice with Mott as often as you'd like to become as skilled as you'd like. And if you stole it so that the other two boys couldn't practice with it, then remember that there are several other swords still available for practice. Now I want a confession. Who took it?"

All three of us remained silent. Conner couldn't possibly believe that the thief would confess. None of us was that stupid.

"Sage must have taken it, sir," Tobias said.

"Why is that?" Conner asked.

"He's the only one who's already handled the sword."

"Which is evidence of nothing," Conner said.

"It was there while the boys were in horseback lessons yesterday," Mott said. "We know where Sage was at that time, and all of the boys have been supervised since then."

"Where were you and Roden during that time?" Conner asked Tobias.

Tobias hesitated. "After Sage ran off on Windstorm, Cregan was going to follow him. He told us to go to the sword arena and wait for Mott. But after a few minutes, a servant came and told us that Mott had gone to look for Sage too, so we left."

"We left together," Roden said quickly. "If either of us had taken it, the other one would know."

"And what did you do after returning to the house?" Conner asked.

Tobias's eyes fluttered. "I was in the library."

Roden frowned. "I went back to our room."

"And can either of you provide proof that you were there?"

After a very long, very uncomfortable silence, I rocked on my heels and smiled. "For the first time, I think I'm glad that horse ran off with me."

## · EIGHTEEN ·

After being dismissed from Conner's office, Mott walked us back to the courtyard to continue with swordsmanship lessons. Tense feelings of vengeance and silent accusation hung in the air between Roden, Tobias, and me. Mott rotated a pair of us for dueling practice while he worked on skills with the third. The wooden swords Mott gave us were severely tested for durability as they clacked against each other, or, in a lucky moment, hit against an opponent's arm, back, or leg.

Roden was merciless against me and brutal with Tobias. I did very well against Tobias, but Mott said he was disappointed in my performance against Roden.

"This is more than just learning swordplay," Mott said. "You must learn it as Prince Jaron knew it. He challenged a king to a duel at the age of ten. What does that tell you about his attitude in battle?"

"That he was stupid," I said flatly. "If the story's true, he lost that duel."

"It shows his bravery," Roden said, ever eager to please. "And his training. He must have expected to win."

I barked out a laugh. "If he did, add arrogance to his list of worthless traits. It's too bad the prince we're trying to become isn't the older brother, Damon —"

"Darius," Tobias corrected.

"Whatever. It sounds like he had a character worth imitating. Not Jaron."

Mott stepped closer to me. "I find it interesting that you'd say that, Sage, considering you naturally have several character traits in common with Jaron."

I was silent for a moment as emotions I didn't understand filled me. What was it? Shame to acknowledge that Mott was correct? Was I as foolhardy as Jaron seemed to have been? Or was something telling me not to try for the crown? Perhaps in having fewer of Jaron's character flaws, Roden or Tobias would make a better king.

Mott seemed to be waiting for me to say something, so without knowing whether I was correct or not, I shrugged and said, "Jaron was a child when he challenged that king to a duel. Perhaps he learned his lesson and would make wiser choices today."

Mott frowned. "I never thought Jaron's challenge was a sign of weakness. I'm sorry that you do. Now let's continue."

Mott paired me with Roden for another round while he worked with Tobias. I held my own until Roden got me backed into a corner. I lowered my sword to end the duel, but Roden took the opportunity to strike a hard blow at my chest.

I reeled backward, then dropped my sword and lunged at him. One solid punch from me would teach him a much-needed lesson about sportsmanship. Mott pulled me off of him and yelled, "Bad form, Roden! This is a practice, not a match. You should have stopped when Sage lowered his sword."

"Sorry," Roden mumbled. "I didn't mean it. Just had a lot of energy."

Mott turned to me. "And, Sage —"

"I won't apologize," I said, folding my arms.

Mott considered that a moment, then said, "No, I wouldn't either. Shake hands, boys, then I'll take you back."

Roden offered me his hand and I reluctantly took it, but with a simple shake we both shrugged off the anger. While Roden replaced our swords, I watched as Mott brushed his fingers across the empty space where the imitation of Jaron's sword had been. Mott clearly loved that sword. I couldn't understand why.

Roden walked along beside me back to Farthenwood. "No hard feelings, I hope, about the way that match ended."

"Do that to me again and I'll kill you," I said.

He smiled grimly, not sure whether it was a joke or not. I wasn't sure either.

"It's safe to tell me if you took the sword," he said.

Not a bad way of changing the subject, so I played along.

"A secret that is safe between you, me, and Master Conner," I said with a wry sideward glance.

"It's not an accusation," Roden said, then lowered his voice. "It's more likely that Tobias took it anyway."

"Why's that?"

Roden shook his head. "Don't you know? You always seem to have everything figured out before any of the rest of us."

I didn't know, and I told him so.

"You know how bad he is with a sword. I was obviously the best out there, and you're not great, but you're better than he is."

I smiled. "If that were true, I wouldn't have so many bruises."

Roden continued, "Tobias needs the sword to help him look more like the prince."

"Tobias would look foolish wearing a sword at his side that he can't even use properly. So what do you propose?"

"I hope Conner chooses me," Roden said, "but if he doesn't, then I hope he chooses you. Not Tobias. For Carthya's sake, I wouldn't want him as prince, whether Conner is behind the throne or not. If you and I band together, we can sabotage him."

"Then what happens when it's down to you and me? Will you sabotage me as well?"

Roden looked down at the trail. "I might. And I know you might sabotage me too."

"How did we get to this place?" I asked, fully aware there was no answer. "No matter what we do, the devils have us."

Roden playfully knocked me in the side with his shoulder. "The devils had you long ago, Sage."

Tobias had gotten quite a ways ahead of us by this point. He turned and called, "Hurry up, you two! I won't be late for dinner because of your slacking!"

---

Dinner with Conner was uncomfortable at best. Tobias and Roden were seated at his right and left. As a sign of his displeasure with me, I was in the third position, farthest away.

I picked up my dishes and reset them at the far end of the table, so that I'd directly face Conner.

"Why'd you do that?" Conner asked.

"We can't see each other where I was at," I said. "This makes more sense."

"Maybe I have no wish to see you," Conner said.

"If that were true, you'd have had Mott keep me in my room."

"In any event, it was very rude."

"It was princelike," I said. "A prince would never let anyone else determine his seat."

After a brief hesitation, Conner smiled and raised his glass in toast to me. "Indeed."

Conner took several opportunities during dinner to point out the errors I was making in manners. Tobias and Roden weren't making the same mistakes, so they must have had this lesson the night before, while I was lying on the ground by the river. I told him I'd make fewer mistakes if I didn't have to use my right hand for everything. He pointed out that it wasn't likely the prince would switch to the left hand for me, so I'd have to be the one to change. I corrected the errors, and Conner moved on.

Despite my objection that it was a boring topic more suited for Master Graves than dinner conversation, he indulged us with a lecture on the customs of castle life, the daily schedule a king might manage.

"If he's king, why is he tied to a schedule?" I asked. "Why couldn't he tell all his subjects that he's off doing what he wants and they can wait?"

"He could," Conner said. "But his primary responsibility is to his country, not to himself. He is a manager, a decision maker, a leader. Not a child at play."

"But if one of us takes the throne, you'd do most of that for us, wouldn't you?"

Conner shook his head. "I'll be there to help you function in your role. I'll be a counselor, a guide. But you will be king."

Conner went quiet while Imogen and two other servants brought in the next course of our meal. She served Roden instead of me and didn't look at any of us.

When she turned, I got a glimpse of a dark bruise over her left cheek. She'd been wearing her hair to hide it, but when she bent over, the bruise was obvious.

"Where'd you get that?" I asked her. She glanced up at me,

then quickly looked down. So I turned to Conner. "Where'd she get that bruise?"

He waved his hand noncommittally. "She has a reputation for clumsiness. I expect she ran into a cupboard door or a wall, isn't that right, Imogen?"

Imogen looked from Conner to me, then back at Conner and nodded. Nobody in that room could have missed the fear in her eyes.

"Somebody did that to her," I said.

"Nonsense," Conner said. "Imogen, if somebody hurt you, you'd tell me, wouldn't you?" He laughed at his own joke. Obviously, Imogen could not have told him. And I suspected even if she could, she still wouldn't have dared.

"We have business," Conner said to all of the servants in the room. "You may all go."

When they left, Conner said, "You seem very interested in that girl's affairs, Sage."

"Somebody gave her that bruise. We both know it wasn't an accident."

"She's a servant girl, beneath your station now. Let those in her circles look after her interests."

"Those in her circles probably caused it."

Conner brushed off my statement with an empty promise to look into the matter, then said, "Forget the servant girl and remember why you're here. Did you know the prince is already engaged to be married?"

That had Roden's attention. "Already? To who?"

"To *whom*, Roden. The betrothed princess Amarinda of Bultain was chosen at her birth for the crown prince Darius. She is the niece of the king of Bymar, and an alliance between Eckbert's home and hers is necessary for continued peace in Carthya. The betrothal was King Eckbert's idea. His wife, Queen Erin, was from an inconsequential border town in southern Carthya, unknown in any social circles of the upper class. He was expected to choose from amongst the noblemen's daughters, so there was a great controversy when he married. Even today, little is known about her life before the marriage. For all his weakness in defending his borders, he was always a great defender of his wife."

"Why was that necessary?" Tobias asked. "What was she before? Some sort of criminal?"

"Bite those words!" Conner ordered. "She was your queen, Tobias, and a respectable woman, always. My only point is that Eckbert wanted to avoid a similar uproar with his son. Now that Darius has been killed, the betrothal will pass to Prince Jaron, if he is found. If you take the crown, you will one day take Amarinda as your wife."

"But if she was engaged to Darius —" Roden asked.

"She was betrothed to the throne, not the prince. Amarinda will marry the man who becomes king."

"Marry?" Tobias chuckled loudly, echoed by Roden and me.

"Not until you're older, of course," Conner said. "But when the time comes, she will be yours."

"What does she look like?" I asked. Conner raised an eyebrow, and I added, "Seems to me a girl whose marriage is guaranteed might not need to take care of her looks as much as one who has yet to catch a man's eye."

"You shall see for yourself," Conner said. "I have invited her to dinner at the end of this week."

"But if she sees us —" Tobias said.

"You three will be in disguise as servants amongst my staff. She is a betrothed princess and will hardly deign to look at any of you. But I want you to see her, to gain an understanding of her mannerisms and style. It will help you after you take the throne."

"So what is she like?" Roden asked.

"I'll have you judge that for yourselves. But I suspect she will appeal to you boys, and make our contest that much more interesting."

Roden and Tobias perked up at the prospect of seeing her, but I only slumped back in my chair. Conner had collected another victim in this hideous game, and the princess would never even know it.

# · NINETEEN ·

ack in our rooms that night, Roden went straight to bed. Tobias was at his desk, reading another book. I lay on my bed, staring out the window. Tucked beneath my pillow was a spool of thread, a needle, and a small pair of sewing shears. I did have a tear in a shirt from the horse ride, but I wasn't going to repair it. When I had enough privacy, I planned to cut the shirt up and sew a few pockets into the linings of my clothes. The vest I wore in the daytime had only one useless pocket on the outside. I needed a way to hide items inside my clothes, where nobody would think to look.

After verifying the sewing items were well hidden, I sat up and stared out the window near my bed. I pulled a garlin from my vest pocket, stolen from Conner's pocket after dinner, and absentmindedly let it roll over my knuckles. When it reached my pinky finger, I carried it with my thumb back to my forefinger.

"Nice trick," Tobias said.

"It helps me think."

"What are you thinking about?"

"Ways to get you to stop talking to me."

Tobias wasn't fazed. "While I have candlelight in this room, you can't possibly see outside. What are you staring at?"

"Nothing."

"This is what you do during lessons as well. Are you lost in your daydreams?"

"Dreaming of what my life might have been like if I'd made other decisions."

Tobias set his book down flat on the table. "Like what?"

"If I'd stayed with my family."

"Then you'd have become a drunken musician like your father was."

"Probably. But I wouldn't be here." I turned back to him. "Are you content with the choices you've made?"

"I never made any choices," Tobias said. "After my parents died, I was told to live with my grandmother, so I did. After she died, I was told to go to the orphanage, so I did. Then I was told to come here, so I did."

"And when Conner tells you what you'll do as king, you will."

"No!" Tobias took a deep breath, picked up his book again, and then in a calmer voice added, "I have a plan. I know what I'll do after I'm crowned."

I went back to looking out the window. "I hope it works for you."

"It will. I've worked out every detail. Stop staring out that window!"

"Why does it matter to you?"

"Because it's pointless when I know you can't see outside. Perhaps you're using it as a mirror to admire yourself." Then Tobias looked down at his papers and suddenly gathered them all together in a pile.

"I can't see your papers," I said tiredly. "You're being foolish."

"Nevertheless." Tobias took his papers and threw them in the fire. He blew out his candle and said, "I'm going to bed now."

---

It was a long time until he fell asleep. I'd had a hard time outlasting him, but I was determined to get outside Farthenwood tonight.

I inched the window open and crept onto the narrow ledge directly beneath it. There was little room for error, but it was a calm night and there were plenty of places to grip on to the walls. I'd be fine.

A neighing sound in the pasture caught my attention first. Conner's wild mare had returned home. That was good news for me. It would diminish any sting in Conner's anger toward me for having lost her. It was good news for Cregan as well. Time off from his sentence of service to Conner.

It was amazing how much I could learn about Farthenwood from the exterior. With a fair amount of climbing and using the ledges, I could see into many of the windows. I only saw a few people still awake this late at night, and there were windows in nearly every room. The more-favored servants' quarters were on the main floor in the corners of the house. A few of the windows were covered in curtains. The rooms with curtained windows likely belonged to Imogen and other female servants, but I never tried to see into them. The idea of being caught staring into a room of sleeping women was not a pleasant one. They'd mark me as a Peeping Tom with no idea that it was the farthest thought from my mind. The center of the main floor was living space such as Conner's office, the library, the music room, a dance hall, and the dining room. The kitchen and other servant areas were in the back. Bedrooms were on the upper floor. Conner's room was on the opposite side of the house from ours. There were other rooms between them, few of which interested me.

I wasn't sure yet how to get onto the top floor of Farthenwood, which was only a third of the area of the other floors. The nursery/schoolroom where Roden and I took lessons was up there, but I wasn't sure of what else. Likely, there were apartments for a governess and possibly more bedrooms. I might eventually find my way up to that level, but I wasn't trying too hard. It didn't seem that anything interesting was up there.

I shinnied down a drainpipe to reach solid ground — always a nice feeling — and set about exploring the grounds. I passed through the stables, the archery courtyard, a wide vegetable garden, and then another carefully tended flower garden. The thought nagged at me again to just run.

But I knew I wouldn't dare. The assurance of that confirmed my worst suspicions about myself. That deep inside, I really was a coward.

The crescent moon had shifted in the sky before I decided to return to my bedroom, where Conner so smugly believed he held us prisoner. It was dark enough that I had to feel for the edges of the window to find the small gap to open it again.

But there was no gap. The window was shut tight. I pressed on it, but it was either locked or stuck beyond my ability to open it.

I wondered what I should do. Tap on the window and get Roden and Tobias to let me in? They'd certainly tell Mott or Conner and I'd face a terrific punishment for that.

As it turned out, I didn't have that decision to make. Tobias sat up in bed and looked directly at me, then a wicked smile spread across his face. He arched his eyebrows, as if asking what I intended to do about this problem.

I held out both hands, then pointed to the window. He shook his head slowly, then rolled over and lay back down again.

I looked at Roden, but if he was awake I couldn't tell. He wasn't facing me and wasn't moving, except for a slow rise and fall of his body. I wondered if he was a part of Tobias's trick. Roden and I had agreed to sabotage Tobias. Maybe Roden also made an agreement with Tobias to sabotage me. If so, it would leave him free of both of us as threats. It would be a clever plan, and I almost regretted that I had not thought of it.

I leaned my head against the stone wall of Farthenwood and balanced my feet on the narrow ledge. It wouldn't be long before the morning servants would awaken to begin preparing the house for a daytime routine. I was running out of time.

# · TWENTY ·

A few of the servants' windows were open, but it didn't seem like a good idea to go through any of them. Too many people, most of whom would be waking up soon. Besides, then I'd have to get all the way upstairs and past Mott or whoever stood guard outside our room at night, all without being seen.

Conner's window was slightly open. That would at least get me on the right floor. Then I could keep watch and hope for a sleeping servant guarding my door, or an easily distracted one. As risky as it was to use his room, it was my best choice. Maybe my only choice.

Conner had a small balcony outside his room. The door was bolted shut to keep it from blowing open during a wind gust, but the window beside the balcony was opened enough to let a slight breeze through. The window gave easily when I pressed on it. It was much larger than the window by my bed, so there was no difficulty in sliding my body into his room.

I stood still for a very long time to be sure of the rhythm of his sleep, the depth of his breaths and their cycle. He snored softly, which I appreciated because it gave me some cover for any sound I might make.

His wide canopy bed was draped in so much fabric, it was difficult to see his body. The sounds of his snoring would have to be enough to assure me I was safe.

Back in Mrs. Turbeldy's orphanage, I'd spent more nights than days roaming through the rooms. I knew how to test for a floor's squeak before placing my weight on it. I knew how to open a door, a closet, or a drawer so that it didn't create a sense of movement in the room. And I knew how to stay invisible.

At least, I knew how to do it there.

Here, it was a little more complicated. I wasn't familiar with the layout of Conner's room, and there wasn't much light to work with.

Conner's room was larger than our bedroom. Ridiculously large for only one man, but he was the master here, so if this was the room he wanted, it was his. On one end of the room, to my left, was his bed and several large wardrobes along the far wall for his many fine clothes. Near me was a cushioned chair where he could look out over the balcony onto the back lawn while he sipped a morning tea. To my right were rows of shelves filled with books. He had so many more in his office below that I couldn't help but wonder if he'd actually read all these books, or were they merely for show? Probably he'd read them. Conner was a thorough man. I was briefly curious about the titles, about what books he studied. Then Conner mumbled something unintelligible in his sleep and rolled over. It was time to go.

The door into the hallway was shut tight. One of the problems that concerned me was not knowing what I'd find on the other side. Was his room guarded or waited on by a night servant? A nobleman's often is, but I wouldn't know until I opened the door, and there was a stiff penalty for guessing wrong.

Then in the moonlight, something caught my eye, hinting at a possibility I'd suspected, but not yet proved. The fringe on a hanging tapestry was pinched between walls. Conner had told us earlier that he knew all the secrets to Farthenwood. I hoped this was what he had meant. Either the interior walls were uncommonly thick or Farthenwood had secret passageways.

I took my time crossing the floor of Conner's bedroom. Wood floors are notorious for their creaks, and I didn't want to cause the creak that woke him. Once I reached the wall, finding the way to open the door into the passageway was remarkably easy. Three finger holes were carved into the wall, but hidden by the border of the tapestry.

I opened the door to the passage as slowly as possible and no wider than necessary. In a bind, I can get through small spaces. This was a very big bind and I allowed myself only a very small space to enter.

Once inside, I saw that the passage was barely lit, with oil lamps set in sconces and spaced far enough apart that a person could make his way through. It was narrow and poorly marked for any exit points, except for a small handle on the wall that released the hidden door to open. I took a few wrong turns, entering other guest rooms that were fortunately empty.

When I came to our room, I immediately saw why Conner had chosen to put us here. There was a small hole at the base of the wall that I'd previously mistaken for a mouse hole. It was no such thing. Conner had given us a room where, if he wanted to, he could listen to our conversations.

Conner still used the tunnels, or one of his surrogates did. That's why oil lamps were kept burning all the time. I would have to use great caution if I chose to return here.

I silently pressed open the secret door, letting myself back into our room. Tobias and Roden were both asleep in their beds. I watched each of them for a while, wondering if in different circumstances any of us might have become friends. Then I shook it off. It had been a long time since I dared call anyone a friend. The concept was only theoretical to me now.

Tobias woke up early that morning to find me sound asleep in my bed, and nobody the wiser. He stared at me openmouthed when I finally woke up, until I rolled over to fall asleep again. Tobias never asked me the story of how I got back into our room. And I never offered it.

# · TWENTY-ONE ·

E rrol entered my room that morning with the clothes I'd
worn when Conner first brought me here.

"Finally," I said. "Why the delay?"

Errol hesitated, finally deciding that instead of answering,
he'd ask whether I had any reward for him.

"I don't know what you're talking about," I said lightly.
"But if you're ever in the library, there's a small bump in the
pages of Conner's family history. You might straighten it out."

Errol grinned. "No offense, sir, but all three of you came in
here empty-handed. It might be wise for me to ask where that
coin came from."

I shook my head. "The truth is, Errol, that it would not be
wise at all. Thanks for returning my clothes. Now get out and
leave me alone."

"I can put those clothes away, sir."

"So can I. Close the door behind you."

When he left, I unfolded the clothes to inspect them.
They'd been washed, and a rip in the side of my shirt was
mended, but otherwise they seemed the same as before. These

were so much more like me. I didn't belong in the silks and fine weaves Conner costumed us in. They weren't comfortable. I didn't feel like a gentleman while wearing them, and certainly not like a prince. I felt like a fraud. Which in the truest definition of the word, I was.

Before folding the trousers, I checked the pockets. My eyes widened and I yelled for Errol to come back into the room.

"I had something in this pocket," I said. "Where is it?"

Errol shook his head, but he clearly knew the answer. "You had nothing of value in there, sir."

I moved closer to him and his face paled. "Did you throw it out, then?"

In almost a whisper, Errol said, "Conner heard you wanted these back. He insisted on inspecting them before they were returned to you. If anything is missing, sir, you should ask him."

Minutes later, I stormed into Conner's small dining room, slamming the door against the wall. "Where's my gold?"

"Where's Mott?" Conner asked. "He should have escorted you."

"He doesn't know I left. Where is it?"

"I can't imagine what you're talking about. Now come, sit, and have some breakfast." He gestured to a seat near Roden and Tobias, who were both staring at me as if I'd gone completely insane.

I had no intention of sitting. "The gold. In the pockets of the clothes I wore before coming here. You took it."

"That's what this is about?" Conner laughed. "Stupid boy. That rock you carried wasn't gold."

"Yes, it is and it's mine."

Conner shook his head. "It's imitator's gold, Sage. You probably bought it from a swindler in the marketplace."

"It was a gift, and it's real. I want it back."

"No." Conner folded his hands together. "You're training to become a prince, even a king. A king wouldn't carry imitator's gold in his pocket. Study hard to become royalty, and I'll see that you carry real gold wherever you go."

"We're all imitators here. So if you're right about the gold, then there's no more appropriate thing for me to carry than that rock. Where is it?"

"It's mine now," Conner said. "I'm sure I'll find a useful purpose for it one day, maybe as a skipping stone in the nearby river. Now please sit down. We were about to discuss the royal lineage."

"You discuss it," I said. "I've got better things to do." And I stormed out.

---

I didn't make it to the reading or history lessons that morning. Tobias, Roden, and I were on our way out to the stables that afternoon when Mott and Cregan strode toward us. I was eating an apple swiped from the kitchen, but from the expressions on their faces, I didn't think I'd get to finish it.

"They look angry," Tobias said to me. "What did you do?"

"Is it always something I've done?" I asked. "Don't you and Roden ever do anything worth their attention?"

"It's always something you've done," Roden agreed.

Although I was tempted, there was no point in running. We were trapped between the stables and the house, so they'd catch me anyway. Besides, whatever punishment was coming my way, I didn't need to complicate it further.

Cregan placed both hands on my chest and shoved me to the ground. Sure enough, the apple rolled out of my hand and into the dirt. "Where is that rock?" he asked.

The fall to the ground knocked the breath from me, but I still muttered, "It's gold."

"You stole it from the master."

"Who stole it from me. What I did only set the universe back in order."

"You don't want this fight, Sage," Mott warned. "Now please, where's the rock?"

I set my jaw forward and dug the heel of my boot into the dirt. Maybe he was right, but I wasn't going to admit it.

"Take him," Mott said to Cregan, who pulled out his knife and ordered me to stand. When I did, he pressed the knife to my neck and grabbed my arm. With Cregan by my side, and Mott on my heels, we walked back to Farthenwood.

Conner was waiting for me in his office, standing behind his wide oak desk. Cregan threw me into the chair in front of the desk, and he and Mott stood on opposite sides of me.

"Where is the rock?" Conner asked coldly.

"Isn't it in your desk where you left it?" I countered with an equal coolness to my voice.

That set Conner off. He nodded at Cregan, who slapped me hard across my cheek. I tasted blood in my mouth and closed my eyes a moment before the sting eased enough that I could open them.

"I bought you from the orphanage!" Conner yelled. "That means I own you, which means I own everything that belonged to you! That rock is mine."

"If it's not real gold, then why do you want it?" I asked.

"Because I don't want you to have it! I will not present someone to the court who carries imitator's gold in his pocket. Where is it?"

"Maybe you lost it," I said.

Cregan slapped me again, harder this time.

"Take him to the dungeon," Conner whispered. "Do what you must, but leave no scars."

"No, wait!" My eyes widened as fear gripped me. I knew what would happen there. "Don't do this, Conner! It's just a rock. Is that what you want to hear?"

Conner pressed both hands flat on his desk as he leaned toward me. "What I want, Sage, is for you to bend to my will. If I tell you to jump from a cliff, I want you to jump. If I tell you to swim to the far side of the ocean, I want you to swim. I don't care about the rock. But if I tell you that it's no longer yours, then I will have your loyalty, respect, and obedience. I'll give you one last chance. Where is it?"

My heart pounded so loudly in my ears that I barely heard him. All I knew was that he would *not* get that rock even if my life depended on it. And I suspected that it did.

"Take him," Conner said. Mott and Cregan grabbed each of my arms and literally dragged me, kicking and screaming, out the door.

# · TWENTY~TWO ·

Conner's dungeon smelled of rotting urine. I vaguely wondered who else had been brought here and how long ago. The dungeon was only a single room surrounded by rough-hewn rock walls and rusty iron bars. There were no windows and no lights except for the few lit candles in sconces on the wall outside the bars. It was damp down here, and I shivered in the cold air. Except it wasn't that cold. I was terrified.

When Cregan used a hand to open the barred door, I wrenched an arm free of his grasp and got in one good punch on his neck. Mott grabbed my arm and wrested it behind me with the other, pinching them tightly together.

"I'll make you pay for that," Cregan hissed. Once we were inside, he sliced off my shirt and shackled my wrists with a chain that hung from the ceiling. When he raised the chain, I could only barely touch the floor with my arms suspended above me.

Mott had gone to the far corner of the room, but now he approached me. In his hands was some sort of whip. It had a long handle, with a thick leather strap on the end that he held tightly bundled.

"Conner said not to leave scars." It was impossible to control the tremble in my voice as I spoke.

Cregan's grin revealed his eagerness for that whip to fly. "He said nothing about bruises. As long as he hits you with the broad side of this strap, you'll feel the pain, but it shouldn't cut you."

"Please don't do this, Mott." I wasn't above begging.

"You chose this!" he yelled. "Didn't I warn you before?"

"What's so important about the rock?" Cregan asked.

"It's not about the rock," Mott said. "The boy just wants to win. This is his way of proving that Conner doesn't own him."

"He doesn't own me," I said.

That elicited Mott's first snap of the whip. I'd prepared myself for pain, but not as great as this. A scream burst from my lips that didn't sound like me. Mott snapped it again and then a third time. My legs collapsed beneath me, which pulled hard at my shoulders.

"Where's the rock?" Mott asked.

Without waiting for an answer, he snapped the whip again. I felt myself separating from the pain, as if a part of me had stepped aside to watch it happen. That part of me cringed at the sound of strap hitting flesh. The other part continued to scream.

"He doesn't own me," I whispered. "It's my gold."

The whip snapped again, ripping like a claw into my skin, then Mott scowled. "Get a towel."

"Conner said not to draw blood!" Cregan said.

"He said not to leave scars. Get me the bandages and then we'll leave him alone. We'll give him time to think about his next answer."

Cregan disappeared for a moment while Mott cursed and threw the whip back into the corner of the room. A minute later, Cregan returned with a bottle of clear liquid and a cloth.

"I'll take care of this," Mott said. "Don't tell Conner anything more than you have to."

"Give me five minutes alone with him," Cregan said with a growl. "I'll find out where the rock is."

"Get out!" Mott commanded.

When we were alone, Mott unscrewed the bottle. I caught a whiff of it and shook my head. "Don't. No more."

"This sting won't be much better than the whip," Mott warned.

He poured the liquid onto the cloth, then pressed it to my back. I howled again and kicked Mott in the knee, and he stumbled backward.

"You'll get infected if I don't clean this," he said angrily. "I'm the only friend you've got right now, so don't upset me."

"If you're my friend, then who are my enemies?"

"You are your own enemy, Sage. Look in the mirror for the cause of your problems. Do you think I wanted to hold that whip?"

He patted my back again with the cloth and I cursed at him.

"Watch your mouth, or Conner will have me whip that out of you too."

"It hurts!" My back was on fire and every nerve in my body felt it.

"I don't know why Conner hasn't killed you already," Mott said. "He sees something in you worth keeping, but his patience won't last forever. Give him the rock, Sage."

"No."

Mott wrapped the wet cloth around my side and knotted it tightly. "You're a fool," he said. "If this is your strategy to become prince, it's a terrible one. Bow to Conner, boy. And give him the rock."

Before he left, he blew out both candles, leaving me suspended from the ceiling, half-naked, injured, and in complete darkness.

# · TWENTY-THREE ·

They came to check on me two more times that day. The first time, Cregan brought a bowl of steaming soup. He said he knew I hadn't eaten much that day and that I must be starved by now. All I had to do was tell them where the rock was hidden and they'd let me go.

I told him the soup smelled awful and I'd rather lick the dungeon floors. Cregan said that could be arranged. Then he leaned against the wall and ate the soup. When he was full, he threw the remains on me and laughed.

"I asked Conner to let me kill you right now," he said.

"If you make it quick, then go ahead." And I meant it.

Cregan got so close to me that I could smell the onions from the soup on his breath. "Oh no, I wouldn't make it quick. I'd take my time with you. Guess I have to be patient, though, because unfortunately, the master wants to keep you around a little while longer."

"Go away, then."

He seemed amused at my attempt to order him, and tried an order of his own. "Where's the rock?"

I turned my face away from him and was rewarded with a punch to the stomach.

"I can do that all I want," he said. "It won't leave scars."

"Keep it up," I said when I recovered my breath. "After I'm king, it will lessen my guilt for having you executed."

Cregan glared at me, issued a few threats for what he'd do the next time he came down, and stomped back up the stairs.

Any number of hours later, Mott came with a rock that he said was as shiny as the one I'd had before. He pointed out that it was a little bigger than the other one and looked more valuable. I could have this rock. I only had to return the other one to Conner.

"That's imitator's gold," I said, irritated at his attempt to patronize me. "Mine was real."

"Yours was just a worthless rock," Mott said. "Even I could tell that."

"Why does Conner want it, then?"

"Why do you want it?" Mott said. "Neither of you could possibly care for what any other person wouldn't even bother to pick up off the side of the road. Conner wants it because you want it, and you want it to defy Conner. If you think this fight proves anything, you're wrong."

"Tell Conner he needs me to be his prince," I said. "Neither Roden nor Tobias will be able to convince the regents. But I can, and he knows it."

"I'll tell him," Mott said. "But I think Conner would be a

fool to pass you off as the prince. First chance after that crown landed on your head, you'd take a royal revenge on him."

"Just tell him. Tell him I'll be his prince."

The next time I heard footsteps on the stairs, I expected it to be Mott or Cregan. But the footsteps fell too lightly. It was impenetrably dark in here, and when the glow from a candle rounded the corner, its dim light was harsh on my eyes.

I squinted, and my dry voice was hoarse as I asked, "Who's there?"

There was no answer. The door to the dungeon opened, and only then did I recognize Imogen. She held a finger to her lips to silence any further questions, then withdrew a flask from her skirt. She raised it to my mouth and let me gulp in cool water until I shook my head that I'd had enough. Also hidden beneath her skirt was a warm roll. She helped me eat it, then wiped my mouth with her fingers so there would be no sign of food or water.

"Thank you," I said.

After a slight hesitation, she whispered, "You look awful."

My eyes widened. "You talk?"

Her voice was soft and low. "You must keep two secrets for me. That I can talk, and that I came here tonight."

"Why did you come?"

"It's been more than a day since they brought you here. I don't know how much longer Conner will keep you here. Can't you give him what he wants?"

I shook my head. "He wants to own me. If I give in to him on this, then there's nothing left of me."

She offered me more water, which I gratefully accepted. "I should have brought you more to eat," she said. "But I was afraid they'd notice."

I closed my eyes to rest them for a moment, then opened them and asked, "That bruise I saw the other night, was it my fault?"

"I had troubles before you came, and they'll continue after you're gone. Besides, right now you should worry more about yourself."

"Who hurts you?"

"Do you know how ridiculous that question is, coming from someone in your position?" The encouraging smile she had forced onto her face faded. "I'm fine. Some days are harder than others, that's all. And it's easy for them to pick on me, because they know I'll never tell."

"Why do you pretend to be a mute?"

She lowered her eyes, then looked back into mine. "It turned Conner's attention away. It's better this way, trust me."

We fell silent for a moment, then Imogen tilted the flask. "It's finished. I'll bring you more later if I can get away."

"Don't risk it. He'll let me go soon. He has to."

Imogen exited the dungeon, fastening the door as it had been before. Looking back through the bars, she said, "Don't give up, Sage, and don't give in to him. Please. A lot of us are watching you, and we need to see that it's possible to win."

She disappeared as quickly and quietly as she had come. With just the bit of food in my stomach, I was able to relax a little. And for the first time ever, I learned to sleep standing up.

# · TWENTY~FOUR ·

I t was impossible to know what time it was when Mott and Cregan returned for me again. It didn't feel as if I'd had any rest, but my arms ached so badly, I was sure I'd slept for some time. Whatever food Imogen gave me had long ceased to offer any comfort.

Cregan reached the dungeon first and got directly in my face. With a snarl, he asked, "Where's the rock?"

"Gold," I mumbled.

"Enough!" Mott pulled Cregan's outstretched arm down. "This is between the boy and the master. Not you."

Cregan grabbed my hair to force me to look at him. "You're not the prince yet, so I can tell you this. I'm going to do everything in my power to see that Conner chooses one of the other two boys. Because after they ride off to the castle, I'm going to kill you myself. And you will beg for mercy, but you'll come to understand just how merciless I can be."

"I said, enough," Mott repeated. "Let him down, Cregan."

They released the chains and I crumpled to the floor like a rag doll. Cregan kicked me lightly until I let him have the satisfaction of a groan, and then dropped an armful of clothes on me. "The master wishes to speak with you. Get dressed."

I didn't move until Mott finally crouched to the floor and began dressing me. Then he cursed and said to Cregan, "He's bled through on his bandages. Get me some more."

"I'll have to get them from upstairs," Cregan said. "We didn't have much down here before."

"Then get them."

Cregan's footsteps pounded up the stairs. While I lay face-down on the filthy floor, Mott worked silently to remove my bandages. One of them pulled where dried sweat and blood had bonded it to my skin. I cringed and Mott breathed an apology.

With tears in my eyes I said, "You have to help me. Please, Mott. I can't do this."

"I work for Conner, not you." Then after a moment, he sighed tiredly and added, "After all this, the master is still considering you. That says a lot. It's time to stop thinking of yourself as an orphan and look at yourself as a prince."

"I will always be an orphan now." And for the first time in as long as I could remember, I cried. I cried for my lost family, and for every circumstance in my life that had led me here. Mott held my forehead until calm slowly returned to me.

"Forgive me," I mumbled.

"You're half-starved and exhausted," he said. "Forgive me that it was my job to bring this upon you."

Moments later, Cregan returned. He handed the new

bandage to Mott and then stood back as Mott carefully peeled away the rest of the old one.

"Give me a light," he directed Cregan.

Cregan handed him a candle, which they held close to me. "It's going to scar," Mott said. "It cut deeper than I had thought. But I think, so far, we saved it from any infection." They poured more of the liquid onto the cut. I clawed at the floor for relief from the pain but made little sound. There was no energy for that.

The sting passed and they wrapped me in a new bandage. It took both Mott's and Cregan's help to get me dressed, then they walked me up the stairs. The early morning light was fierce on my eyes and I stumbled backward, anything to get away from so much sun.

"Get him some water," Mott said to someone nearby while still holding me firmly.

A cup appeared and Mott pressed it to my lips. I took a few sips, then turned my head away. The light didn't hurt so badly now. I faintly realized how much I'd missed seeing it.

"We can't delay any longer," Mott said. "Let's take him to Conner."

---

They sat me in a chair facing Conner's desk. Conner stared at me for what seemed like an eternity, and then said, "You look terrible."

I said nothing.

"If you learn nothing else during your time here, Sage, perhaps you will learn not to defy me. You were two nights down there; did you know it's been so long? I hope you had time to reflect that disobedience to me will bring you nothing but misery."

Again, I had no response. It occurred to me that obedience to him offered its own form of misery, but I wasn't going to tell him that. Besides, it hurt to talk.

Conner nodded at Mott, who brought out a tray and set it on Conner's desk. It was filled with items I recognized as having come from various hiding places around my bed and my drawers.

Conner picked up a few things that I'd pickpocketed over the last few days: a butter knife, a gold cuff link, several coins. "No need to ask about these," he said. "You've obviously managed to find time amongst your other studies to steal from me and those in this household."

Yes, that was obvious, so I remained silent.

Then Conner picked up some papers. "But I must ask about these. Do you know what's on them?"

"I don't know what you're looking at," I mumbled.

"They're notes someone made. Whoever wrote them seems to have detailed some strange plans. They may be interpreted as ways to get rid of me should he become king. Everything from the rather nonoffensive appointing me as a foreign ambassador to poisoning my wine. Who wrote this, Sage?"

I shook my head. "Is your name on it?"

"Of course not. As I said, this is only my interpretation of the notes. Tell me who wrote them so I can ask about it."

"I wanted to practice writing with my right hand. I found these in a bin, set for fire kindling."

"I must ask you directly, did you write these notes?"

I started to laugh, then choked on it as a pain thumped in my side. "You can't think I'm that foolish."

"Roden couldn't have made these notes either," Conner said. "It must be Tobias."

"Ask him, then."

"I think not," Conner said. "I believe I'll let Tobias rest secure in the belief that he's in the lead for my decision. The more confident he is, if he authored these pages, that overconfidence will guide him to expose himself." Conner chuckled, and then added, "I'm sure this secret is safe between you and me, correct?"

He didn't wait for a response and I offered none. Conner stood and walked over to me. He lifted my face and inspected it for cuts or bruises. "You're none the worse after a stay in my dungeons. I hope the experience humbled you."

He took the blank expression on my face as an answer and continued, "You're a difficult young man, Sage, but I suspect that comes from your lack of discipline and supervision, which means I can train it out of you. I've heard that down in the dungeons, you told Mott you would be my prince. Is that so?"

"You need me."

"Why is that?"

It took a few seconds to collect my breath to answer. "Tobias and Roden can't convince the regents. I can."

"So you'll be *their* prince," Conner said. "But will you be *my* prince?"

Slowly, I nodded. Conner smiled and said, "You have one more week to prove it to me. Sleep today and you'll resume lessons tomorrow. Now go get some rest."

He never asked me about the rock, but he got what he really wanted. I had promised to be his prince.

# · TWENTY-FIVE ·

Once they got me into bed, Errol attempted to take care of my back, but I fought him so much that at one point after I awoke, it was Imogen who sat beside me.

I mumbled a hello to her. She shifted her eyes to identify Errol in the room, standing against a wall and looking irritated. So I closed my eyes and went back to sleep.

The next time I awoke, Imogen was using a warm damp cloth to clean my face. It was getting darker outside, though only a few lamps were lit yet. I looked around the room, but we appeared to be alone.

"Where's Errol?" I asked.

"Gone. For now."

"So they let you out of the kitchen to play nursemaid?"

"No one else would come. Not after the way Errol described all the trouble you were giving him."

"He made it hurt worse."

She frowned. "I'll try to do better. Let me look at it."

"Don't. It'll look bad and then you'll have to pour this stuff on it."

"That stuff is alcohol and it'll keep infection away." She helped me roll onto my stomach, then lifted up my shirt and pulled at the bandage. There was silence as she looked at my back. It didn't even sound as if she was still breathing. "Oh, Sage."

"It's just the one cut."

"Which looks awful. But you're covered with bruises too." She lightly traced a finger across my back.

"Your hand is cold," I mumbled.

"Your skin is hot." She unknotted and loosened the bandage, then said, "The wound has sealed, which is good, but I've still got to use the alcohol."

I groaned and buried my face in my pillow. She applied alcohol to a towel and pressed it against my back, apologizing the entire time. When she finished, I focused on steadying my breathing while she reknotted the bandage.

"The servants say you did this for some little rock," she said. "They had us search everywhere, but nobody can find it. Where'd you put it?"

"What's your reward if I answer that?"

Imogen drew back, offended. I apologized, but the damage was done. "I'm no spy. It was just a question."

"If you knew, maybe they'd try to get the answer from you too."

"You're the only one in the entire world — Conner included — who truly gives a devil's inch about that rock."

"Gold."

"Whatever it was, you're crazy to defy Conner that way."

"Only one week more. Then everything will change."

"Didn't you learn anything in the dungeon? Nothing will change as long as you're living under Conner's rules. You've got to find a way to get out of here."

"If he chooses me this week, I could get you away from here too."

She hesitated, then said, "You're delirious with exhaustion."

"I'm not."

"You *are*," she insisted. "Sage, you are, trust me on that."

"If I were the prince —"

"Whatever title they give you, you'll always be a servant to Conner. You'll always belong to him in some way, which means you're in no position to make that offer. Now enough of this; you have to eat something. Can you sit up?"

With Imogen's help, I got to a sitting position. She offered to feed me, but I said I'd rather do it.

"After becoming prince, I could trick Conner," I said after I'd taken a few sips of a warm vegetable broth. "Free myself of his influence. Then you could —"

We were interrupted by Tobias and Roden returning to the room. They stopped in the doorway and stared awkwardly at me.

"Thought you'd never see me again?" I asked.

"It's like looking at the dead," Roden said.

"We didn't think Conner would bring you back here," Tobias said. "Not after what you did."

"It's okay for him to steal from me, but not for me to take it back?"

They didn't answer and stared at Imogen as if they wanted her to leave before anything more was said. I finished the rest of my soup and handed it to Imogen. She shook her head stiffly at me, then gathered up any items not needed and quickly left the room.

"It's irrelevant for you now anyway," Tobias said, sitting at the desk. "You've missed so much of the lessons, there's no way you can catch up, not even to Roden. Conner will choose me."

"How do you know that?" I asked.

"No, it's true," Roden said, obviously dismayed. "Conner made it very clear at supper tonight that I've been a disappointment to him and you're too unstable. He didn't say anything at all about Tobias. If he had any problem with him, he'd certainly have said so."

"Tobias isn't strong enough to be king," I said. "You and I have proven ourselves. Has he?"

"I will." Tobias's face was already red, and I suspected it was going to get redder before he was finished. "Don't challenge me on that and don't get in my way."

Pretending I couldn't detect the threatening tone in his voice, I casually leaned my head against the wall. "This is your chance with Conner, then. Be strong. Be bold. Tell him about all the notes you've made. Show them to him and prove just how smart you've become."

Tobias glanced over at his stack of papers. Worry lines creased his forehead as he asked, "Have you been in my papers?"

"What good would that do me? I just think those notes would show off the results of your studies, prove to him that you have plans of your own."

Tobias grabbed his papers and threw them into the fire. He marched over to my bed and stuck a finger in my face, then yelled, "You think you're so clever, but if you push me any further you'll see how foolish you are."

"I never denied being a fool," I said, lying back down on my bed. "That's the difference between us."

# · TWENTY~SIX ·

I slept the rest of that evening and through the night, waking up only when Imogen came to check on my bandages. There was so much I wanted to ask her, but someone else was always in the room with us, and any real conversation was impossible.

I was more careful this time to let her do her job without giving her any particular attention, though I still felt the entire charade was ridiculous. Most of these servants came to Farthenwood in better circumstances than I had. And right now, I was much more like the servants than Conner. My friendships with Imogen or Errol or Mott shouldn't have threatened any of them.

Morning brought stiffness to my muscles. I must've been too tired the day before to notice how sore they were, or maybe it was that I didn't have to move around much before now. Errol insisted on helping me dress, even brought Mott into the room to ensure I accepted that help. It wasn't necessary. Standing there with my arms out while Errol dressed me was about as much as I could do.

With considerable struggle, I managed to stay awake that day and even paid a semblance of attention to the morning tutors. Master Graves made it very clear that they had moved on without me and had no time to return to the lessons of the previous few days, so I would have to catch up as best as I could.

"It's been a week since you came to Farthenwood, Sage, and you're no further along than the first day we started."

I told him that was probably because I'd only had two of his lessons and, in all fairness to myself, hadn't really bothered to pay attention to either of them. This only darkened his glares at me, and he focused the rest of the lesson on Roden.

Mistress Havala also said there wasn't enough time to review what had been discussed while I was — she generously used the word *indisposed* — but gave me two books that she said contained much of the same information.

"You probably can't read them without help," she said. "Perhaps Tobias will help you in the evenings."

"I'm certain that Tobias has already given me too much help," I said.

Tobias gripped the sides of his chair and said whatever he might do to please Master Conner would please him.

Roden and Tobias did horseback and sword-fighting lessons that afternoon. I was excused from participating, but Mott insisted I watch them. I watched the horseback lessons until they rode too far away for me to see them and I fell asleep. The sword-fighting lesson was somewhat more interesting. Tobias was still a disaster with a sword, but Roden had improved significantly. I wondered if he was naturally talented or if he'd been putting in a lot of extra hours of practice.

Mott commented on it too. Roden shrugged and said Cregan had offered to help him during free hours.

"Cregan is skilled with a sword, but he's self-taught," Mott warned. "With him as your teacher, you will learn to fight, but your style will not reflect the training of a prince."

"My lessons with you will help me pass for the prince," Roden said. "But Cregan's lessons will keep me alive."

Dinner that evening was relatively quiet. Conner vaguely inquired after our progress but said he'd already had full reports from all our instructors. He asked me what I was doing to try to catch up.

I shrugged and said I planned to study Tobias's notes after he was asleep. Tobias shot me a glare, but Conner laughed.

"And what is your response to that?" Conner asked Tobias.

Tobias shook his head. "I have no notes, sir. And Sage couldn't read them if I did."

"If you did have notes, Sage could get them and perhaps even read them. You had better be careful, Tobias, or Sage will end up as my choice."

"That would be a mistake, sir," Tobias mumbled.

"*Your* mistake," Conner corrected, "is that you are more interested in pleasing me than in becoming like the boy Prince Jaron was. Learn to fight back, Tobias. Be strong!" His eyes drifted to me, and he shook his head. "Don't be smug about that, Sage. Jaron didn't seek fights either, the way you do. I can see you all still have much to learn about who the prince really was."

After we returned to our room that night, I fell onto my bed, not caring what clothes I slept in, as long as I could sleep. But Tobias sat at the desk, turning his chair to stare directly at me.

Finally, I muttered, "You obviously have something to say, Tobias. So what is it?"

His eyes narrowed. "I am strong enough to stop you, Sage. You too, Roden. I'm warning you both not to push me any further."

"Conner said the prince never sought out fights," I reminded him.

"This isn't about being like Jaron," he said. "It's about stopping you. And I will if I have to."

Grimacing with the sting in my back, I rolled over to face the wall. Before closing my eyes, I said, "Conner will choose me this week and you know it. You wouldn't dare to stop me."

As tired as I was, I forced myself to stay awake for nearly an hour after that until I was sure both Roden and Tobias were asleep. Because no matter what I said, it was becoming increasingly obvious that Tobias would at some point carry out his threat.

# · TWENTY~SEVEN ·

**M**ott was waiting for us after lessons the next day to tell us there would be no horseback riding that afternoon, nor sword fighting. "Cregan says you're all good enough on horseback to pass initial scrutiny, and Conner has other plans for you this afternoon."

Those other plans were dancing lessons in Conner's great hall. So Conner apparently had other ways to torture us beyond his dungeon walls.

I grabbed my side and sat in a chair near the door. "I'm not dancing. It'll hurt."

"Today is the only time we can spare for these lessons," Conner said, walking in ahead of a small group of women. "Surely, a handsome young prince would never be so tired that he couldn't enjoy a dance with a lovely young lady."

Reluctantly, I stood, though swallowing a laugh when I saw our three dancing partners. None of them were young, and lovely was a kind exaggeration. They were dressed in clothes similar to his other servants and had the rougher skin of women accustomed to physical labor.

Roden shared a grin with me. Tobias straightened his spine, but looked a little nervous.

"Don't be shy, boys," Conner said. "You don't have to romance them. It's just some dancing, and all of them are fine dancers."

We walked forward and made the decision of who our partner would be based on which lady happened to be standing closest to us. My partner was a woman in her forties who whispered to me that her name was Jean. She had curly hair that was probably once a pretty brown before it had grayed and faded. Her eyes were wide, contrasting with her thin lips and nose. Not a pretty face, but it was an interesting one.

Conner began instructing us in a basic minuet, demonstrating the steps himself with Roden's partner, then clapping his hands to a beat as we imitated him. Jean was pleasant and helpful. And forgiving with every mistake I made.

"You're doing fine," she said. It was a lie and we both knew it. But I appreciated it nonetheless.

Neither Tobias nor Roden seemed to be doing much better. Conner remained patient with us, though, and after several tries, we all began to make the steps in a respectable manner.

At a break between dances, Conner asked if my father was a musician.

"As I've told you on more than one occasion, sir."

"Surely you play an instrument, then."

"I've also told you my father was a poor musician. You cannot believe the student could rise higher than his teacher."

Conner walked to the corner of the room, where a small instrument case was propped. He pulled out a fippler and fitted the pieces together. "I'd like to hear you play, Sage. *If* you were taught by your musician father."

"I'd leave my lovely dance partner alone, sir."

"I'll dance with her, if you play something we can dance to."

I eyed Conner. "Is this a test?"

With a tilt of his head, Conner said, "Everything is a test."

So I took the fippler. It needed a bit of tuning, which was awkward for me at first. I'd actually never played a fippler, but it was a basic wind instrument, and with only a little trouble at first, I could guess at the fingering. "What I don't remember must be improvised," I warned them. "Forgive me if I fail to do this song justice."

Then I began to play. It wasn't a song for dancing but was instead a sad melody that had always given me images of loneliness on a forgotten beach in the night. It was a tune that used to make my mother cry, and after a while, my father no longer played it. After a while, he no longer played any songs at all. But I never forgot the tune.

When I finished, there was a hush in the room. I handed the fippler back to Conner, who solemnly said, "You were right, Sage. The student cannot rise higher than his master. I believe we need to dance again."

I caught Conner's eye a few times over the next dance,

wondering what he had intended by asking me to play. If I'd been lying about my father's hobby, all I would have had to say was that he never taught me.

After the dance finished, Conner told us to rest a moment, then folded his arms and chuckled. "None of you will ever be great dancers," he said. "But at least you won't humiliate yourselves either. We'll work a bit longer, then I'll have each of you boys go and change clothes. You'll work in the kitchen tonight, learning from the servants there about what is expected in serving guests. You'll need to learn these roles because I'll have you serving the betrothed princess Amarinda tomorrow evening."

"When does she arrive, sir?" Tobias asked.

"I expect to receive her sometime late this evening, though she isn't planning to dine with us until tomorrow. Sage, have you been working on your accent? If you are called upon to speak to her, I won't have you replying with an Avenian accent."

"I happened to be alone quite a bit in recent days," I said in a Carthyan accent. "It gave me a great deal of time to practice."

"Not bad," Conner said with a smile. "But you're still too soft on your consonant sounds. Tighten them up, and never let me hear the Avenian accent again."

I acknowledged Conner's request with a nod. Then Conner said, "I think we'll practice a waltz now. Take your partners by the hand, please."

Kitchen duty that afternoon was tedious. Our escort in the kitchen happened to be my dance partner, Jean, who I learned was more a supervisor than a servant. Conner had a large kitchen, and Jean took great pride in showing us how smoothly it operated.

"The master occasionally has unexpected guests, so we always have a plan for last-minute meals," Jean said. "We've enjoyed this week since you boys came. We're preparing a lot more food than usual, and our serving dishes come back empty."

"Everything tastes so good here," Roden said. Tobias and I both smiled at that. It wasn't her decision who was made prince, so neither of us could figure out what he hoped to gain by complimenting her.

Roden answered that question a moment later when he noticed our grins. "It really does taste good," he whispered. "You should have seen what they fed us at my orphanage. I don't even think it was food half the time."

Jean instructed us on the proper way to hold a tray and how to serve or retrieve dishes on the table. She showed us how to pour a drink, and even let us sample a taste of Conner's best wine. I was interested in a detached sort of way and so was Roden. It was nice to know, but did me little good. However, Tobias leaned over to us at one point and whispered, "If Conner hadn't pulled us from the orphanages, this would likely have been our futures."

"Not mine," I said firmly. Nothing in me could accept a life like this. Roden quickly agreed.

"You know what little you must," Jean finally said. "Now make yourselves useful in here. There is always too much to do, and if we have you on loan, we'll use you."

She showed us a pile of dishes that needed to be washed. I pointed out there was really only room for two dishwashers and assigned myself the job of kneading dough at the other side of the room. Roden and Tobias didn't seem to care, so Jean gave in and waved me away.

I wandered over to the wood counter in the corner and picked up a lump of dough. After a minute, Imogen entered the kitchen, and Jean directed her to come over and help me. To my surprise, she didn't seem to object, and only moved a set of kitchen knives out of my way, giving herself room beside me to knead another lump of dough.

"I've done this before," I said, working my fingers into the warm dough. "It was one of the jobs at the orphanage. But the dough here is much better. We ate from a lot of charity ingredients before, which almost always meant whatever was unfit for the upper classes." She glanced at me and I continued. "I don't see why the upper classes object to food with weevils in it. They're very nutritious."

That finally earned a real smile, even though it was far from the funniest thing I'd ever said to her. Then I realized the smile wasn't about me; something in her had changed.

"You're different," I said quietly.

Without looking up at me, she nodded. She couldn't tell me what it was, but she didn't need to. There was less fear in her than before.

"Imogen!" a tall, square-cut man shouted from the far end of the kitchen. Based on his clothing, he was one of Conner's chefs. "Lazy girl!"

Imogen swung around. I started forward, but she grabbed my wrist to hold me back.

"Isn't that dough ready yet?" he said. "I've got to have it baked by this evening!"

"How could she have finished?" I scowled. "Every time she walked in here, you sent her out with another job!"

The chef crossed to me and shoved me against the brick wall. Pain lit across my bruised back and throughout my body. But I somehow held my tongue. "Don't tell me how to operate in my kitchen!" he snarled.

"Let him go!" Mott said, entering the kitchen. He grabbed my shirt and yanked me away from the chef's grasp, then motioned for Tobias and Roden to follow him. "We're finished here." As we walked out, he said to me, "Can't you go anywhere without causing a problem?"

"Is that who gives Imogen her bruises?" I asked.

Mott clenched his jaw. "It's clear that if you work from the kitchen tonight, one of you will end up killing the other. I'll assign you different duties." Then with a parting glare, he walked ahead of us.

Tobias and Roden caught up to me as we followed Mott.

"He hurt your back," Roden said. "I can tell by the way you're walking."

"My back is fine." It wasn't true, but I felt braver for saying it.

"It's your own fault if he did hurt it," Tobias said. "Why do you do it?"

I shrugged. "What?"

"Aggravate people the way you do. You seem bent on making enemies here."

"And you insist on making false friends. They're no different. Don't you ever get tired of pretending to be something you're not?"

"Like the prince?" Tobias arched his head. "No, I could pretend to be him for the rest of my life. Don't judge me just because you're not able to do the same."

His words hit me too close, and I fell behind him and Roden as we walked back to our rooms. We both knew he'd won that round.

# · TWENTY~EIGHT ·

We were secluded in our room when the betrothed princess arrived later that night. Roden suggested I sneak out and bring back a report of what she was like, which I was perfectly willing to do, but Tobias said he'd tell Mott if I left.

"You can't have the advantage of seeing the princess before we do," Tobias said. "Knowing you, you'll convince her tonight that you are the prince, and she'll have you crowned at the castle before Roden and I are awake tomorrow."

I snorted, and then said, "Now that you're onto me, I'll have to figure out an even cleverer plan." Mocking Tobias was risky, and probably unfair. But it was usually too hard to resist. I grabbed one of the books off his desk and brought it back to my bed, letting it fall open somewhere in the middle.

"What are you doing?"

"Mistress Havala said I'd have to study on my own to catch up. That's what I'm doing."

"You can't read."

"I said I can't read well. But I paid very close attention to Master Graves this morning, and I hope to read well enough to understand this book."

Tobias folded his arms. "Do you even know what it's about?"

I shook my head and flipped to another page. "It would help if there were more pictures in it."

"It's on early Carthyan history. If you are going to study, you might choose a topic more relevant for convincing anyone you're a prince."

"Great. Give me one of those kinds of books."

"They're in the library and we're not allowed to leave this room."

I turned several more pages of the book. "Then I'll have to content myself with reading this one."

Roden chuckled and grabbed another book off Tobias's table. "Me too."

"Now you're a reader also?" Rising anger tinged Tobias's voice.

"It'll be good practice." Roden settled onto his bed with a book.

Tobias's face reddened. "You think this will convince Conner of anything? I'm twice as smart as either of you."

"And half as strong as me or Roden, even if we're asleep," I said. "You have to do better, Tobias."

"Is that a challenge?" he asked.

"I'd never challenge an inferior. Now go to sleep. You'll need rest before whatever humiliation comes your way tomorrow."

"You sleep," Tobias said. "You'll need some strength for sneaking out later tonight."

I laughed and tossed the book on the floor before lying down. But I didn't go to sleep. That was a luxury I couldn't afford. It was much later in the night before I finally decided to sneak out, this time through the secret passages. Climbing across the exterior walls of Farthenwood was a bad idea since I still felt so weak, but as long as nobody else was in the passages, it would be a fine way to explore.

I was gradually learning the exit points of the passages. They ran throughout Farthenwood, or at least to areas where Farthenwood's architect felt a person might want to secretly travel. One of my favorite exits took me into the hallway around the corner from my room. It helped to see what was happening on the outside when everyone thought we were safely inside. I left the passages and entered the hallway, using that door.

As always at this time of night, there were only a few servants wandering the halls, so as long as I was careful to find the shadows in Conner's home, I had access to most of the places I wanted to go. This time, I even got a glance down the hallway at who was guarding our room each night. I practically choked with laughter when I saw him. He might have been younger than the three of us, and he'd fallen asleep. He wore a sword, but the smallest buckle of the belt still hung loose around his waist. Clearly, Conner no longer considered any of us as at risk for running.

The one well-guarded room wasn't far from Conner's. The vigils in front of the door were unfamiliar to me and they stood very alert. It had to be the guest bedroom for the betrothed princess Amarinda.

It was impossible to continue any farther through the hallway without risking the attention of her vigils, so I slipped back into the passages. Somewhere in there was a door leading directly into Amarinda's room, but using it for any reason was a terrible idea. It did occur to me that there might at least be some way to peek into the room without entering it. The curiosity of what Amarinda looked like was very strong.

While feeling around for any place to view into the room, I felt a hand on my arm and the point of a knife at my back. It had been only a matter of time before the others discovered the passages too.

"Is this how I have to prove my strength?" Tobias's voice was thick and he sniffed loudly. I wondered if he was crying.

"Where'd you get the knife?" I asked calmly. Calm was important here.

"I stole it from the kitchen." He pressed the long end of the blade into my back and I stiffened as I felt it cut. It was a razor-sharp knife. "If the whipping before wasn't enough, maybe I can stop you."

"From what?" I said, gasping. Blood trickled down my back, though I couldn't tell if he'd opened the old wound or created a new one.

"Stop you from being considered. I saw Conner's admiration for you while we practiced our dancing. But how can he? You're the least worthy of the title, the lowest of us three."

"And you're the biggest coward," I hissed, then caught my breath in my throat as his blade cut deeper.

"Don't call me a coward," Tobias said. "I'm not!"

"Have you come here to kill me?" I asked. "Because I'll scream when you do and it'll wake up the princess and probably a whole lot of other people, and you'll get into trouble."

"You'll be dead."

"Yes, but you'll be in trouble."

Tobias lightened the pressure on the blade. "This is just a warning for you to back down. I will be king."

"If you don't want to kill me, then lower the knife."

Tobias released my arm, then said, "Don't try anything with me. I'll keep this knife ready if you do."

I stumbled away from him, my head spinning. "What am I going to try in here? You know that if you're this paranoid as king, it'll eat you alive."

"Maybe King Eckbert should've been more paranoid. Then he wouldn't be dead right now."

I stopped and grabbed on to the wall for support. It took every bit of my concentration not to be sick all over him.

"You okay?" Tobias asked. Not that he cared. When I

began walking again, he followed, adding, "What's the point of wandering around here every night?"

The sting gradually eased. It was still fierce, but the whipping had hurt worse. Maybe he hadn't cut me as badly as I first thought.

"Conner has you and Roden in his control," I said. "Not me."

"Not me either," Tobias quickly said, but from the tone of his voice, it was obvious that even he didn't believe it.

"I'd like to go to our room now," I said. "I'm tired and you hurt my back."

"I'm not apologizing for that. I'd rather keep you weak."

"What a person of honor you are."

Tobias snorted. "A statement like that, coming from you?"

That brought a faint smile to my face. "Then let's hope Conner chooses Roden, so that Carthya has some hope of an honorable king."

Tobias didn't like that and he strutted ahead of me. "Roden would have this kingdom destroyed in a generation, with or without Conner's lead. He has no thought that someone else hasn't put there. I shudder to think either of you has any chance of being chosen."

"If Conner's choice was that obvious, my back wouldn't hurt so much right now."

"My warning is real," Tobias said. "And if you try to tell anyone about this, I'll see that Roden takes the blame. I know how to persuade Conner."

"You have no control over Conner. You may wear the crown one day, but he'll be king."

"I'll let him think he has control, then get rid of him. Where are we?"

Despite the pain I still felt, I couldn't help but smile wickedly. "Conner's room is on the other side of this wall. Pray he is a deep sleeper, or else he heard every word you just said."

Tobias made a sound in his throat and put his ear to the wall, to see if he could hear Conner on the other side. I used the moment to grab his arm and twist it behind his back, and then withdrew my own knife from inside my clothes.

"Where'd that come from?"

"You're not the only one who stole from the kitchen." I withdrew his knife from his belt and whispered in his ear, "You're in a lot of trouble, Tobias. Conner knows about the notes you made, your plans to get rid of him. You've already lost. In a few days, he's going to kill you."

Then I hit him over the back of the head with the butt of my knife and he fell unconscious.

# · TWENTY-NINE ·

Tobias was asleep in bed when I woke up, so he must have found his way back to our room sometime in the night. The idea that I'd slept through his walking freely around the room made me uncomfortable. Usually, I was a light sleeper, and I didn't like the idea of wondering what he might have been tempted to do to me in my sleep.

Roden was already awake and still working on the book he'd taken off Tobias's desk the night before. "I can figure out a lot of these words," he said. "You should've paid more attention to Master Graves. I think he could've helped you."

"I can't pretend to be interested in someone who's so boring," I muttered.

Roden rolled his eyes and went back to his book while I got out of bed and began to get dressed. It would irritate Errol, I knew, but lately that fact was more motivation than deterrent.

"There's blood all over your shirt!" Roden said.

"Noticed that, did you?"

Roden closed the book and came closer to me. "It looks like your shirt was cut too. What happened?"

"Do I need a bandage?"

"How should I know? Let me call Errol."

I pulled off my shirt and threw it into the fireplace, which still bore a few smoldering ashes. The alcohol that Imogen had used for me was in the corner of our room. I poured just enough of it onto the shirt to stir up the fire again.

"What did you do that for?" Roden asked.

He made enough noise that Errol and the other two servants took it as a sign that it was time to enter from the hallway. I was never sure what time they arrived each morning, but they always came in when they heard us talking.

"I'll help you finish dressing, sir." Errol said the words as if he were tired of speaking them. He knew I didn't want his help, and that was especially true right now.

I turned so that my back was facing the wall. "I'll dress myself and I'll do it privately."

Tobias opened his eyes. "Will everyone speak quieter? I have a terrible headache here!"

"Sage's back is bleeding again," Roden said to Errol.

Everyone's eyes turned to me. Errol walked between me and the wall. A gasp escaped his lips, then he said, "This is a new wound. Where did it come from?"

I shrugged, not yet ready with an explanation. Whatever I said, it'd have to be a lie. Although the truth would ruin Tobias's last hope to become the prince, it did me no favors either.

Errol gave up asking for details and said, "The cut isn't so deep, but we have to take care of it."

"Just give me a bandage and I'll wrap it myself," I said.

Errol shook his head and left the room. It was a good thing the two weeks were almost ended. I doubted whether he could tolerate me for much longer.

"I'm already dressed." Roden scowled at his servant, who was tugging at his shirt. "Get out!"

"You're dismissed too," Tobias told his man, a new servant who avoided me as often as possible. "We need to talk in private. Shut the door behind you."

Immediately after we were alone, Roden leapt across the room, grabbed Tobias by the shoulders, and shoved him hard against the wall. "You did that to him? Were you going after me next?"

"Check me for a knife if you think I did it." Tobias looked sideways at me. "I don't have anything that could make a wound like that, do I, Sage?"

"You're afraid of what Roden would find if he searched?" I asked.

Tobias threw up his hands, and Roden pulled back Tobias's blanket and checked his pillow. Then he lifted Tobias's mattress and gasped.

Tobias's face paled as Roden withdrew the knife Tobias had used against me the night before. Dried blood still stained the tip of the blade. I'd made sure of that.

"How'd that get there?" Tobias whispered. His eyes narrowed as they met mine. "Oh, of course. Well, Sage has a knife too."

"Do you think so?" I said. "I'm sure the kitchen staff will find there's only one knife missing." But I let Roden search my things anyway. No knife was there, and Tobias's face paled even further.

"I've got to tell Conner," Roden said. "This goes too far, Tobias."

"Please don't," Tobias begged. "Conner already thinks I have a plan to get rid of him. If he thinks I tried to do anything to Sage — he'll have my head."

"Conner should punish you," I said. "Being chosen as the prince is the least of your worries now."

Tobias's eyes filled with tears. "Help me, then."

"You nearly killed me last night. Should I care what happens to you now?"

"Please. I'll do anything."

"You're asking me to lie for you? Then I'd be the one in trouble. Why would I do that?"

His voice raised in pitch. "Please, Sage. Anything you want. Help me, and I'll fight for you."

He looked terrified, probably exactly as I had looked when Conner told Mott to take me to his dungeon. Tobias had played into my hands, but I felt sorry for him nonetheless. "I'll help you, but at this price. It's time to fail. You will be less intelligent, less impressive, and certainly less princelike."

"Is what you told me last night true?" Tobias asked. "Does he really know about the notes?" I nodded and watched as tears filled his eyes. "Then he's going to kill me anyway."

"What if I promise that he won't?" I said. "Back off and I promise that you will live, or else I'll die trying to save you." Now not only was Tobias out of the competition, but someone at Farthenwood owed me his life.

Errol returned to our room, accompanied by Imogen and Mott. Luckily, no attention was on Roden, who quickly hid Tobias's knife back under the mattress.

Mott strode across our long room in less than a half dozen long steps. He turned me around to examine my back, then cursed loudly. "The master must hear of this. Tell me how this happened or I'll take you to him for questioning. You know how that will end."

I glanced at Tobias, who nodded his agreement to my terms.

"It's embarrassing," I said. "I tried to sneak out last night through the window. I got caught on the window frame and it impaled my back."

"This is more than a scrape on your skin, Sage. You've been cut."

"The window has a jagged edge," I insisted. "I'm lucky not to be hurt worse. But it's my own fault because I should never have been out there." For an extra touch, I shrugged innocently and added, "I hoped nobody would notice."

"How could you think we wouldn't notice a wound like that?" Mott cursed under his breath. "Was this your attempt at obeying the master's rules?"

"All I wanted was to look outside," I said. "It would've been hard to go anywhere off that ledge."

"It'd be impossible," Mott said. "But you might have fallen to your death in the attempt." He inhaled, then added, "Not a word of this to the master, then, but I must punish you. I hesitate because I know how weak you must be from the last few days, but you'll miss today's meals."

I started to protest, then Mott arched his eyebrows and said, "Or shall we leave it to the master to choose a punishment?"

"I wasn't hungry anyway," I said.

---

Princess Amarinda had sent word that she would remain in her bedroom all morning. So Mott called Tobias and Roden to accompany him to breakfast with Conner and brought in Imogen to take care of my wound. She immediately went to work on washing away the blood. Her manner was cool and businesslike, but her touch as she cleaned my back was as gentle as ever.

"He knows you're lying," she whispered.

"Am I such a bad liar?"

"I'll have to wait until you tell the truth so I can compare the differences." She paused when I drew in a sharp gasp, and when she continued, the cloth was pressed so lightly on my back I could barely feel it. "How did it really happen?"

"A knife."

"Who held that knife?" I hesitated and she added, "One of the other two boys, obviously. It isn't a stab wound, though. This was done with the long edge of the blade."

"You know your knife wounds."

"I heard the chef say this morning that one of his knives has gone missing. He keeps them sharp. That's why you were kneading bread, to get close to the knife block."

"Actually, it was to keep Tobias away from the knives. He'd already stolen one, and that was as much damage as I wanted him able to cause me."

I thought that would at least get a smile or a chuckle, but she continued as if she hadn't heard me. "I checked first thing this morning. The knife you took is back in its place, and I found a few drops of blood on the floor."

"I thought I had them all cleaned up."

Frustrated, Imogen slapped at my bed. "Sage, please! Someone tried to kill you last night!"

"Not really. He just wanted me to think he could."

"Why must you play these games?"

"Because now there are only two people competing to become the prince."

Even without seeing her, I knew Imogen was frowning in disapproval. But she only said, "You know what I have to do now. It's going to sting."

"I'm getting used to —" I started to say before she pressed the wet towel to my back and made me howl.

Apparently, I'd reached the end of her sympathies. "Maybe you want Errol back," she said.

"Maybe I do," I moaned. "At least he wouldn't scold me the whole time."

"Someone should be scolding you," she said. "If you're not strong enough to handle all these injuries, you should stop getting them! You'll never convince anyone you're a prince this way."

Imogen began to wrap a new bandage around me. This one had to go diagonally over my shoulder and down below the older bandage. After she knotted it, she noticed the change in my mood and said more softly, "I'm sorry, I didn't mean that. You'll do fine in convincing them."

I remained facing the wall. "What if I don't? What if after Conner chooses me, they look at me and only see Sage?"

"Would that be so bad, just to be who you are?"

This time I looked back at her, grinning. "You mean other than being executed for stealing the crown?"

She laughed. "Yes, other than that."

Then I grew serious again. "What about you? If you were in the court when I'm presented, would you bow to me?"

After a moment, she slowly shook her head. "I hope Conner chooses you, and I think if he does that you'll be able to convince them. You'll be a fine king one day, but I know too much. And I won't bow to a fraud."

I turned away as she left the room. Unfortunately, I understood exactly how she felt. Nobody should have to bow to a false prince.

# · THIRTY ·

As the day progressed, it became evident that I would eat better on this period of punishment from Mott than I'd eaten yet since coming to Farthenwood.

Tobias snuck me back better than half of his breakfast, and Errol left some food in my room while cleaning up, expressing false dismay after I ate that "it was food intended for somebody else."

We were to remain in our room in private study because of Princess Amarinda being in the house, but after lunch was brought to us, Tobias gave me all of his lunch and Roden shared half.

"You owe me nothing," I said to Roden.

"Not now, but if Conner does choose you, then I hope you'll make the same promise to me that you did with Tobias, to save my life."

"And will you make that promise to me as well?" I asked him.

Roden shrugged. "I can't make Conner do what I want. Not even if I were king."

I clapped Roden on the shoulder. "Then, for the sake of my life, I'll have to continue hoping to be named the prince."

Near us, Tobias's feet dropped to the floor and he banged on the door for his servant. When he arrived, Tobias said he had to use the toilet, the only reason we could be allowed out of the room. Even our lessons would be held in this room for the day.

"Do you think Tobias is so angry that he'll try to kill you again?" Roden asked after Tobias had gone.

"He wasn't trying to kill me last night. He just wanted me to think he could."

"Same thing, as far as I'm concerned. Though I guess in the end, it worked out better for you. Oh." Roden's eyes widened. "Did you plan for that to happen?"

"Tobias was getting desperate. Once he took the knife when we were in the kitchen, I knew something was bound to happen soon."

"Why didn't you just report that he had a knife?"

"There's forgiveness for that. But Conner wouldn't forgive what he did last night, and Tobias knows it, so he had to agree to my terms."

Roden slowly shook his head. "You let him cut you."

A smile spread across my mouth. "Well, I let him make the first cut. I thought that'd scare him into stopping. I wish it had, because it really did hurt."

Roden laughed and shook his head incredulously. "You're the craziest person I've ever met. Tobias may be more educated than you, but he's not the smartest of us." I chuckled, but Roden turned serious and added, "It really is down to you and me, Sage. I've still got to try to win, you know that."

"It's cruel, this game of ours," I said. "Between us, you're Conner's favorite now."

Roden nodded. "You can bait me all you want. I won't try to kill you."

"You could, though," I said. "I've seen you out practicing swords with Cregan."

"Cregan hopes Conner chooses me, and he wants me to be ready for when he does." Roden's voice raised in pitch. "What's wrong with that?"

"Nothing. I'm just glad to hear you're practicing for Conner's benefit and not mine. I'm running out of places to get hurt."

"I don't see why that's funny. I think you must like the pain, because you're constantly pushing people until they hurt you."

"I definitely don't like the pain," I said firmly. "So if you do decide to kill me, make it quick."

Roden's laugh came without humor and we finished lunch with little more conversation. When Tobias returned a few minutes later, Master Graves had already arrived and begun a particularly dreary lesson on the great books and fine art of Carthya. Tobias lay on his bed for the entire lesson, causing Master Graves to remark that he never thought he'd see a lazier student than me. I felt a little sorry for Tobias, watching him pretend to be less than he was. But unfortunately, that was his situation now.

Errol and the other two servants came in mid-afternoon to get us ready for the charade of being servants to Princess Amarinda that evening.

"Why so early?" Roden asked.

"You may have been clean orphans this week," his servant told him, "but you're still orphans. It'll take a bit more cleaning up to make you worthy of the betrothed princess."

"Have you seen her?" I asked.

If he had, the servant wouldn't acknowledge it. But while he gathered my clothes, Errol whispered to me, "I've seen her. She looks as beautiful as any princess could. You should feel lucky to be able to serve her tonight."

I was too tired to feel lucky, or to care what the princess looked like. I told Errol he could take my place tonight, which he said was fine if I'd do the laundry in his place. That was the end of our bargaining.

Making us worthy servants included trimming the uneven ends of our hair so that it would tie back neatly, filing our nails, and lecturing us on the importance of always standing up straight around anyone we served.

Unfortunately for Errol's best efforts on my behalf, the shorter side of my hair refused to stay out of my face. Finally, he gave up and told me to keep it pushed back whenever I was around the princess. We both knew I probably wouldn't.

When we were finished, they placed us in front of mirrors.

Our white undershirts were cut closer to the arms, to avoid the sleeves touching any of the food as it was served. The vests we wore over them were simple, earth-colored, and laced up the front, and the boots were low and secondhand.

I snorted a laugh. "Everything here is about costumes. We don't know the first thing about being servants, but they've certainly dressed us for the part."

"This is my part," Tobias mumbled beside me. "Now."

"I like them." Roden twisted in an attempt to see how he looked from the back. "It's easier to move in these than the clothes Conner has had us in all week."

Mott entered the room and surveyed each of us. I wondered if he'd polished his bald head. It looked shinier than usual, and he wore clothes nearly as fancy as Conner's. He was to be distinguished tonight as something more than a servant, though still not worthy to sit at the table. With a very stern voice, he said, "As long as none of you does anything stupid, I believe tonight will be successful. Here are some things each of you must remember. Never address a master first and never look them in the eye unless they are speaking specifically to you. You follow my directions and never take any initiative with the princess unless I order it." Looking straight at me, Mott added, "You three must remember that you are in disguise. The worst thing that could happen would be for the princess to remember meeting you here tonight after you are presented at court. That cut is still evident on your face, Sage."

"It'll be healed by the time I'm presented at court," I said. "Besides, Imogen once served us with a bruise on her cheek, so this should only help me fit in better with the other servants."

Mott didn't rise to my remark. "And how are the wounds on your back, specifically the one caused by the . . . window?"

"If I'd had more to eat today, they'd probably be healing faster."

Mott smirked and glanced at Errol for an answer. "No signs of infection, sir," Errol reported.

"That's good," Mott said. "Because I'd expect a dirty window to have caused infection. I did hear that a knife was missing from the kitchen last night, one of the chef's sharpest blades. Those are kept very clean."

"Only one knife was missing?" Tobias glanced at me and then quickly looked away when I tilted my head in response to his silent question. He whispered something under his breath, I'm sure some sort of curse aimed at me. That wasn't a problem. The devils were used to receiving curses with my name on them.

"One knife," Mott said, walking over to stand directly in front of Tobias. "With a blade about as long as Sage's wound. Do you know anything about it?"

Tobias took a step backward, and his eyes darted around as he searched for a response, but I spoke up. "None of us would know where the chef misplaced the knife. And fortunately, I have no intention of going out that particular window again, so there should be no injuries in the future."

Mott scoffed, making it clear he didn't believe me, but all he said was, "Line up behind your servants, boys. The dinner will be ready soon."

# · THIRTY~ONE ·

Conner's dinner that night was served in the great hall, not the dining room where we'd eaten all week. Several guests were already there, but the princess and her parents, who apparently had accompanied her to Farthenwood, had not yet entered.

I was assigned as a door servant, with no apparent function other than to stand beside the doors of the great hall and observe as other servants came and went. Tobias's and Roden's assignment was no better. They stood at the far end of the room, tasked with the job of closing the curtains if the setting sun got in anyone's eyes.

Mott announced Princess Amarinda's arrival, along with the entrance of her parents and some of their courtiers.

Amarinda was as beautiful as Conner had described her, with chestnut brown hair swept away from her face and falling in thick curls down her back, and piercing brown eyes that absorbed her surroundings. As she recognized Conner, her entire face lit up with a smile that was warm and inviting.

Here, in Conner's home, the guest had made the owner feel welcome.

Conner stood, along with the others at his table, and bowed to Princess Amarinda and to her parents. Master Graves had told us about them, and how Amarinda came to be the betrothed princess.

The alliance between Amarinda and the house of King Eckbert was made at her birth. She was three years younger than Darius, and the product of a lengthy search by Eckbert. He wanted a foreign girl whose connections were powerful enough to forge a marriage that would create a bond between her country and Carthya, but not a direct heir to the throne, who would have political ambitions of her own.

Amarinda was a niece to the king of Bymar. Before she was even old enough to crawl as an infant, her parents had promised her to whoever inherited Eckbert's throne, most likely Darius. And although she'd never been given a choice in marriage, the older Amarinda became, the more her admiration for Darius grew. Both were said to be eager for the time when she would be of age and they could marry.

Amarinda stopped when she passed me beside the door. "What are you staring at?"

Whatever rules Mott had given us blurred in my head. I could speak to her if she was addressing me, but she was only addressing me because I'd looked right at her, which was not allowed.

"Forgive him, Highness," Mott said, stepping forward.

"No forgiveness is requested. I merely wondered what a servant found so interesting."

I looked to Mott to see if I should answer. With a stern warning in his eyes, he nodded permission at me, and I said, "You've got dirt on your face."

She arched her eyebrows. "Is that a joke?"

"No, Your Highness. On your cheek."

Amarinda turned to her attendant, who flushed and wiped the dirt off. "Why didn't you tell me before I walked in here?" Amarinda asked her.

"You led the way, Highness. I didn't see it."

"But he did and he's only a servant." She turned back to me apologetically. "Before leaving my room, I had the window open and paused to look out. I must have gotten some dirt on my face then."

"I never said the dirt detracted from your beauty, Highness," I told her. "Only that it was there."

With a somewhat embarrassed smile, she nodded at me in return, and then continued on, taking her seat. Out of the corner of my eye, I caught Conner looking at me, though his expression was so controlled I couldn't tell whether he was amused, relieved, or furious.

Dinner smelled so good as it was served that it took considerable willpower not to reveal that I was in disguise at that moment and to sit down to eat with the others. A large roast had been prepared, with boiled carrots and potatoes, hot bread, and some sort of imported cheese, the name of which I didn't recognize when Conner offered it to Amarinda.

Imogen was one of the servants of the meal. I noticed a cut on her forehead and wondered if Conner would dismiss that as yet another clumsy moment. No matter how long I stared at her as she served, she avoided my eye each time she entered or exited the room. Had I offended her somehow? Or was she keeping herself away from the increasing danger that surrounded Conner's plans?

Across the room, Tobias was disinterested and lackluster. He stared at the floor and soon faded into the background. Roden looked hungry, and I caught him staring at the princess with a powerful expression of admiration.

The conversation at the table began with shallow pleasantries. Conner described his life in the country, away from the politics of Drylliad. Amarinda discussed her travels as she toured Carthya in the recent weeks. Her parents understood that as an heir to the throne, she was far more important than they were, and deferred to her in leading the conversation.

After the main course was served, Conner steered the conversation directly to the topic I was sure he had intended for us to hear: the plans for her eventual wedding and ascension to the throne.

Amarinda pressed her lips together, then said, "Perhaps there will never be a wedding." She glanced over at Conner, who feigned appropriate concern. After a moment, she added, "There is a rumor that came to me only a few days ago regarding the king and queen, and their son."

"Oh?" Conner's wide eyes actually looked curious. He knew exactly what that rumor was, and I couldn't help but respect his acting skills.

"You haven't heard it?"

"I was told the king and queen and their son are touring the northern country, which they often do at this time of year."

"And may I ask when you last saw them?"

"It's been a few weeks," Conner said. "Before their trip to Gelyn."

"And they were well?"

"Certainly."

Amarinda's father spoke up. "Then the rumor cannot be true." He heaved a sigh of relief and took his wife's hand. She also looked relieved.

"Rumors have always surrounded the royal family," Conner said, as if the matter were settled. "It's the cheapest entertainment for everyday folk."

There was laughter at the table, except for Amarinda, whose solemn voice took control of the room. "I heard they're dead. Murdered." The laughter fell silent, and she continued, "All three of them, poisoned during supper and dead by morning."

Mott glanced at me from his position and shook his head, warning me not to react. I forced a disinterested, blank expression onto my face, despite the churning in my stomach. If I reacted, Conner would change the subject. But I needed them to continue talking about it, because no matter how easily he could avoid giving us more details, he'd have a harder time dodging the princess. However, the one question at the top of my mind was one I knew she'd never ask: Would the person who steps in as the prince become the next victim?

Conner leaned forward and clasped his hands together. "Highness, you are scheduled to be at the castle in Drylliad tomorrow, correct?" When she nodded, he said, "Let the rumor lie until then. Whether it's true or false, it will be verified once you're there."

"Waiting is more easily said than done." Amarinda's voice was heavy with sadness. "If there's no heir, there's no betrothed princess. I'll be a widow without having married."

"Even if the rumor is true, there may be another way," Conner said. "Perhaps all is not lost for you, or for Carthya."

Amarinda arched an eyebrow, curious. Conner waited several seconds to continue, which I knew was to increase her anticipation. It was heartless, even cruel. Finally, he said, "What if Prince Jaron were alive?"

Amarinda froze. Everyone at the table did, except Conner, who was enjoying this moment far too well. He manipulated those around him as though we were all pawns in his twisted game. I hated that my life had become entwined with his.

Finally, Amarinda's mother said, "Everyone knows Prince

Jaron was killed by pirates four years ago. Are you telling us this is not so?"

"I'm only saying that there is always hope." Conner then addressed himself to Amarinda. "Highness, perhaps you may soon claim the throne after all."

"Am I that shallow?" Amarinda stood, angry. "Do you think I cared about the throne and not the prince? You talk about Jaron's return as if it would solve all our problems, but it's Darius who concerns me. I need to know if *he* is alive!" She closed her eyes a moment, regaining calm, then said more softly, "You must forgive me, but I'd like to return to my room. I have a headache."

Her father rose to escort her out, but she raised a hand to stop him. "No, Father, you should stay and continue the evening. My ladies will accompany me."

"My man will see you to your room," Conner said, gesturing at Mott.

Amarinda eyed me, and I lowered my head, willing her to look anywhere else. "That boy can see me there."

Conner hesitated, then smiled and nodded his permission at her. I wondered if perhaps he wasn't allowed to refuse her, or maybe he liked her suggestion. I didn't.

"I don't know the way, Highness," I said. It was a stupid lie and poorly told. Hers was the room where I had bathed on my first day at Farthenwood.

"I do. All I ask is for an escort."

Conner waved me away, so I bowed to her and we walked out into Conner's great hallway. I led the way up the master staircase, which seemed endless on this trip. All I wanted was to take her to her room, then get away.

Behind me, Amarinda said, "You've obviously never escorted royalty before. Do you expect me to keep up with you at this speed? I set the pace, boy."

I stopped, but did not turn around. "My apologies," I mumbled.

"You do not have my forgiveness yet. Let's see how you do from here."

When she was close behind me, I continued walking, slower this time. "What is your name?" she asked.

"Sage."

"That's it?"

"I'm a servant, Highness. Do I require more of a name?"

"I am known to most only as Amarinda. Am I a servant as well?" She supplied her own answer. "Of course I am. I exist only to ensure there is a reputable queen for Carthya when the time comes. Have you heard of Prince Darius?"

"Of course."

"Have you heard the rumors of his death?"

"I've heard them." And they weren't rumors.

She touched my arm to get my attention. I stopped, but kept my gaze low. "Is he really dead, Sage? If you know, you must tell me. Perhaps you know someone who works in the castle at Drylliad. Surely, you servants talk with one another."

For the first time, I turned to face her, though I didn't dare look her in the eyes. "The servants wonder what Amarinda will do if she has to marry Prince Jaron to gain the throne. If he is alive, of course."

Amarinda didn't answer for a very long time. Finally, she said, "You speak too boldly for a servant."

I continued walking again. Amarinda caught up to me and said, "Is Jaron really alive? Whether the king's family is living or dead, if Jaron is alive, he must be presented at court."

I stopped in front of Amarinda's door, still keeping my eyes on the floor. "Here's your room, m'lady."

"You told me you didn't know where it was."

And quickly realized what a stupid lie it had been. Rather than respond to her, I asked, "Is there anything else you need?"

"Do you wonder why I asked you to escort me, Sage?"

I shook my head and might have sighed a little too loudly. My back hurt from so much standing, I hadn't eaten yet, and I was tired of pretending. Beyond that, I didn't want to hear that a girl who'd have to marry me one day, if I was declared Prince Jaron, really loved the prince's older brother.

"I asked you here because you spoke honestly to me before. If I'd entered that room with a face smeared in mud and asked another servant how I looked, he'd have bowed and told me I looked as beautiful as ever. When you're in my position, Sage, you come to realize how few people you can trust." She waited, expecting me to respond. When met with silence, she went on,

"So I trust your opinion on my dilemma. Should I continue on to Drylliad, hoping Prince Darius will greet me there but knowing in my heart that something is wrong? Or shall I stay away, knowing that if there is no Darius, I am no longer a betrothed princess and have no place in Drylliad?"

This time I looked directly at her, although her eyes were so perceptive, I immediately looked away again. "You should go to the castle, Highness. You should always choose on the side of hope."

"That's good advice. I have less of a headache now than before, Sage. Thank you for that." She smiled sadly. "Do you envy me, as a royal?"

I shook my head. The closer I got to the castle in Drylliad myself, the more I dreaded it.

"Many do. I'm glad you can appreciate your station in life as a servant. I'm a servant too, you know. Perhaps with finer clothes and servants of my own, but few choices about my life belong to me. We're not so different, you and I."

She was closer to the truth than she realized, but I held my tongue and stared at the ground.

"Will you not look at me?"

"No, my lady. If I cannot look at you as an equal, I will not look at all."

She placed a hand on my cheek and softly kissed the other one, then whispered, "Remember this moment, then, Sage, when someone of my status offered a kindness to someone of yours.

Because next time we meet, if Darius is dead, I will no longer be anyone of importance."

Then she entered the room with her ladies in tow. Only after her door was shut did I look up again. Darius was dead, and very soon she and I would meet as equals. But I had the feeling it wouldn't be a day she ended up celebrating.

# · THIRTY-TWO ·

Where are you going?" Mott asked as I began walking away. He was never far behind.

"To my room. My back hurts."

"How will it look to everyone at dinner if the servant who left with Amarinda fails to return?"

"How will it look if that servant's bandages bleed through and he drips blood on Conner's dining table?"

"Come on," Mott said with a sigh. "I'll walk you to your room."

"You don't have to. I know the way."

"Saving you from getting lost is not the reason I'm here. Tell me, what did you think of the betrothed princess?"

"I think she loves Darius."

"There's plenty of time for her to learn to love Jaron. Besides, this is the way of life for royals. They do their duty to their country, and if they are very lucky, it will sometimes bring them happiness."

"I don't want anyone to do their duty for me," I grumbled. "A charade like that is not for her."

"Conner is preparing you to wear a mask for the rest of your life," Mott said. "It's better that your queen pretends to love you, because if she truly did, she would only love a lie."

That hardly made me feel better.

Errol was sitting on the bench just outside my bedroom door. He stood as he saw us coming. "Are you ill?" he asked me.

"Get me some dinner," I growled, pushing past him to enter my room. "And no, I don't need help dressing."

Ironically, I did need help. My shoulders and back had stiffened over the past few hours of standing, and with every movement, I felt like my wounds might tear open again. When Errol returned with a tray of food several minutes later, he found me sitting on the floor with an unbuttoned shirt and vest.

Errol set the tray on Tobias's desk, and then silently went to the wardrobe to gather my nightclothes. He was able to pull off my shirt without causing me too much pain and, without asking, checked my bandages. "Imogen is occupied at the dinner downstairs," he said. "You must let me clean those wounds. They look hot."

I leaned forward, which took less work than arguing. He soaked a towel in the alcohol and pressed it to my back. I arched it with the inevitable sting, then relaxed as it slowly passed.

"Every servant at Farthenwood knows Tobias cut you," Errol murmured. "I'd be surprised if the master doesn't hear of it soon."

"The servants are mistaken. I was trying to climb out a window."

"We hear things, Sage. More than anyone knows."

"Then you obviously know why Roden and Tobias and I are here. Are Conner's servants loyal to him, to this plan?"

"Shortly after you came, Conner impressed upon us the sacred nature of what he's doing, how important it is to Carthya. To be sure, he threatened us dearly if word of his plan leaks outside Farthenwood. But he shouldn't worry, nor should you. This is a secret we will all carry to our graves. If you are chosen as prince, I will treat you just as I would a true royal."

With that, he finished bandaging me up. He pulled my nightclothes on and even fastened them in front, which I was more than capable of doing.

When he stood to leave, I said, "Thanks for helping tonight, Errol. Thanks for helping every night. I know I'm difficult."

"I'll take that as an apology, sir. Your dinner is on the desk there. Good night."

---

I was in bed when Roden and Tobias came into the room. Tobias entered more quietly than usual and lay down on his bed indifferently. Roden crossed over to me and said, "Conner was furious that you didn't return to the dining room tonight. I heard him ask Mott to come get you right now."

I groaned. "How can he expect us to see ourselves as royalty when he treats us as slaves?"

Errol entered the room and began rummaging through my drawers. "I'm sorry, Sage, but it's true. Conner has asked to see you. Mott is waiting outside to take you to see him."

I winced as I rolled out of bed. Errol held up clothes for me, but I shook my head. "If he asks for me at night, he'll find me in nightclothes."

"It's inappropriate," Errol said.

"And it's indecent of him to summon me when he knows I'm asleep!"

I opened the door to leave, but Mott blocked the doorway and shook his head at me. "I won't bring you to the master like that. Allow Errol to dress you, or I'll do it."

I shut the door in his face and held out my arms to Errol, who hurried forward, clothes in hand. Minutes later, Mott was walking me, fully dressed, down to Conner's office.

"Am I in trouble?" I asked.

"That depends on your answers to his questions."

Conner was in the middle of writing something when we entered his office. Mott directed me to stand in front of his desk, but I sat. A minute or two passed before Conner even acknowledged I was there. Finally, he set the quill down and looked up at me.

"What did you think of her?"

"The princess?" I shrugged. "She's beautiful. I'd heard the betrothed princess was more horse than woman."

"Bite your words," Conner hissed. "You're speaking of the future queen of Carthya. That is, if the prince is found. And yes, she has most unexpectedly become a beautiful young woman. Why did she choose you to escort her out?"

"Because I told her about the spot of dirt on her face before. I think she appreciated the honesty."

"You're lucky she did. She might as easily have had you whipped for being disrespectful."

"I've already been whipped."

"And stabbed, I hear."

"Mott has my story on that incident, sir."

"A story which is probably a lie."

"At Farthenwood, lies and truth blur together."

"Only lies in pursuit of the truth, Sage."

My body ached with tiredness. All I wanted was to finish this pointless conversation and go back to sleep. But there was one question I needed answered. "Why did you allow me to go with her? When you bring me to court, she'll recognize me."

"*If* I bring you to court. Don't mistake my tolerance for you as any sort of favoritism. Quite the contrary."

"My question stands, sir. Why did you allow me to go with her?"

"The possibility of her recognizing you did concern me for a moment. Then I decided you can easily explain that I kept you in hiding here until you could be presented at court. The fact that you two already met could be seen as an advantage. Now I have some questions for you."

"I have a few more questions first."

Conner arched an eyebrow. "Oh?"

"What if Prince Jaron is alive? Then he returns to the castle to find me sitting on his throne? I don't think he'll appreciate that."

"Jaron is dead. I told you once before that I have proof of it. Besides, the pirates off the coast of Avenia are ruthless. The reason no body was ever found is because they likely destroyed everything identifiable about him. Whatever trouble he may have caused his family, the king and queen loved Jaron. The queen in particular never gave up searching for any trace of him in the years that followed. It was all in vain. I doubt he was even alive by the time his ship sunk."

"What's your proof?"

"I present that to the boy I choose as prince and to nobody else."

"If you can prove Jaron's dead, then can you also prove to the regents that Jaron survived?"

"At court, Jaron will confess that he has been hiding all these years in an orphanage, right under their noses. He went by the name of Sage or Roden or Tobias, but he has come back now to claim the throne."

"What if another orphan steps forward to say he knew us before Jaron was killed?"

"We would say they are mistaken, and perhaps one night that orphan would disappear. Thrones have been claimed over thinner evidence than we have, Sage. Besides, my prince will have evidence of his identity."

"What?"

Conner shook his head slightly. "I'll save that answer until my prince is chosen, but rest assured, it is something that will identify my choice as the prince without doubt. Now to my questions. What did Princess Amarinda talk with you about after you two left?"

"She's worried that the king's family is dead, despite your assurances that she shouldn't worry. She doesn't seem to believe there's any hope of Jaron being alive, and I don't think she'd want him even if he were. She's afraid, sir."

Conner smiled. "We can use that to our advantage. Use her fear to make her more apt to accept the prince when I present him. So that even if she has doubts, she'll accept him because she needs it to be true."

I couldn't hide my disdain as I glared at him. It was disgusting that he'd think so quickly of how he might benefit from her pain.

"Don't make that face at me!" Conner cried. "How convenient it must be for you to play the pious victim when it benefits you, or to be the prince, or the servant, or the orphan! Yet I must at all times be the keeper of this unholy plan. I do not celebrate my role in Carthya's future, but I've accepted it. Have you?"

Any expression vanished from my face. "Yes, sir, I have. I am your prince."

"You think too highly of yourself. Tobias can no longer be trusted, but Roden presents some fine advantages. I believe he has been underestimated this week. He has learned more than any of you in such a short time."

There was nothing I could say to that. He had.

Conner continued, "What I wonder is if you *want* to be the prince. I sense you battling that decision internally, perhaps because you're afraid of the consequences of being caught, perhaps because you cannot picture yourself sitting on the throne. And yet here you are, telling me to my face that you are my prince."

I threw out a hand, then immediately regretted the gesture when the movement pinched in my back. "Would you choose Roden, who rushes toward the throne with no thought of the consequences? He has no idea what he's accepting. I have thought about it, Conner. And I am your prince."

Conner clasped his hands together and a glint of triumph flickered in his eyes. "I believe that what I suspected all along was true. All you ever needed was the proper discipline and the right motivation. I can see that you are finally bending to my will, and that pleases me."

It did not please me. Tired as I was, I still had plenty of energy to be angry with his smugness. However, I simply asked, "Can I go now?"

He hesitated a moment, then nodded, and I left without looking at him. As Mott escorted me back to my room, he tried to make conversation, but I ignored him. Conner's words still rang in my ears. With every step closer to the throne I took, I felt myself bending too. I only hoped I could get to the end before Conner broke me completely.

marinda left with her entourage early the next morning and our tutoring schedule resumed. Roden's reading wasn't fluent, but he was amazing, considering how recently he'd begun learning. I thought he would be good enough to get by if Conner chose him as prince.

Mott pulled me out of Mistress Havala's class to work on sword fighting with him, even though I insisted I couldn't fight with my back in bandages.

"If we wait for a full healing, it'll be too late," he said. "We'll both use wooden swords today." He took one for himself and tossed me the other. I jumped away from it and it landed in the dirt.

"Afraid of a wooden sword?" Mott teased.

"Just demonstrating my skills in evading an attack," I said, a grin tugging at the edge of my mouth. "Impressed?"

"No. Pick it up."

When I complied, Mott stepped me through the basic defensive moves. "If you can't attack like Jaron, at least I can teach you to defend yourself."

He thrust his sword at me. I moved mine in an attempt to block it, but his went right past mine and jabbed my ribs.

"You're worse than when I last saw you," Mott said.

"You shouldn't have whipped me so hard."

"You shouldn't have let yourself get stabbed."

I smiled and swung my sword low to the left, getting in a swat on his thigh.

"Not bad," Mott said, "but you lack the discipline that would be expected of a prince."

"I could always say that I'm out of practice."

"Nonsense. Prince Jaron was an amazing swordsman for his age before he disappeared. You cannot be as pathetic as you are now and hope to pass for him. Why do you think his sword was made?"

I blocked his attempt to graze my shoulder. "Maybe to encourage him to take his studies more seriously."

"Jaron always took sword fighting seriously. He is known to have once declared in front of the entire court that he intended to lead the Carthyan armies in war one day."

"Then he sounds like a fool," I said, thrusting forward. Mott dodged me and easily blocked my move. "Mistress Havala said that Eckbert was a peaceable ruler, at all costs. Carthya has avoided war for generations."

"Carthya has enemies, Sage. Darius understood that. Perhaps Jaron did as well. Their father never did."

"Are you saying Eckbert was a bad king?"

"He wasn't evil. Just naïve. Each year, his enemies have grown stronger, forged alliances, stockpiled their weapons. Eckbert failed to see their hungry eyes as they looked toward Carthya." Mott shrugged. "He failed to see the enemies within his own castle."

I used the opportunity to jab at his side, then followed it with a slice that threw his sword off balance. Mott backed up two steps and readjusted his grip. "Good move, Sage. Very unexpected."

"I fought better with Jaron's sword," I said.

"You fought better because it was a superior sword, even as an imitation. It's too bad that it's been taken. Conner now believes it wasn't any of you three boys. He thinks one of the servants took it to sell, knowing you boys would get the blame for it."

"Cregan probably took it to help train Roden."

"Unlikely. You dislike Cregan, Sage, but he serves Conner well. He'd do anything Conner asked."

"So would you."

Mott stopped and lowered his sword. "I wouldn't kill for him. That's my limit."

I couldn't let that go unanswered. "Then your limits are meaningless. Cregan killed Latamer on Conner's orders, and you helped it happen. That's the same thing."

Something flickered in Mott's eyes. He pressed his lips together and said, "Our lesson is over. Hang up your sword and I'll walk you back to the house."

The rest of the day was taken up with lessons. So much information was being pushed into our heads that it's a wonder none of them exploded. Tobias was eventually sent back to our room as punishment for sleeping during the lesson, and he was clearly relieved to be going. That gave a burst of energy to Roden, who saw it as his chance to be the star student. After all, I wasn't much more interested than Tobias had been.

Tobias stopped me in the hall as we were being escorted to dinner with Conner that evening. "You remember your promise to me, right? You'll make sure I live through this?"

"That's still my promise," I said.

Tobias exhaled a sigh of relief. "Then let me help you become the prince. What do you need?"

"I want nothing from you, Tobias. Just loyalty, if I'm chosen."

Tobias lowered his voice further. "I wasn't going to kill you the other night. I never had any intention of doing that. The knife was sharper than I thought. What I thought was only a surface wound —"

"It will heal."

"I think Mott suspects the truth. Maybe Conner too."

"You have my promise, Tobias. You will live."

"I trust you." Tobias paused, as if he were weighing his own words. "I do, Sage. I trust you."

"Keep up, you two," Mott called back to us. "Conner is waiting."

We caught up to Roden and Mott shortly before we arrived at the dining room. Once there, Mott opened the door to allow Roden and Tobias in, but he put a hand on my shoulder to hold me back and shut the door again.

My heart raced, but I tried to keep my expression calm. Mott looked very serious and I had no trouble thinking of any number of reasons why he might be about to punish me.

"Whatever you think I've done —" I began, but he shook his head to silence me.

"I didn't know he was going to kill Latamer," Mott said in a low voice. "You had it figured out before I did."

The memory of Latamer turning just before he was struck with Cregan's arrow was burned into my mind. It was relentless in my dreams at night and haunted my steps in the day. If only I'd realized what was happening a few seconds earlier, it might have been enough to save him.

"Why are you telling me this?" I asked.

He shrugged. "I guess I just wanted you to know that I remember what you said down in the dungeons. Conner doesn't own me either."

---

Conner had news for us that evening. "Do you remember when we spoke of the prime regent, Veldergrath? He is the one who aspires to become king, the one we must prevent from taking the throne because of the damage he will do to Carthya. I received an interesting letter from him tonight, which is both distressing and encouraging." To illustrate, Conner held up a few papers, which I assumed was Veldergrath's letter. "The encouraging news is that he has heard the rumor that Prince Jaron may be alive. I knew he was meeting Princess Amarinda earlier today, to travel with her as far as Eberstein on the outskirts of Drylliad, where he maintains a home. I expect she told him. This bodes well for my prince's acceptance at court, if it is less of a surprise when I announce him."

"And the bad news?" I asked.

"The bad news is that word is also spreading of the king's and queen's deaths. A decision cannot be made as to who will take the throne until the end of this week, but Veldergrath will use the fear of their deaths to build up more support for himself. He wrote to ask me whether I have any solid information as to Prince Jaron's whereabouts. My response to him was nonspecific, which will test his patience, but it does buy us another day."

"Another day for what?" Tobias asked.

Conner took a deep breath, and then said, "I will choose my prince in two days' time, then we will leave immediately for Drylliad."

Tobias, Roden, and I looked at one another. There was surprisingly little enthusiasm from any of us, and Conner noticed.

"I might have expected some excitement," he said.

"What will become of the two boys who aren't chosen?" I asked.

Conner paused, then he said, "I haven't decided that yet."

Everyone in the room knew that was a lie.

# · THIRTY~FOUR ·

The night passed without incident. If Tobias and Roden knew I'd snuck out during the night, neither of them mentioned it the next morning. After breakfast, Mott entered the room and said Conner had new plans for us that day.

He carried something in his arms, which he unwrapped and set on an easel in front of us. It was a painting of a boy standing beside a tall hedge in a springtime garden. He had light brown hair with darker streaks underneath, a mischievous smile, and a hint of trouble in his bright green eyes. None of us had his innocence, his naïveté.

"Is that Jaron?" Roden asked.

"The last known picture of him," Mott said. "Painted more than five years ago, when the prince was nine years old."

I couldn't help but stare, comparing myself to every detail of the painting. Roden and Tobias were studying it as carefully, no doubt doing the same thing. Each of us had features that looked similar to the prince's, but Roden groaned in disgust.

"Sage looks more like him than Tobias and I. Conner led me to believe just the opposite."

"Do you see a resemblance?" Mott asked me.

I shrugged. "My face is longer, and my hair is the wrong color. If anyone compares me to that picture, the regents won't believe I'm him."

This brought on even louder complaints from Roden, as well as a few objections from Tobias, that none of us was enough like the picture to be convincing.

Mott shushed us, then continued, "Conner's plan this morning is for each of you to undergo whatever transformation you can to look like the prince. Your hair will be cut to match his — Sage, we have a hair dye that may work for you. You will each be measured and clothes will be prepared for the one Conner chooses. By the time one of you is chosen tomorrow morning, he will look like the prince."

While Roden and Tobias got their hair cut, Errol led me outside to work the dye through my hair.

"It will look like I've used hair dye," I said. "And what about when my hair grows back into its color again?"

"Master Conner believes you can use less and less dye each time," Errol said. "Within a year, it will appear as if your hair has naturally changed color."

"He thinks of everything," I said without any hint of admiration.

I had no mirror to see myself once the dye was washed out sometime later, but Errol smiled when he looked at me and seemed pleased. "It's amazing how that one thing has brought your appearance so much closer to the prince's. I'm certain Conner will choose you. Most of us servants believe that."

Which would have been comforting if we hadn't passed Conner in his office with Roden as we walked back in. Roden was kneeling before Conner at his desk. His hair was styled just as Jaron's had been and he looked very nice. If there were inconsistencies between his look and Jaron's, they could easily be explained by the changes in a face over time.

"I am exceptionally impressed," Conner was saying to him. "You have surprised me, Roden, and pleased me. Tobias, any similarities between you and the prince have vanished. Do not consider your chances of being chosen tomorrow to be good."

"No, sir," Tobias said. I hadn't even seen him in the room. He must have been beyond our vantage point.

"Ah, Sage," Conner said, noticing us at the door. "It seems that once again you're behind the others. I still find myself looking at an orphan, albeit one with the same hair color as the prince."

"I am your prince," I told Conner, then walked on past his office.

Errol caught up to me and whispered, "Perhaps I was wrong to have said that Conner would choose you. You might be too late."

With my hair cut and styled an hour later, I gasped when Errol handed me a mirror. Errol's wide eyes hinted at his equal amazement. "The resemblance is so strong, you could almost be Jaron's twin," he said.

I couldn't stop staring. Was this really me? I was too accustomed to hiding my eyes behind my hair and feeling dirty and grimy. Had Conner known this was possible when he first took me? Had he seen through all that?

"Take me to see Conner," I said.

"You walk differently," Errol observed as he followed me down the hallway a moment later. "You are different, Sage."

"Let's hope Conner sees things the same way."

Conner's office door, which was usually open, was closed this time. "I think we should come back," Errol said.

I rolled my eyes and knocked on the door.

"Enter," Conner said from his office.

I opened the door. Mott was sitting on the chair in front of Conner at his desk, but turned to see who had come. He stood when I entered, as did Conner.

Conner said nothing for several seconds. His eyes scanned me up and down, and his mouth hung open.

"It can't be," he said. "More than I'd hoped for."

"I told him he could be the prince's twin," Errol said.

Conner's eyes flashed at Errol. "Get out."

Errol nodded and vanished from the doorway. He'd made a mistake by openly acknowledging that he knew about the plan. It didn't matter that Conner was the one who'd told them about it in the first place.

"Kneel, please," Conner said. "I wish to study you better."

"Come as close to me as you'd like," I answered. "Study me here, on my feet."

"You won't kneel?"

"Would a prince?"

Conner raised his voice. "You're not a prince until I say so."

"I don't need you to say so, sir. As you see me standing here, I am the prince of Carthya." I turned to walk out of the room, but Cregan flew past me through the doorway.

"Master Conner," he said in breathless words. "You were right. Veldergrath is coming."

"How far away did you see him?" Mott asked.

"Several miles off, but he wasn't alone. He has an entire company of men with him."

"Soldiers?"

"Not in uniform. But they're armed."

Conner nodded. I could almost see plans forming in his mind like storm clouds gathering. "He wants to intimidate us, not fight. So we must welcome him in with all hospitality. Get word to the staff to prepare a meal large enough for him and his company. And remind them not to speak of my plans unless they all want to hang for treason." Then he turned to Mott. "Find the three boys. Hide them in my secret tunnels."

"I know about them, sir," I said. "I can take us there."

Conner looked surprised only for a moment, then he nodded and said, "Sage, you must find Roden and Tobias and hide in the deepest of my tunnels. I don't need to tell you what will happen if you are found. Mott, go to their room. Destroy any trace of the boys' presence here."

I began to leave, but Conner said, "Wait!" He opened the bottom drawer of his desk and withdrew a small locked box decorated in emeralds. "Take this with you. Do not open it and do not let it get into Veldergrath's hands."

Cregan, Mott, and I each ran our separate ways. In the library, I found Tobias and Roden, who stood when I entered. "You look so . . . different," Tobias said. "I admit I couldn't see the resemblance to the prince before, but now —"

"Veldergrath is coming," I said. "You must come with me at once."

"What's the hurry?" Tobias said, putting his book away. "Conner can declare you or Roden as prince and resolve his plan today."

As they followed me upstairs, I answered them. "Veldergrath is the last person in this kingdom who wants to see Prince Jaron return. If he finds us, we're all dead."

## THIRTY-FIVE

I led Tobias and Roden to an area of the tunnels I had discovered on my last trip. They went deeper than any others and, in one area, placed us beneath Farthenwood's main entrance. The rock foundation of the house was showing its age. Using small gaps in the mortar, we had a limited view outside.

Since finding the tunnels, I'd felt Farthenwood was designed for a paranoid man who expected enemies to enter his walls. If Conner's father had built this house, he had no doubt made his son just as paranoid.

From where we stood, we could see the approach of Veldergrath and his men. They were at least fifty in number, and each carried a sword. But they were still too far away for us to tell which of them was Veldergrath.

"It's an act of war for Veldergrath to do this," Tobias said.

"Only if Conner doesn't invite him in, which he's going to do," Roden said.

"Conner thinks the army is only for intimidation," I said. "We have no means to fight him, so, hopefully, Veldergrath only intends this to be a show of power, maybe to persuade Conner to join him if Carthya does fall to civil war."

"If Veldergrath wants the throne this badly, he won't give it up easily," Roden said. "Whomever Conner declares as prince will eventually have to face Veldergrath."

A moment of silence followed. That idea didn't appeal to any of us. Finally, Tobias said, "If you hadn't already forced me out of the plan, Sage, I would've withdrawn right now."

Ignoring Tobias, Roden angled forward to get a better look. "That's got to be him," Roden said. "There in the center."

It was obvious by his fine clothes and the men who surrounded him that this was Veldergrath. He had hair the color of midnight, which he wore pulled behind his head so tightly that I wondered how he could blink. His face was constructed of hard angles and long lines. I tried to imagine him as king of Carthya. If a person could be judged solely on appearances, this man was a tyrant.

Conner walked out to Veldergrath, and they greeted each other with courteous bows. "My old friend," Conner called out, loudly enough that we were able to hear him. "To what do I owe the honor of your visit?"

"I've heard troubling news about you, old friend." The way Veldergrath voiced "old friend," it was clear he considered Conner anything but that. "May we speak in private?"

"Certainly. In anticipation of your arrival, I've had my chef make up some soup for your traveling companions. They must be hungry."

"Perhaps we should eat first," Veldergrath said. "I antici-pate you'll feel less hospitable to me after we talk business."

With that, Conner led Veldergrath and a few men inside, while the rest dismounted as Conner's servants assisted them in caring for their horses.

"Why does Conner help them?" Roden asked. "I'd send them on their way."

"I'd give them soup," Tobias said, then grinned. "I'd use the rottenest meat in my stores and hope they all got sick on it."

"It's diplomacy," I said, irritated they couldn't see that. "It's all Conner can do right now, and for all of our sakes, let's hope it works. C'mon."

They followed me up another bend in the tunnels to the main floor. We were near a secret door behind a tapestry in Conner's office, where they were certain to have their private meeting. Although their voices would be muffled, we could hear them from where we stood.

Tobias whispered, "If they eat first, it'll be a while."

So we waited. It was impossible to determine the passing of time from here, although with the sting in my back and ache in my legs, it probably felt longer than it really was. Tobias and Roden wanted to sit, but I reminded them that any position they took now, they would have to maintain after Conner and Veldergrath entered, or risk making a noise that would give us away. So we all stood in silence.

After a very long time, we heard Conner's voice as he

entered the office. "I always feel bad news is better handled on a full stomach. Don't you agree?"

"It's only bad news if you're up to something you shouldn't be." My fists clenched at Veldergrath's arrogance. Even if he was correct in his suspicions, Veldergrath wasn't king yet and had no right to question Conner.

We heard the squeak of Conner's chair as he sat, and his invitation for Veldergrath to sit as well. Then Conner said, "You should explain yourself. Am I accused of doing something wrong?"

"The betrothed princess was here for dinner last night, correct?"

"Yes. She is a lovely young woman."

"A bit distressed, though, at having heard news about the deaths of the king, queen, and Prince Darius."

"She heard it only as a rumor."

Veldergrath huffed. "A rumor you and I both know to be fact. Obviously, you could not confirm or deny that to her, but she told me something else you said. Something that I find remarkable. You told her that Prince Jaron may be alive."

"I believe he is."

"We've sent three regents to Isel to determine this. Have you heard any news from them?"

"No."

"Then how have you come to this stunning conclusion?"

Conner hesitated a moment, then said, "Old friend, you seem distressed at the possibility. Don't you see what a great advantage it would be to the kingdom if Prince Jaron were alive? Eckbert's line would continue and Carthya would be saved from certain war. Surely, there could be no better news, yet you don't appear to welcome it."

"Er, of course." Veldergrath seemed to be taken by surprise, but he recovered quickly. "Of course I hope the prince is alive, but you and I both know how impossible that is. My question is not whether we should hope for that news, but how you have come to be so certain of it?"

"Obviously, an accusation follows this question, so why don't we move straight to it."

"As you wish," Veldergrath said. "Master Conner, I'm told you had a sword made, a replica of the one Prince Jaron used to carry."

"It was an imitation, not a replica. Sadly, I've recently lost it, or I could show it to you. I had it made, intending it as a gift for the queen's next birthday, in honor of her lost son."

"There's more. I'm told in the previous week, you scoured the orphanages of Carthya and even collected a few boys. Why is that?"

"Indentured field laborers. My crops are planted and I needed them."

"Where are they?"

"Ran away the first time my back was turned. If you know of their whereabouts, please tell me and I will have them punished." Lies fell from his lips as gracefully as raindrops from a cloud.

"There's one last thing. You sat with the king's family at supper the night they died."

"Many regents did."

"But you were given the honor of pouring their drinks."

Conner's voice remained calm, despite Veldergrath's clear insinuation that Conner was the one who had poisoned them. "And you dished up their pudding, sir. Is there a point to these questions?"

"Perhaps not. Are you aware that there is something missing from the residential quarters of the castle, a box covered with emeralds?"

My fingers rubbed over those emeralds. Conner must have stolen this box from the king and queen, either shortly before or shortly after their death. I didn't know what was in it, but whatever this box contained, it was probably going to be used as proof that one of us was Prince Jaron.

"You ask that as if you think I have it," Conner said.

"I'm certain that you'd never steal from the king, even a dead one," Veldergrath said. "But we have friends who are less certain of your character. So to appease the other nobles, who are suspicious of you, I ask your permission to search Farthenwood."

Conner laughed. "An estate of this size and you hope to find an emerald-covered box?"

"A box, or a prince. Do I have your permission?"

"Several of your men are rough-looking. They will frighten my staff."

"No harm will befall any innocents here." Veldergrath's insertion of the word *innocents* was calculated. "That is my promise."

Conner's voice was grim as he spoke. "Do what you will, Veldergrath. Waste your time in my dusty corners and crowded cellars if you must. You'll find nothing."

We didn't dare move until after Veldergrath had left the room. Then Tobias turned to me and hissed, "You know these tunnels. Are they safe?"

All I could do was shrug. I didn't know.

# · THIRTY-SIX ·

Veldergrath's men decided to begin in the dungeons and work their way up. So we made our way to the upper floor, keeping ourselves as far from the men as possible.

"This is a terrible idea," Tobias whispered as we walked. "If they do get into the tunnels, we'll be trapped."

"Then we go onto the roof and make our escape there," I said.

Roden's eyes widened, but he nodded his agreement. Tobias seemed even more anxious. "The roof? And fall to our deaths?"

"I've been there," I said. "We won't fall."

"Then let's go now," Roden whispered.

"There's too much chance of us being spotted if he's sent men to search the grounds or guard the doors. Veldergrath is no fool, so we must expect that he's done that. Going onto the roof is our last option."

We reached the upper floor using a tunnel that put us near the nursemaid's bedroom. I wondered if any children who once lived here had used the tunnels to play tricks on their caregivers. It's what I would've done.

Temporarily safe from Veldergrath's men, Roden nodded at the emerald box in my hands. "Is that the box Veldergrath was talking about?"

"Probably."

"What's in it?"

"It's locked."

"You don't seem curious," Tobias said.

"I'd have to break the box to get into it here, and I won't do that. Whatever its contents, we'll find out soon enough."

There was a moment of silence, and then Roden asked, "Sage, did you know you looked so much like the prince?"

"I always felt I looked more like myself than anyone else." I grinned, then shrugged. "I'm too scarred for a prince. Too many calluses and rough edges. A similar face may not be enough. Besides, what we saw is only a painting, an artist's interpretation of what Jaron looked like. Have either of you ever seen the royal family in person?"

Neither of them had. Roden observed, quite accurately, that royalty rarely visited orphanages, or invited poor orphans to state dinners.

"The king came through Carchar about a year ago," I said. "So I stood on the street to see him. He looked right at me as he passed — I could've sworn he did. Everyone was supposed to bow to him, but I didn't."

"Why not?" Tobias asked. "Honestly, Sage, have you no respect?"

"An Avenian bow to a Carthyan king? Wouldn't that dishonor the king of Avenia?"

Tobias's groan was muffled by Roden, who asked, "So what happened?"

"A soldier clubbed me across my calves. That sent me to my knees, and I was in no hurry to get up again. For a moment I thought King Eckbert would stop the entire procession, but he didn't. He only shook his head and continued on."

Roden chuckled softly. "It's a wonder you've lived so long. If Conner doesn't choose you, it will only be because you're too reckless to trust on the throne."

"I can't deny that. My point is that people don't always look the same in real life as they do in their paintings. My resemblance to a five-year-old painting doesn't matter. Facing the regents is the real test."

We immediately fell silent when footsteps clambered up the stairs near us.

"How many?" Tobias mouthed.

I shook my head. Maybe four or five men, but it was impossible to tell for sure. We heard several other men still on the floor below us.

They spread out, each of them taking one area of the upper floor to search. One of Conner's servants was with them to open any locked door or cupboard.

"There's a lot of storage up here," one man said.

"All the better for a hiding place," another said. "Check every trunk, beneath every bed."

"He wouldn't hide a prince in a dusty room like this."

"We search everywhere," the first man ordered.

My spirits lifted a little. There was no mention of secret passageways, which there would have been if any entrances had been found downstairs. It didn't appear they even suspected these tunnels were in the house.

Suddenly, Tobias grabbed my arm. He leaned very close to me and whispered, "I hid papers in our room. If they find them, they'll know we're here."

I threw out my hands in a gesture to ask him where the papers were.

He leaned in again. "I cut a small hole in the side of my mattress. If they move it, feathers will fall out and they'll see the hole."

He drew back with an apologetic look on his face, but I could only shake my head. Judging by the thoroughness of the search on this floor, it was too much a risk that they might find those papers.

I motioned for them to stay where they were. My feet would move quietly enough that I could pass through the tunnel undetected. Tobias and Roden might not.

I crept down the narrow stairs of the tunnel. One of the steps was loose, and I was concerned that when I pulled off the wood plank it would make too much noise, like it had before. There were a few small squeaks, but I moved so slowly they didn't seem to draw any attention.

The imitation of Prince Jaron's sword was lodged inside. I hoped I wouldn't have to use it, but I wasn't about to go out there without a weapon of some sort. With the sword in my hand, I inched open the door to our bedroom. A few men still remained on our floor, but they seemed to be nearer to Conner's room. I didn't think they'd come my way yet.

Our bedroom had been scrubbed of any evidence of our having been here. Now it looked like a little-used guest room. The wardrobes were empty, our books were gone, and the beds were pushed into a line of three near the wall.

Tobias's bed was the farthest from my hiding place.

I crept along the floor, hardly suitable for a gentleman or whatever Conner had turned me into, but very familiar from my life as an orphan. Once in a conversation with Mrs. Turbeldy, I compared myself to a caterpillar that went wherever I wanted with barely any notice. She compared me to a cockroach instead, who ran about freely in the darkness and scattered in the light. It was meant as an insult, but I thought it was a fair comparison, even a compliment judging by how hard they are to catch.

I crawled beneath what had been my old bed and then Roden's. Finally, to Tobias's, the last in the line. I was about to reach my arm up to feel around his mattress, and then froze. Footsteps were coming down the stairs.

"We're going to search this floor now," the man in charge of the others said.

"Julston! We need your men in here now," someone called from the hallway near Conner's room. "There's a lot of heavy furniture in here."

"So we get the sore backs and he gets the glory in whatever we find," someone outside my bedroom complained. But they went anyway.

I only had a few minutes. It was simple to find the hole in Tobias's mattress. He'd cut it well, so that it would always remain covered and so that no feathers would fall from it unless the mattress were overturned. The papers were right inside, tightly folded. I tucked them into my pocket and then crawled back to the doors. I was about to dart safely into the tunnels when a voice said, "Did anyone hear that? Like footsteps inside the walls."

I rolled my eyes. Was it Roden's or Tobias's carelessness that would reveal us?

It sounded as if the man began to call out someone's name, then he cried out in pain. I pressed myself against the wall, and only a second later, Imogen ran into my room, looking for a place to hide. In her hands was a fireplace poker. She must have hit the man with it.

My heart pounded. Imogen had successfully distracted him from the tunnels, but she was about to pay dearly for having saved us.

# · THIRTY~SEVEN ·

**W**here are you?" the man growled. Imogen back-stepped as he entered the room, holding the poker like it was a sword.

He was a big man, with a belt that had been stretched to its limits to fit around him. Even to protect us, Imogen never should have attacked him. She had no chance against this man.

He advanced and she swung at him, but this time he grabbed the poker. With one twist, he pulled it from her hands and yanked her toward him. "Who are you hiding here?" he asked. "Veldergrath will want to talk to you."

Imogen tried to resist his grip, but it was pointless. Finally, she wrenched up her face, then stomped on his foot with all her strength. He released her only for a second and she tried to run, but he grabbed her again and shook her by the shoulders.

"Oh no, you're coming with me," he snarled.

By that time, I had crept to within only a few feet from

him, my sword out and ready. Imogen didn't mean to betray me. She glanced my way for only a second, but it was enough. The man pushed her to the floor and with surprising agility swung around with the poker, swiping hard enough to make a swishing noise in the air.

I ducked to avoid his attack and thrust my blade deep into his gut. He gasped as blood leaked from his wound, then for the first time really looked at me. "Prince Jaron?" he whispered.

"Perhaps soon," I said as he toppled over.

Imogen ran into my arms, holding me so tightly that she nearly knocked me over. Her entire body was shaking, so I put my arm around her to try to calm her. One hand clawed into my wounded back, which I couldn't have tolerated if it was anybody but her causing me the pain.

Then she darted back from me, hearing a sound behind us. I swung around, ready with the sword, then lowered it when I saw Mott in the doorway.

Mott's eyes went from the man on the floor to the sword to me. "Drop the sword and get out of here," he whispered. "Now."

I gently set the sword on the floor, then took Imogen's hand and pulled her into the tunnel. Before I shut the door behind us, I saw Mott use the dead man's knife to stab himself in the arm. Reeling, he pulled the knife out, then fell on the floor.

Several of Veldergrath's men ran into the room. "What happened here?" one of them, a leader of the group, asked.

Mott rolled over. Whether he was exaggerating his pain or not, I believed his performance. "Your man attacked me," he mumbled. "I might have startled him when I came in, but it was only to assist him with unlocking these doors."

One of Veldergrath's men knelt down to examine Mott's injury. "You're lucky it wasn't deeper, or in a more vital area."

"I tried to dodge out of the way. He was aiming for my chest. I had to defend myself."

"You must have provoked him!"

Mott shook his head. "You saw me walk in here. I had no reason to attack this man. Perhaps I should report to your master and mine exactly how this search is going."

"Get rid of that body," the leader said. "Veldergrath doesn't want damage done to Conner's property. One of you clean up this blood."

A few men went to look for cleaning supplies, and after wrapping him in sheets from Roden's bed, it took most of the rest of them to haul the body out of the room. Mott assured them he could get himself bandaged and was soon left alone.

He glanced at the crack of the opened passage door I'd been staring through, then nodded at me.

I closed the door tightly and sank against the wall with my arms wrapped around my knees. Imogen sat silently beside me. I vaguely felt her presence, but took no notice of it. As it was, all

I could do was stare into the darkness and try to keep breathing.

Conner said he would let the devils have his soul if it meant succeeding with his plan. I had the feeling that when he did, the souls of all the rest of us would go to the devils too.

# · THIRTY-EIGHT ·

Imogen and I remained there until the search ended and Veldergrath's company of men left. Conner himself came to claim us in the tunnels. He found Tobias and Roden first, and then they walked downstairs through the tunnels to find us.

Conner offered me a hand from where I still sat on the floor, numb. I'd never killed before, not even accidentally or for defense or for whatever label they would attach to it tonight. My only intention had been to stop him from harming Imogen, and without alerting anyone else in the house to my presence. That at least had been accomplished, but it had come at a heavy price.

And as hard as I tried to avoid the comparison, in that moment, I had seen myself as Cregan, sending a deadly arrow into Latamer's chest, all to protect Conner's unholy plan. Every feeling within me was pain, so I hollowed it out and barely acknowledged Conner's greeting when he saw me.

I took his hand, but he did more work in pulling me up than I did with any effort to lift myself. I could tell from there that the imitation of Prince Jaron's sword was gone. Mott must have taken it with him when he went to get bandaged. Conner led us into the bedroom, where I sat on my bed. Roden sat next to me, Tobias took a stool for himself, and Imogen stood, keeping herself apart from the rest of us. Mott was already in the room when we entered. His arm was bandaged and his face was grim. It was obvious where the floor had been scrubbed of blood.

Conner addressed Imogen first. "May I assume that you were in the tunnels because you were somehow involved in the death of that man?"

Imogen nodded, slowly.

"It was my fault," I said. "I thought I struck him low enough to avoid any major damage."

"It was for good reason," Mott said. "We all know what would've happened if you hadn't acted, not only to Imogen but to you boys as well."

I knew, yet even that was not enough to make me feel better.

"But why were you out of the tunnels in the first place?" Conner asked. "You so easily might have been found."

Imogen drew in a breath and opened her mouth. She would speak to take the blame, but reveal the one secret that had protected her ever since coming to Farthenwood.

Cutting her off, I withdrew Tobias's papers. "These were left in this room, and if found, would have been damaging evidence about us."

Mott took the papers and handed them to Conner. He opened them, read a little, then said, "You wrote these, Tobias?"

"Yes, sir." His voice trembled when he spoke, and I wondered what was in them.

"You are a thorough record keeper. More fit to be a king's scribe than a king, I think."

Tobias lowered his eyes. "Yes, sir."

Then Conner turned to me, his expression different from before. Was it respect? Gratitude? I'd so rarely been looked at in any favorable way, I couldn't recognize it. He said, "If these papers had been found, none of us would be here tonight. Veldergrath's men were exceptionally thorough, but Mott was able to cover up your presence through his own brave act. Veldergrath left here embarrassed and disgusted when his most tedious search turned up no evidence of either you or that emerald box."

"But he was right," I mumbled. "You are plotting a false ascension to the throne, and you did steal that box from King Eckbert."

"Neither of which I make any apologies for." Conner's expression cooled. "Do you want the throne, Sage? Do you want me to choose you?"

It wasn't in me to care how I answered. "I accept the throne if the alternative is for Veldergrath to take it." My voice sounded as tired as I felt.

"That's not the same thing. Tell me that you will be a good

and noble king, that you want to claim the hand of the betrothed princess, and that you are glad I've done this for you. Lie if you must, but tell me that you want it."

I stared at him with a blank expression. "Aren't you tired of lies? I am."

Conner sighed heavily. "I would choose you, Sage, but for that. There is one thing that you must never tire of, not for the rest of your life, and that is the lie. The person I choose must have the lie so settled in his heart that he truly believes he is king, that he ceases to think of his own name and answers only to Jaron's. He must become so convinced of his lies that, were his own mother to appear at his side and call to him, without shedding a single tear he would tell her he is sorry she's lost her son, but he is the child of Eckbert and Erin. The person I choose must recall memories of a royal upbringing that never happened. And he must do all these things, every day, for the rest of his life, never once regretting the lie that brought him there."

I barely heard him and only stared at the scrubbed area on the floor. Imogen caught my eye and offered a grateful and sympathetic smile. At least she was safe.

Conner turned to Roden. "Can you tell the lie, Roden, for the rest of your life?"

He sat up straighter. "I can, sir."

Conner motioned to Imogen. "Bring the boys a supper here in their room. Each of you get a good night's sleep because morning will come early. Roden, you are my prince. You and I depart for Drylliad after breakfast."

# · THIRTY-NINE ·

O nce I'm named as king, I'll ask Conner not to kill either of you," Roden said as we lay on our beds that night. "Maybe I can get him to exile you to another country or something and make you promise not to return."

"By the time you've had the chance to talk with him, Cregan will already have carried out his orders," Tobias said. "He'll be quick with me, but what about Sage?"

He'd be anything but quick with me. Cregan had made that clear.

I arose from my bed and pressed open the secret door. "Where are you going?" Roden asked.

"If you're running away, let me come," Tobias said.

"I'm not running away and it's none of your business where I'm going," I snapped. "But I won't lie here while we all talk about our deaths."

Roden was still awake when I came back sometime later. He was sitting up in bed, staring forward but seeing little. "Why didn't you run?" he asked. His tone was flat and lifeless. "You had your chance."

I pulled off my boots and sat on my bed. My fingers found a garlin in my pocket, which I ran over my knuckles. "You think Conner's going to have Tobias and me killed in the morning?"

Softly, Roden said, "It's not personal, Sage, but I've decided not to ask him to save you two."

Not a big surprise, but I still asked him why.

Finally, he looked at me. Deep creases lined his forehead. "You know my answer. You and Tobias are threats to me now. There's only one way to guarantee you'll never come back to expose me."

"We're also the only protection you have from Conner."

Roden finger-combed his hair off his face, then leaned against the wall. "I'll have to deal with that eventually, but until then, I've got to do what's in my own best interest, and Carthya's best interest. I hope you two will forgive me."

I flipped the garlin at him before I lay on my bed. "There's your alm of forgiveness, Roden. Pay it to the gods or devils, or to Conner, whatever altar you bow to. But don't ask it from me."

---

Errol and the other two servants awoke us shortly before dawn. It was clear as we looked at one another that none of us had slept well, but the bags under Roden's eyes were so dark I wondered if he'd slept at all.

Particular care was taken with Roden's bath and dressing that morning, requiring all three servants to help. Tobias and I were left mostly to ourselves, other than Errol briefly slipping away from Roden's care to check my back.

"In another day or two, you can remove those bandages," he said.

"I'll be as healthy as any other dead man," I said lightly.

Errol frowned and lowered his eyes. Obviously, he didn't think my impending death was very funny.

Once we were ready, Errol pronounced me as similar to Prince Jaron in appearance as he'd seen the night before, but then loudly told Roden that he also had many features that reminded him of the prince.

Looking at Roden, I hoped he planned on eating only a little. He didn't appear to be in a state to handle a full stomach.

Mott came to collect Roden for breakfast. "You understand that the master may wish to reserve some conversations for himself and the prince alone," he said to Tobias and me. "Your breakfast will be served in here, and I will come for you later to say your good-byes."

"We're tired of eating in here," I complained, but Mott only frowned at me as he led Roden out of the room.

When the door shut, Tobias went to the window. "You can get us out of here, right? It's time to run."

"Run to where?" I asked. "Where would you go?"

"You could take us back to Avenia. We could hide there."

Out of the corner of my eye, I saw the garlin that I'd tossed to Roden last night. It had been left on the floor beside his bed. A day ago, he wouldn't have been so casual about leaving behind any amount of money, but he was Conner's prince now. Money was the least of his concerns.

I picked up the garlin, rolled it over my knuckles, then deposited it in my pocket. Tobias had retreated to his bed, defeated. I sat beside him and said, "We're not running away and this isn't over yet. When I said I wouldn't let Conner kill you, I meant it."

Tobias gave a halfhearted smile. "Thanks for that, Sage, but at this point, you should start worrying about your own neck."

Breakfast arrived soon after. I was as hungry as always, but Tobias barely ate a bite. Mott returned for us before I'd gotten too far into his meal.

"What's going to happen to Sage and me now?" Tobias asked.

"The master has given no orders," Mott said.

"Maybe not to you," I said. "Where's Cregan?"

Mott's face darkened. "Why didn't you tell Conner you'd lie for him, Sage? He stood right here and said he'd make you his prince. All you had to do was say you would lie."

I set my jaw forward, but said nothing. Even if I were inclined to explain myself, which I wasn't, I had no answer to give him.

Finally, Mott waved us to our feet. "It's too late to go back now anyway. Come with me and bid the prince and the master farewell."

We followed him into the entrance hall. Roden looked

pale and terrified. I leaned against the wall and withdrew the garlin from my pocket and began rolling it over my knuckles. It was a nervous habit, and I admit that I felt a little nervous.

Tobias tried a different tactic. He fell on his knees before Conner, begging mercy.

"Please don't have us killed," he said. "Please, sir. Give me your word that we can leave here safely."

"You ask for the word of a liar?" I asked. "Would you feel any better if Conner did promise us our lives?"

Tobias shrank even lower, but Conner stared at me, frozen. "What is that trick you're doing?" he asked.

The knuckle roll came so automatically to me that it barely required my attention. "Sir?"

Conner's hand flew to his mouth. "How can I have been so foolish? The devils must be laughing, for I nearly ruined everything!"

## · FORTY ·

Roden opened his mouth to speak, but Conner hushed him and walked over to me, never taking his eyes off the coin in my hand. "Where did you learn to do that?"

I shrugged. "Any pickpocket can do it." To demonstrate, I dropped the coin in Conner's coat pocket. With my thumb and forefinger I withdrew the coin, then rolled it over my knuckles and into my palm. "It's a good way to steal a coin because you can sneak it away without having to make a fist."

Conner turned to Roden. "Can you do it?"

Roden shook his head. Tobias also shook his head before he could be asked.

"I notice you do that with your left hand," Conner said. "Just as you prefer to use a fork or write your letters. Can you do it with your right?"

I tossed the coin to my right hand and demonstrated the knuckle roll with equal agility.

"And can you write and eat with the right hand as well?"

"When I was young, my father insisted I learn to use my

right hand for everything. He didn't want me to appear different in that way. I was out of practice before but have remembered that habit since coming here."

Conner walked toward his office. "Sage, I will speak with you in private."

It was an order, not a request, and I followed him into his office, where he shut the door behind me.

"You don't have to lie for the rest of your life." There was a desperation in Conner's eyes I'd never seen before. "There is another way."

"Oh?"

"Claim the throne now as Prince Jaron. Be him for a year or two, any respectable length of time. Then assign the throne to anyone you want. You may leave and return to a private life, albeit one of wealth and luxury."

"What are you asking, sir?" I knew, but I wanted to make him say it.

"Be the prince, Sage. I'm convinced now that it can only be you."

"What about Roden?"

"Prince Jaron was famous for his ability to roll a coin over his knuckles. As I've rehearsed this plan in my mind, I anticipated everything the regents might ask in accepting or rejecting you. I considered qualities of his personality and what might remain in his character as he grew and changed. Jaron was trained throughout his childhood in the royal tradition, so my choice would have to display some semblance of that training as well. But until I saw you there, I forgot that this coin roll was an occasional habit of his, a parlor trick, but one few others could do as well. Sooner or later, the regents would expect to see the prince do that."

I sat down in one of the chairs and crossed one leg over the other. "Roden can be taught to do it."

"Not in time, and not as well as that. He'd look like he'd just been taught. Sage, you must be the prince."

I didn't answer right away, admittedly partially because I knew how desperate Conner was for my response. Finally, I looked back at him. "No."

Conner exploded. "What? Has this all been a game to you? Just a test to see if you could get this far and then reject me?"

"No, sir. But I got to thinking last night while we were in the tunnels. Veldergrath's men would have killed me if they'd found me, right? Somebody did kill the king and queen and Prince Darius. They'll kill me too, eventually. I don't want power or wealth, Conner. I want to stay alive."

"Veldergrath won't dare harm you once you're seated on the throne. If the high chamberlain, Lord Kerwyn, accepts you as Prince Jaron, then Veldergrath will too. As for the royal family, you don't have to worry about the same threat."

"Why not?"

"They were killed for political reasons. If you use different politics, there will be no motive."

My eyes narrowed. "How do you know that, Conner? Do you know who killed them?"

"Is that an accusation?" he boomed, then lowered his voice, struggling to keep his temper. "Regardless of who killed them, I know who their enemies were and they're no threat to you. I can guarantee your safety on the throne, Sage. And I'll guarantee your death here if you refuse me."

"You won't kill me," I said. "I'm the only hope for your plan to succeed. Let's not pretend otherwise."

Conner sat in the other chair facing his desk, his eyes pleading with me to accept his offer. "Sage, no harm will come to you upon that throne, and you can reign only for as long as you want to."

"Then I can hand the throne over to you."

Conner's face reddened and he stood, yelling again. "Hand the throne to anyone you choose, just make it to someone you trust. I am not a villain in this story, no matter how many times you've attempted to frame me that way!"

"Are you a hero, then?"

"I'm just a man trying to do what I think is best for my country. If I've made mistakes along the way, they were made out of a desire to do the right thing."

"I have terms," I said.

"You're insufferable," Conner said. "Have you waited for this moment since we met? To force me into a situation where I must give in to your whims or else see everything I've worked for all this time go to waste?"

"Tobias and Roden must accompany us to the castle."

"Why?"

"I promised that if you chose me, I wouldn't allow you to kill them. It's the only way I'll be able to keep that promise."

"It's a foolish idea. They're a threat to you now."

"If you had left with Roden just now, Tobias and I were going to be killed, correct?"

Conner waved a hand in the air. "I can't deny that, nor will I apologize for it. The two boys not chosen know everything. They can use that knowledge to blackmail you, harass you, and intimidate you for the rest of your life. Information is a dangerous thing in the wrong hands, Sage. As of this moment, *they* are the greatest threat to you."

"But I will decide how to manage that threat. There's more. Imogen will come to Drylliad as well."

"Fool boy! May I remind you of the betrothed princess Amarinda? Imogen has no future connected with you."

"Once I'm made prince, I'll pay off her debt to you, then set her free. Either all of them come with us, or I don't."

Conner cursed, then grabbed a small marble statue off his desk and threw it at me. It whisked past my shoulder, hit the far wall of his office, and cracked the wood paneling. He probably intended to miss, but maybe not. "You are not the king yet!" he growled. "I'll bring them with us, only to get your stubborn head into the carriage with me. But until you are crowned, I am the master, and if I see a need to dispose of them, I will."

"Fair enough," I said, then a mischievous grin snuck onto my face. "So do you want to bow to me now or wait until we reach Drylliad?"

Conner brushed past me and into the entrance hall. He shouted orders for a carriage to be prepared for seven travelers. Cregan would now be our driver.

"Hail His Majesty, the scourge of my life," Conner said to Roden and Tobias as he stomped up the stairs. "I fear the devils no longer, because I have the worst of them right here in my home!"

# · FORTY-ONE ·

Since Conner's traveling group had now swelled from only himself, Mott, and Roden to a group of seven, we were informed that there would be a delay before we could be ready to leave. Tobias looked pleased and relieved, but Roden's expression was almost murderous as he stomped away. I wasn't sure where he was going, but knew he'd return when it was time to leave. He couldn't risk being left behind.

After changing into riding clothes upstairs, I told Mott that I wanted to go for a ride. "This may be my last chance to be truly alone, perhaps ever," I explained. "Let me have that time with my thoughts."

Mott gave a permissive bow of his head. "Be careful. You're Conner's prize now."

"I'm never careful," I said, grinning. Mott didn't smile back.

I walked past the kitchen toward the back door of Farthenwood that would lead me to the stables, and was only barely outside before someone punched me in the arm. Not a hard punch, compared to most hits I've taken, but an angry one.

Imogen had been standing just outside the door. She'd probably seen me in riding clothes and came out to wait for me.

"What was that for?" I asked, rubbing my arm.

She glanced around to make sure we were alone, then hissed, "How dare you, Sage? How dare you interfere with my life?"

Genuinely confused, I took her by the elbow and led her farther away from the door, beside a tall hedge where we would not be easily seen. "What are you talking about?" I asked. "What have I done?"

"You're the prince now?"

"Looks that way."

Tears welled in her eyes, though she was obviously trying hard to push them back. "And you're bringing me to Drylliad with you?"

"I can get you away from here, from whoever treats you so badly."

"And then what, Sage? What happens to me in Drylliad?"

I shrugged, unable to understand why she was so angry. "You go free. Once I'm made prince, I'll have access to the treasury. I'll pay off your mother's debt to Conner and you're free."

She shook her head stiffly. "I won't have your charity. Not from an orphan and certainly not from a prince."

"It's not charity. You're my friend, and I want to help."

If possible, that made her even angrier. "Do you think this is helpful? I had a place here, Sage. I understood my life."

"You have no life here. I'm giving it back to you."

"No, you're not. I know what this is."

I folded my arms as I faced her. "Oh?"

"You're afraid to go to Drylliad, correct?"

A little anxious perhaps, but that didn't explain her anger. "What if I am?" I replied. "You don't understand what —"

"I understand perfectly. You played Conner's game and won, but now that his decision is made, you're afraid no one will believe the lies. You want help in convincing the court. You think by bringing me to Drylliad, I'll feel obligated to lie for you."

Strong emotions rose in me. Not exactly anger, though that's how it sounded when I spoke. "You think that's my plan, that I'd use you in such a way? I had no idea I was such a horrible person."

Her face softened somewhat. "You're not horrible, Sage. But look at what Conner's turning you into. Don't you see it? I've watched you go from this orphan boy who might've become my friend to Conner's prince, who'll never be anything but his costumed servant."

"I'm nobody's servant."

"Yes, you are." She shook her head sadly. "You gave in to him. You let Conner win. I didn't think you would."

"Imogen, there is so much more happening than you know."

"And does any of it matter more than your freedom?" After a slight hesitation, she added, "I'm disappointed in you. I'd rather you had run. That would be better than this."

"Run?" Truly angry now, I started to walk away, then

turned back to her. "Then you'd condemn Tobias to death, make Roden a puppet king, and doom yourself to a life here. Conner's held you down for so long, you've forgotten what it's like to breathe free air."

"And you've given your life to his control forever. You'll never breathe free again."

I started to answer, to say whatever was necessary to make her understand. But in the end, I hesitated too long and finally only managed to suggest she should pack her things before Conner was ready to leave.

She shook her head, then hurried back into the house. As much as I wanted to follow her, gut instinct told me that would only make things worse. She could believe whatever she wanted about me, but she was still coming to Drylliad.

There were a few stable boys tending to the horses when I arrived there a few minutes later. No sign of Cregan, who was probably now having to get ready for our journey. The longer I avoided him, the better. Cregan had wanted Roden to be chosen. He'd be furious with me for winning out at the last minute.

I chose a quarterhorse named Poco for the ride. The stable boy seemed reluctant to let me have it without direct orders from Conner, so I began preparing the saddle myself. Finally, he said he'd do it before I ruined my clothes and got us both in trouble.

Riding Poco through the open field was refreshing. I'd

found spots of time alone over the past two weeks, but nothing of freedom. Poco was an excellent horse, instinctively obedient and eager to be tested. It wasn't long before Farthenwood was lost behind a wooded hill, and all was silent except for the gentle river nearby with birds chirping overhead. A slight breeze rustled the leaves of the tall trees over my head. I lifted my face to the sky and let the wind and the sun caress my skin. This was freedom.

As much as I'd ever know again, anyway. If Imogen had been right about anything she accused me of back at the house, this was it.

I slid off Poco's back and walked him to the edge of the river. This wasn't far from where Windstorm had left me several days ago, and the memory forced a smile to my face. I wished for a friend or a father I could tell the story to and make them laugh. Either with me or at me, I didn't care. Several smooth rocks lay along the bank of the river. I grabbed a fistful and flung them one by one into the water, watching them skip a time or two before disappearing. One rock I kept for myself.

It was little surprise only a few minutes later when another horse snorted in the background. Mott had come, no doubt. I'd seen him watching me from a distance when I was in the stables. And by the time I reached the arch of the eastern hill, Mott was in the stables. It must have killed him to wait this long before finally approaching me.

"Do you mind a little company?" he asked.

"Yes."

It didn't matter. He dismounted and walked over to me. We stood side by side for a long while, watching the river.

Eventually, Mott asked, "Did you know he'd pick you, because of that trick you can do with the coin?"

"I don't think anyone can predict what Conner will do. It's what makes him so dangerous."

"But you must have guessed it, or else you would have escaped this morning. Using the passages, it would have been an easy thing to run."

"Look what happened to Latamer when he tried to run."

That brought on an uncomfortable silence. Finally, Mott said, "Conner wants you to know that we're ready to leave soon. Errol is waiting to help you change into traveling clothes."

"You'd think they'd make traveling clothes more comfortable," I muttered. "I believe when I'm king, my first order will be to let everyone wear whatever clothes they want."

Mott chuckled. "Fashion. What a mighty beginning that will be for your reign." After another pause, he added, "What kind of king will you be, Sage? Tyrannical and fierce, like Veldergrath would be? Complacent and indifferent, like your father?"

I turned to him. "Like Eckbert, you mean?"

"Of course." With a cough, Mott added, "Get used to it. If you are Jaron, then Eckbert is your father."

I let that pass. "If I'm the prince, then you have a higher loyalty to me than to Conner, correct?"

"Yes."

"Then tell me this, did Conner kill my family?"

"I can't answer that, Sage."

"Can't, or won't?"

"You haven't been declared the prince yet."

I held out my arms to Mott. "Who do you see now, Sage or Jaron?"

Mott studied me for a long time before answering. "The bigger question may be, who do you see?"

"I don't know. It's not easy to be one type of person when you've worked so hard to be a very different type of person."

Mott's reply came so fast I wondered if he'd been waiting for just that type of opening. "And tell me, Sage, which person have you worked so hard to be? The orphan or the prince?"

He walked to his horse and untied a bundle on its back, unwrapping it as he carried it to me. Then he set the imitation of Prince Jaron's sword in my hands. My thumb rubbed over the rubies in the pommel.

"Thinking of how much you could get for them at market?" Mott asked.

"No." I held the sword out to him. "I don't understand."

"I thought you must want it. You stole it before, didn't you?" He didn't wait for an answer. We both knew the truth. "Which means you must have controlled that foul mare Cregan gave you long enough to get to and from the sword arena without being seen."

"I wouldn't say I ever controlled her," I admitted with a grin. "I was so worn out at the end, she really did dump me into the river."

Mott smiled and tapped the sword. "I figured you must want it back now, before we leave for Drylliad."

"Are you giving it to me? Is it mine now?"

Mott nodded. Without giving it a second glance, I hurled it into the deepest bend of the river.

Mott started forward, as if to rescue it, then turned back to me. "What did you do that for?"

I arched my head to look at him. "The prince of Carthya will never wear a cheap copy of a sword at his side. That sword is an insult to him."

"Is that why you stole it?" He didn't wait for an answer, which was good because I couldn't admit that aloud. "It would have helped you look more authentic."

"Do you really think I needed *that*, Mott, to help me?"

Mott nodded, very slowly. Not in response to my question but as if he had finally settled something in his mind. "No, you will not need that sword, Your Highness."

"Then you think I can convince them that I'm the prince?"

After a deep breath, Mott lowered himself to one knee and bowed his head. "What I think, if you forgive me of my blindness before, is that I never was looking at Sage the orphan. I kneel before the living prince of Carthya. You are Prince Jaron."

# · FORTY~TWO ·

J aron Artolius Eckbert III of Carthya was the second son of Eckbert and Erin, King and Queen of Carthya. All of the regents agreed it would have been better if this child had been a daughter rather than a son. A daughter could have married into the kingdom of Gelyn, as a measure of preserving peace.

Nor was the young prince particularly impressive as a royal. He was smaller in stature than his brother had been, had a talent for causing trouble, and appeared to favor his left hand, a quality frowned upon for Carthyan royalty.

Privately, Erin cherished her second son. The older child, Darius, was already being trained as a future king. He had belonged to the state from the moment of his birth, and fit the role well. He was decisive, controlled, and detached, at least to his mother. But less was expected of Jaron, and he could always be a little bit more hers.

Erin never had felt comfortable as queen of Carthya. It required her to hide much of her true spirit and zest for adventure. Indeed, engaging in a secret romance with young Eckbert had been the greatest adventure in her youth. She hadn't paused to consider the consequences until it was too late and she was in love.

Erin had served drinks in a small tavern at Pyrth for a year, working off the debts her father had acquired after becoming seriously ill while at sea. It was humiliating work. Until then, their family had enjoyed a fair social status and she had enough education to know how far they had sunk. But Erin endured it, and eventually the tavern began to prosper under her guidance.

Eckbert spotted her one night when he and his attendants traveled through Pyrth. He returned the second night in disguise, enchanted by her beauty, charm, and loyalty to her family. By the third night, Erin had figured out who Eckbert really was. He begged her to keep his secret, only so that he could continue to see her again.

At the end of a week, Eckbert paid off her father's debts, with extra to the tavern owner on a royal command that he must never reveal Erin's humble origins. He brought Erin back with him to Drylliad and made her his queen.

In marriage, Eckbert and Erin were happy, but as king and queen they disagreed on how to rule Carthya. Erin saw enemies in the faces of those Eckbert sought to appease with favorable trade laws and by ignoring clear violations of treaties. Their older son, Darius, would one day have to bear the consequences of Eckbert's fear of conflict. Jaron would be given more freedom to pursue his own desires. And Erin loved him for that.

Jaron was still very young when it became clear that he was his mother's child more than his father's. The fire he set in the throne room was not malicious. He had taken a bet from a friend, a castle page, that tapestries could burn. He intended to prove it by burning only a hidden corner of the tapestry. Over three hundred years of threaded history went up in flames before servants were able to put the fire out.

Commoners also loved the story of Jaron, at age ten, challenging the king of Mendenwal to a duel. None of them knew that Jaron had overheard the king accuse Queen Erin of not being a true royal. They only laughed at the image of a ten-year-old boy facing off with a king four times his age. The Mendenwal king humorously obliged Jaron and undoubtedly restrained himself during the duel. Although the king easily won the match, Jaron satisfied himself that he did give the king a nasty cut on the thigh. And he practiced his sword fighting twice as hard from then on.

As Jaron grew, Eckbert became increasingly angry and embarrassed by his son's antics. Instead of compressing himself into a model royal, as his father wished, Jaron rebelled further. He snuck out of his bedroom window at night, as often as the weather permitted and on too many occasions when the bad weather should have discouraged him. Heights never bothered Jaron, not even after the time he fell more than ten feet from a tower and had his life saved by an acroterion at the edge of the gable. He learned to scale the exterior rock walls with his bare hands and feet. Few people ever knew of that, because the only person to ever catch Jaron was his older brother. Jaron never understood why Darius kept his many offenses quiet. Perhaps because Darius knew he'd one day be king and hoped Jaron wouldn't embarrass him as well. Or because Darius wanted to spare his father the rumors that would swell throughout Carthya and abroad over how a king who couldn't control his own son could possibly control a kingdom. It never occurred to Jaron that Darius loved him. Protected him so that he could have the life Darius never could.

In fact, Jaron never fully understood that anyone in his family, other than his mother, truly loved him. Until it was too late and they were all dead.

Shortly before his eleventh birthday, Jaron's parents called him for a private council. Both Gelyn and Avenia pressed at Carthya's borders, threatening war. The regents were in an uproar, threatening to depose Eckbert if he didn't push their enemies back. Jaron was a distraction for the country and something had to be done. Eckbert had found a school up north in the country of Bymar for Jaron to attend. It would give him an excellent education and teach him proper decorum for a prince.

Jaron angrily protested. He swore to his father that if he tried to send him to Bymar, he would run away and never be found again. Eckbert retaliated, telling Jaron that if he did not go, it could mean the end for Carthya. He had to prove to both his own country and to the enemies at his border that he could be decisive. He would send his own son away and end the embarrassment.

Erin pled with Jaron to accept Eckbert's decision. To do it for Carthya. To do it for her.

"I will do it for you, Mother," Jaron had said. "I'll leave you for your own sake. But you will never see me again."

He hadn't meant those words. He was angry and felt horrible even as the threat tumbled from his mouth. But he also hurt in a way he couldn't describe. Enemies weren't at Carthyan borders because of him. They were there because his father had looked the other way for too long. Perhaps there were Carthyans who laughed at the prince's latest antics, but they would stand by their king when he called them.

Jaron left the very next day, rather quietly. There was no farewell supper, no grand entourage to accompany him to the docks at Isel. Only a few officers would journey with him to Avenia, then across the Eranbole Sea to the gates of Bymar.

Jaron got onboard the ship and immediately complained of rolling seasickness, despite the fact that the ship had not even left the harbor. A calming medicine was offered to him, and it was recommended that Jaron go to his room belowdecks to rest.

Jaron never took the medicine, and it was no easy matter for him to slip out the small porthole of his room. Still, he had a smaller build than most ten-year-old boys, and after he worked his shoulders free, the rest was simple. Unaware that Jaron had left, the ship set sail without him. The ship was attacked by pirates late that afternoon.

When news of the piracy returned to Carthya, a search was made for any survivors. There were none, all of them killed in fighting the pirates or drowned at sea. Because Jaron's body was never found, a search was made throughout Avenia and Carthya for any hope of his survival. Before long, most people believed he had joined dozens of others in the ship at the bottom of the sea.

Safely on land, Jaron quickly found he had skills that enabled him to blend in with Avenians. He was good with accents and had studied enough of foreign cultures to move amongst them like a native. He pickpocketed for spare coins or worked odd jobs wherever he found them.

Still, he went hungry most days and spent his nights huddled in the shadows, hoping to go unnoticed by the street thugs who patrolled the darkness.

It was Darius who found Jaron first. Jaron had dropped a coin in an offerings dish at a church. The priest there recognized the young prince and sent word to Darius, who was known to be searching for his brother in a nearby town. To stall for time, the priest kindly told Jaron he had some extra food, and if Jaron agreed to wash the church steps, he could stay the night. Darius arrived early the next morning, alone. Over a small breakfast with Jaron, Darius described the suffering of their parents, who had tortured themselves over having lost their son.

Jaron dissolved into tears and said he would gladly return

home if his parents would allow him to come. Darius told him to stay at the church and he would ask their father what should be done.

Darius left Jaron in his room, thanked the priest for his services but informed him that, sadly, the young boy was not the lost prince of Carthya. However, he expressed his pity for the boy and paid the priest to continue to watch over him for another week.

One week later, Jaron would finally begin to understand his role in the future of Carthya.

# · FORTY-THREE ·

At the end of the week, a man came to meet with Jaron in the church. If anyone had asked, the priest would have said he did not know who the man was, only that he had the air of someone of great importance. But nobody asked. As far as they knew, the boy living in the church was an orphan.

Jaron recognized his father immediately, despite his extravagant attempts at disguise. They did not embrace. It was not his father's way. But there were tears in his father's eyes, and for the first time, Jaron saw his father as a man, not as a king.

They sat in the center of the pews and received little attention from the few patrons who had come that day. It was awkward at first, for although they sat close together, father and son had grown miles apart.

"When I was your age, I wanted to be a musician," Eckbert said. It was a poor attempt at connecting with his son, but it was all he had. "Did you know that?"

Jaron nodded. His mother had told him that once. And when he was very young, his father would occasionally show him how to play some of his favorite instruments, although he was careful never to do so when there were servants around. His father thought it would be an embarrassment.

Eckbert smiled at the memories of his own youth. "I enjoyed playing the fippler, and although I confess I wasn't very good, it brought me a lot of joy. Do you remember when you were younger? I taught you a song or two, I believe."

"I remember one of them," Jaron whispered. "Mother's favorite."

Eckbert folded his arms together and leaned against the bench of the church. "My father, your grandfather, couldn't tolerate the squeaks and pitches of my music and discouraged me from playing. He said music was a useless education for a future king, and a waste of my time. Although I didn't understand it then, he was right."

Jaron listened quietly. It was hard to picture his father as ever having been a boy, as ever having any desire unconnected with the throne.

"You and I are not so different as you might think, Jaron. I spent much of my own childhood wishing I could have been someone other than a crown prince."

"I'm not a crown prince," Jaron reminded him. "Just a prince. Darius will take the throne."

"As he should. And he'll be a fine king one day. But what about you? What do you want for your life? Being a prince doesn't seem to suit you."

His father had intended to mean that Jaron was capable of anything, even beyond the castle walls. Jaron took it that his father felt he was unfit for his title and offered nothing more than a shrug in response.

"How has your life as a commoner been these past weeks?" Eckbert asked.

"I've managed."

"I knew you would. And I know you can."

Jaron glanced up at his father with questioning eyes. What did he mean by that?

Eckbert sighed. "Still, there will be hard lessons. If you are not Jaron, then you are nobody to the world. They will not care if you go hungry, if you are cold, if you lie beaten on the streets. I'll do the best I can for you, and beg your forgiveness that I can't do more."

"I want to come home," Jaron said softly. It was difficult for him to admit, but whether he was good enough to be a prince or not, he couldn't take another day on his own. His mother would want him back, probably Darius too. He wasn't sure about his father.

"You cannot come back" came his father's solemn answer.

Jaron set his jaw forward, the way he often did when he fought against his anger. "This is my punishment for running away? To be disowned?"

"You're not disowned and it's not a punishment. It's what your country demands of you now."

Jaron rolled his eyes. His father couldn't shove the blame away from himself so easily. "I'm to become a commoner, then? Shall I call you King Eckbert, or forget your name entirely?"

That hurt his father. But Jaron hurt too, so he felt justified in his words.

"You are always my son," Eckbert answered. "But the situation with the pirates has changed everything. Everyone believes you are dead, and I cannot allow that belief to change."

They were silent for several seconds. Finally, Jaron spoke. "If I came home, would you declare war on Avenia for sinking that ship?"

Eckbert sighed heavily. "I would have to, because you could provide the proof that it was Avenian pirates who attacked a ship with a royal onboard. If I start a war with Avenia, Gelyn will almost certainly align with them, and we shall be nearly surrounded by enemies. Carthya could not survive that war."

"And if I remain missing, would you have to declare war?"

"If you remain missing, I can tell my people that I will not declare war until there is proof of your death."

"Then we both know what has to happen." Jaron had said it matter-of-factly. He had considered this possibility, but hoped against it. "What about Darius and Mother?"

"Darius . . . misses you. But he knows there are sacrifices we make for the good of Carthya. Your mother doesn't know you've been found. Obviously, she would want you to come home to her, but she doesn't see the enemies that surround us, not like I do."

"We've always had enemies at our borders."

"But not all at the same time. Since you've been missing, they have backed off our borders. Royal courtesy in our time of mourning for you. But the news is worse. I have enemies within Carthya, within my own castle. There are regents who look at my throne with greedy eyes. If I declare war in vengeance for you, they may not support me. They are the ones I fear."

"Do you think they're a danger to you?"

Eckbert forced a smile onto his face. "Regents are always the greatest threat to a king. But I have Darius. If they get to me, the royal line must continue, or else Carthya will destroy itself in civil war. That's Darius's duty, Jaron. Do you understand yours?"

He understood it far too well for a boy of only ten years. "Mine is to remain missing. To not come back."

"Do you understand that you cannot reveal your true identity out here? You must change everything about yourself that you can. Lighten your hair with some dyes, and grow it out to alter the look of your face. I'm told you speak with an Avenian accent. Keep that."

"I can use my left hand," Jaron offered. "I always preferred it anyway."

"And rid yourself of anything you might have learned in the castle. Of learning, of culture, of skills. There is an orphanage in Carchar, not far from here but back within Carthya's borders. It's run by a woman whose reputation is good, Mrs. Turbeldy. Now you must understand that I cannot have payment made to her for your care. You go there as an orphan, without any advantage over the others. It will be a hard few years until you're of age and can live on your own."

Tears stung Jaron's eyes, but he pushed them away. He wouldn't give his father the satisfaction of seeing his pain.

If Eckbert noticed his son's breaking heart, he didn't acknowledge it. He gave Jaron a handful of silver coins. "Come up with a story to get yourself into the orphanage. Say you stole these or whatever excuse you'd like, but they will buy your way through the front doors."

"I can fake an illness when the coins run out," Jaron said. "Let her think she's got the truth from me."

Eckbert smiled. "You used that trick often enough on your tutors. What an irony that it may keep you alive now. There is always the possibility of Mrs. Turbeldy trying to sell you into servitude, but I don't think she'd find any buyers."

"No," Jaron agreed. "I'm too difficult for anyone to want me."

"Exactly," his father said. The full meaning of Jaron's words probably didn't occur to him, which almost made it hurt worse.

Eckbert untied a small satchel at his waist, which he pressed into Jaron's hand. "I have a gift in there for you, the best of anything I could offer. There is a letter instructing you on how to use it."

Jaron looked in the satchel, then closed it up again. It meant nothing to him.

When Eckbert stood to leave, Jaron placed a hand over his father's arm and whispered, "Stay a little longer."

"If I do, the priest will grow suspicious," Eckbert said.

"This is real, then?" Jaron's heart pounded, though he couldn't tell whether it was from sadness or fear for his future. "When you leave, I'm no longer Prince Jaron. I'll be nothing but a commoner. An orphan."

"You will always be a royal in your heart," Eckbert said tenderly. "There may come a time when you must be Prince Jaron again for your country. You will know if it does come."

"Am I alone?"

Eckbert shook his head. "I will come in disguise on the last day of every month to the church nearest Mrs. Turbeldy's orphanage. If you ever need to see me, I'll be there."

Then he left.

And from that moment on, I became Sage of Avenia. Orphaned son of a failed musician and a barmaid. Who knew little of the king and queen of Carthya, and cared even less.

Completely alone.

# · FORTY~FOUR ·

My head snapped up as our carriage bumped over a rock in the road. Conner, sitting in the seat directly opposite me, watched me with obvious disgust. I knew he hated having to choose me as his prince. But Tobias, who was asleep on my right, was a complete failure, and Roden, sitting up straight on my left, could not convince the regents.

Imogen was on Conner's left. She stared straight ahead, refusing to acknowledge that she saw anything at all. Mott sat on Conner's right and nodded slightly at me when I looked at him.

There had been no point in lying any further to Mott. Back at the river, he hadn't asked whether I was the prince. He knew it. And he knew by my reaction that he was correct. Undoubtedly, he had a hundred questions to ask, and there were so many things I wanted to tell him, just to have somebody to speak openly to. But Conner was anxious for us to leave, and there was no time. All I had asked of Mott was that he keep our secret to himself. Judging by Conner's sour expression, he had obeyed.

I leaned back and closed my eyes again, not to sleep but to be alone with my thoughts. After four years of pretending, of immersing myself so completely in Sage's identity, could I emerge convincingly as Jaron?

Conner's regimen of lessons in the past week actually had been helpful. I had forgotten the names of several court officials and even a few of my ancestors that a prince would be expected to know. As a boy, I had been well trained in both sword fighting and horseback riding, both which were as instinctive to me now as breathing. Although I had practiced whenever possible in the orphanage, those skills had softened over the past four years, and it was good to build them up again.

Even though I was pretending to sleep, I couldn't help but smile at the memory of Cregan's anger when I challenged him to his wildest horse. The horse he'd brought me out from the stables really was beyond my skills to train, and I was barely able to control her enough to steal the fake sword while everyone was distracted elsewhere.

Other things had been a waste of time. Obviously, I could read much better than I let on, though to have confessed that would have been disastrous for my disguise. I'd have to apologize later to Tobias for that lie. He would have secured his papers more carefully if he had known I read every word on them while he slept at night. Of course, my back still stung from where he'd cut me, and that was a far worse crime. I'd agree to forgive him if he forgave me.

There were a lot of things I'd have to ask forgiveness for. And I feared I wouldn't receive half as much of it as I wanted.

Not from Imogen, who had trusted me with the greatest secret of her life, that she could speak. I had trusted her with nothing.

Not from Amarinda, who pled with a broken heart for any truth about whether Darius, the prince she was betrothed to and loved, was alive. Or about the existence of his younger brother, whom she would eventually have to marry if Darius really were dead.

And I'd get no forgiveness, ever, from my mother, who went to her death believing I'd died in an attack by Avenian pirates. Nor from my father.

For most of the past four years, I'd blamed him for keeping me away from the castle. True, I'd accepted his request without argument, but how could I have known then how difficult these recent years would be? He would have known much of what was ahead of me, and still he chose peace for his country over his own son. Maybe it was the right thing to do; I still didn't know for sure. But it didn't diminish my shame that they'd had to send me away in the first place. Nor my anger at my father, who at his first reunion with me in the church, already had a plan to keep me away.

I returned every month to the church near the orphanage

to see my father. But I never let him know I was there. We never spoke again.

It was only after Conner told me that both my parents and my brother had been killed that I began to understand my father in a new way.

He had said that his greatest enemies were the regents. Conner had told me that all three members of the family were intended victims, so that a regent would have to be crowned.

While at Farthenwood, I slowly began to understand that as long as four years ago, my father had foreseen the possibility that all of them could be murdered one day. He didn't keep me away to protect himself from embarrassment, nor was it to avoid having to declare war on Avenia. My father kept me away to keep me alive. After pirates had tried to kill me, he must have worried that the rest of his family's lives were in danger. He had told me in the church that day that the royal line must continue, to save Carthya. So that if the worst happened, and they were all killed, I would remain to claim the throne. He'd even given me a way home. I just never expected to need it.

He had let me think the worst of him for over four years, and I had eagerly done so. For that, I could never have his forgiveness.

When Conner first brought me to Farthenwood, I had thought he knew that Jaron was alive and he was searching for the prince, hoping to use him for some sort of ransom. So I determined that he must never suspect my true identity. That would have been bad, but Conner's real plan was far worse.

He was hoping to fool the entire kingdom with a fraudulent prince. I knew then that the best course of action was to play along with his plan, get him to choose me on my own terms, then return to Drylliad to prove my identity. Conner had his plan and I had mine. Whether either of them would work remained to be seen.

Conner kicked my feet to get my attention. "We're nearly there," he said. "Straighten up and at least try to look like a prince."

"Are we going to the castle this late at night?" I mumbled while glancing out the window into the darkness.

"Of course not. We'll stay at an inn. The choosing ceremony is tomorrow evening."

"If we're going to the inn, then I go as I am." I slouched back into my seat. The charade of being Sage was nearly over. I planned to enjoy it as long as I could.

# · FORTY~FIVE ·

We stopped at a place known simply as the Traveler's Inn. It wasn't far from the castle. Nobles not invited to stay within the castle walls often slept there. I told Conner it was too fancy because they'd only expect people of wealth and influence to stay there. The irony amused me and escaped him.

"I am a person of wealth and influence," Conner said, irritated. "My face is known, so I won't have anyone wonder why I'm staying at a commoner's tavern. And nobody will look at you, if you keep your head down."

Mott stayed with Roden, Tobias, Imogen, and me, while Conner went inside to reserve three rooms for us. I wondered as I stared at Imogen whether she would run away if she had her own room, but then dismissed those thoughts. She had no money to support herself in a strange town, and besides, she would likely consider it dishonorable to run.

"Why bring us along?" Roden asked me after Conner had left. "Will you enjoy having us watch in humiliation as you're declared?"

"He saved our lives," Tobias said. "He brought us along to make sure Conner didn't have us killed back at Farthenwood."

"Tobias is right," Mott said. "Cregan told me his orders were to kill the two boys left behind."

Roden folded his arms and arched his head. "Cregan wouldn't have killed me. He wanted me to become the prince."

"That isn't Cregan's decision to make," Tobias said.

"Besides," Mott added, "you will understand in time that Conner's decision was the right one."

I flashed Mott a glare. That was going too far. He lowered his eyes and said nothing more.

"What's she here for?" Tobias asked, nodding at Imogen. Then he smiled. "Oh. You'll use her to convince the princess. Amarinda would never suspect her of lying."

Imogen flushed and stared at me with hatred in her eyes. It was nearly the same accusation she had already made to me.

"After I'm declared, you're all free to go," I said. "All I ask is if there are any secrets between us, that you keep them."

"I don't believe you," Roden said bitterly. "We're too dangerous with all we know. So you'll excuse me if I wait to see whether we walk free before I celebrate your generosity."

"You're excused," I said, and slumped down again and closed my eyes.

That didn't last. Conner returned only seconds later. "There are no rooms available in all of Drylliad," he said. "It cost me more than three rooms combined to take the reservation of a man who should have arrived by now. Bribing the inn-keeper to claim his messenger never arrived to make the reservation was enormously expensive."

"Only one room?" I asked. "What about Imogen?"

"She'll sleep out here in the carriage," Conner said.

"No, we will," I protested. "A lady won't be treated that way."

"She's no lady," Conner said. "She's my kitchen maid, whom you are in the process of stealing away for yourself!"

"She won't belong to me any more than she should belong to you right now! She takes the room."

A wicked glint sparked in Conner's eyes. He smiled and offered a hand to her. "Very well, my dear. Come with me."

I swatted his hand away and Mott sat forward, saying, "I'll stay in the carriage with Roden and Tobias, to make sure there's enough space in the room. You can give Imogen the second bed and hang a sheet for her privacy. Conner and Sage, you two can share the rest of the room."

It was an acceptable compromise. Imogen didn't seem happy about it, but it was the best of her options. She refused either my hand or Conner's to help her out of the carriage, and followed Conner and me into the inn.

As we walked, I asked Conner why the inn was so full.

"Keep your head down," he hissed. "The rumor of the deaths of the royal family has spread throughout Carthya. Everyone has come to see who the new king will be tomorrow night."

"Are you still confident in your plan?"

"Less confident than I was," Conner whispered. "I didn't anticipate so much competition. You will have to do a very good job tomorrow in convincing them."

A grin spread across my face. "Don't worry. I will."

# · FORTY~SIX ·

It wasn't a large room, but it was clean and pleasant and would be enough for the three of us for one night. Two small beds stood along one wall. I helped Conner push Imogen's bed against the opposite wall, then quickly offered to sleep on the floor.

"I'm still an orphan and you're still a noble," I said to Conner. "You should have the other bed."

"Of course I should. And watch your tongue when saying I'm *still* a noble. I will always be a noble if you hope to remain a prince."

"My mistake," I said, putting on whatever expression of humility he would expect to see.

Imogen and I took a sheet off her bed and hung it from the ceiling. It wasn't a perfect solution for her privacy, but it was the best any of us could hope for. She removed one of the blankets from her bed for me to sleep with on the floor. I put myself directly between hers and Conner's beds.

He noticed. "You think I'd try any mischief with that

disgusting girl? I knew her mother, who was worthless too. Imogen's safe with me, boy. It's you she should worry about."

I let that comment pass. No doubt she was worried about me, but for entirely different reasons.

It was very late at night when I heard her roll off her bed onto her feet. Conner's snoring was ferocious, so it was no surprise that he didn't hear her and wake up. She stepped from behind the hanging sheet and touched my shoulder. I sat up and she put a finger to her lips, then motioned for me to follow her.

In the chance that Conner did awaken, I positioned my blanket so that in the darkness, it would appear someone was here. But I'd learned from more than one time in his presence during the night that he never woke up.

Once on Imogen's side of the makeshift curtain, she pointed to the window.

"Are you too warm?" I asked.

"Can you take me out there?" she whispered. "Is it safe?"

I inched the window open, examined the wall in the moonlight, and nodded. In typical Carthyan style, a ledge had been built directly below the window. I crawled through the window first, and then helped her through.

The night was cool and the breeze had picked up somewhat. But she didn't seem to hate me right now, so it was probably our last chance for any private conversation. We sat on the ledge and leaned against the wall of the inn, letting our legs dangle below.

"Do you often go out on ledges at night?" I asked.

"You do. I saw you once crawling around the walls of Farthenwood." She shrugged and said, "I don't think you saw me watching you, though."

I hadn't seen her. Which was amazing because I'd always watched carefully for anyone below me on the grounds.

"I couldn't sleep," she added. "All I could think about was the carriage ride. Roden is so angry with you."

"Is he? With so much cheerfulness in that ride, I barely noticed."

She ignored that. "Doesn't he understand why you brought him? What would've happened if you'd left him behind?"

I was silent. It was nothing new to have someone mad at me, but Roden's anger bothered me and I couldn't quite figure out why.

"Back at Farthenwood, I said horrible things to you," Imogen continued. "I don't know why I said them."

"Maybe I deserved some of it."

"No, you didn't. I blamed you for my own worries about coming to Drylliad, leaving the safety of Farthenwood. But now that I'm gone, I can't imagine returning there. Anything is better than Farthenwood." She lowered her eyes. "I'm sorry. I should have trusted you."

I deserved no trust, and yet she asked *my* forgiveness? Could she see me in the darkness and know how her words bit into my heart? Or did I have no heart, no soul? Conner had said we must prepare to sacrifice our very souls to bring Prince Jaron to the throne. I had done just that, although not in the way Conner thought.

"Are you nervous about tomorrow, Sage?"

"Yes." Even with the truth on my side, there was so much that could go wrong.

"Don't be. You look so very like him in that painting that they're sure to accept you. I watched you as we rode in the carriage. If I'm not careful, I may begin calling you Jaron myself."

"Would you?" For reasons I couldn't explain, even to myself, I longed to hear someone call me by my real name. I was tired of Sage. There were so many things I disliked about him lately.

She hesitated a moment before smiling. "Right now? What am I supposed to call you, Jaron or Prince or Your Majesty or what?"

I shook my head. "They all sound so wrong for me. But after tomorrow, there will be no more Sage. Only Jaron."

Her smile fell. I could see the curve of her mouth by the light of the midnight sky. "I won't know Jaron. Don't make me give up Sage yet."

There was nothing I could say to that. A wisp of her hair blew in the nighttime breeze. I caught the hair and tucked it behind her ear. She smiled, then reached for a pin and fastened it again, always maintaining her neat servant's braid. I wondered if she could ever learn to see herself as something other than a servant, something greater.

"We should probably go inside." Imogen sat up straight.

"I can't imagine what would happen if Conner found us out here."

"We're not doing anything wrong," I said. "And I'm not afraid of him."

"But I am. Will you help me in?"

I stood, and when my footing was secure I helped her to stand. But instead of turning to reenter the window, she faced me. "Back at Farthenwood, you told me there were more things happening than I understood. What did you mean by that?"

I pressed my lips together, then said, "I meant that there's a big difference between acting like a prince and being a prince. If you see me after I'm crowned, will you try to talk to me as Jaron? Can you do that?"

Without answering, she crouched down to the window. Before she returned to the room, she paused and said, "You'll become a king tomorrow, the most powerful person in the land. But I'll still be Imogen, a servant girl. After tomorrow, it will no longer be appropriate for me to talk to you."

Before I could answer, she disappeared through the window. By the time I climbed through and shut it tightly, she was already back in her bed. Her message was clear. I was a prince now, and she had returned to being Imogen the mute.

# · FORTY-SEVEN ·

Morning came early. I'd barely slept, if at all. One thought after another had tumbled through my mind faster than I could make sense of it. For most of the past four years, I had accepted the idea that I would be Sage for the rest of my life. Letting that go and allowing myself to be Jaron again was more difficult than I had anticipated.

I was already awake when Conner tried to kick me into consciousness, so his foot hit my hands and nothing worse. Then he called for Imogen to wake up and go downstairs to order us a breakfast. Ours was to be served in our room, then she could take something to the boys in the carriage. He gave her no instructions on when she could eat.

"We'll stay here in the room until it's time to leave," Conner said. "I've got only hours left to prepare you for presentation."

"I am prepared," I grumbled.

Conner smirked at me. "I would have expected more humility from you today. Our highest priority is to rehearse the order of action tonight. And don't try to tell me you know about that."

I didn't. "Tell me, then."

"Get dressed and straighten this room first, or else the maids will wonder about our arrangement last night. I have a few duties for Mott to attend to this morning that I must speak with him about."

By the time I dressed and replaced the hanging sheet and my blanket on Imogen's bed, Conner was returning with Imogen behind him. She carried a tray that she set on a table in our room. I wondered if she had risked speaking to the staff to order our breakfast, or if not, how she had communicated our order to them.

"Maybe it was a good thing you brought her along," Conner said. "It's handy to have a traveling servant."

"I thought that's what Mott is for," I said.

"He's more than a common servant. Surely you've noticed that by now."

Imogen left as quickly as she could, and Conner handed me a plate filled with hot cakes, eggs, and thick slices of bacon.

"It's a large breakfast," I said hungrily.

"This is nothing compared to what lies ahead for you," Conner said. "Once you're the prince, you may tell your servants anything you wish to eat and they will provide it. They will feed it to you if you desire."

"I don't. There's no need to tempt me for this position, Conner. You have me. Now tell me about court tonight."

"All twenty of the king's regents will meet in the throne room at five o'clock. Also there will be the king's closest adviser, the high chamberlain, Lord Kerwyn. No need for you to know all of their names. Jaron likely would not have known them, so no one will expect you to."

I didn't know all of them. But there were some I expected to recognize. Kerwyn would know me best. He'd suffered through my childhood beside my family. But would he recognize me after all this time? It was doubtful. I'd changed a lot in four years.

Conner continued, "The first act of the meeting will be to officially announce the deaths of the king, queen, and Crown Prince Darius."

I winced at that. Conner didn't notice. He never had before, either.

"The announcement is merely a formality. Most of the regents have known this from the start. And the others will have heard enough rumors to confirm the likelihood in their minds. Then we'll have a report from the three regents who traveled to Avenia to seek any news as to the life or death of Prince Jaron. They will report a confirmation that he's dead."

"How do you know?" I asked.

"Because he is dead!" Conner snapped. "Who do you think hired the pirates so many years ago?"

The news knocked the wind from my lungs. It overwhelmed any sense of pretense I'd been able to maintain thus far with him. All that kept me from attacking him was the knowledge that I still wanted him with me at the castle tonight.

"Why?" My voice was hoarse. I didn't trust myself to say anything more.

"I thought it'd force us into war with Avenia. Eckbert stood by and did nothing year after year while Avenia inched its way deeper into Carthyan lands. But if Avenian pirates killed his son, he'd be forced to act. Unfortunately, despite the pirates' assurances to me that everyone on that ship went down, Jaron's body was never found. Eckbert was able to appease his critics by saying he wouldn't go to war until he had Jaron's body as evidence in the attack. However, Avenia has backed off since their suspected involvement in Jaron's death, so in a way, my plan worked better than I could have hoped for. Our borders are safer and no war was needed."

Conner paused as if he expected me to say something. What did he want? Congratulations? He seemed to sense my discomfort, then added, "I know this secret is safe with you because you can't reveal it without betraying your own true identity."

"No," I mumbled. "I can't betray my identity." Yet.

Conner brushed his hands together as if the matter were settled. "So let's continue. When the three regents report that Prince Jaron is dead, this will be the time when, as the high chamberlain, Lord Kerwyn will stand and declare that a new king must be chosen. However, before he stands, I will come forward and announce that the regents are wrong about Jaron's death. That's when I will introduce you to the court. There will be a bit of commotion initially, but Kerwyn will have you brought to him. There will be several questions, a careful examination of you. It will take some time, and no matter what they say, you must answer calmly and with confidence. You must keep your sharp tongue under control. And you must not make a single mistake. Can you do it?"

"I can."

That pleased Conner. "Good. We'll work on your answers through much of today, make sure you know everything to say, and of course, I'll be there to assist should you get into any trouble."

I pushed my plate aside, unable to eat anything else. Conner pushed it back to me. "You must have your energy today."

I shoved my chair behind me and stood. "You said you have proof I can offer them. What is it?"

"Later," Conner said. "You don't get that unless I'm certain you are going to be declared prince tonight. You have only a few hours to learn everything else you must. If you've finished eating, are you ready to get started?"

I closed my eyes and tried to control my breathing. My heart raced at the prospect of all that lay ahead of me that day. No matter what Conner told me or tried to teach, one thing was certain. I was not, nor would I ever be, ready. But that wasn't what he wanted to hear. So I looked at him and said, "Okay. Let's begin."

# · FORTY~EIGHT ·

onner drilled me nonstop for four hours. He refused to answer any knock on the door with more than an order of "Go away," and denied my requests for a break to step outside and clear my head. I didn't care about most of what he told me, but I had to remember it for now, word for word, in order to repeat it back to him.

Finally, in the late afternoon, Conner announced I was ready to go before the court. He declared himself an excellent teacher due to the fact that I had learned so much in such a short period of time. Little did he guess how much his student already knew. Yet there were a few things I did not know. Things I had been too young to understand when I left there as a child. Conner had provided me with details of Jaron's early life with such intimacy that I had asked him how he could know so much.

"I read the queen's diaries," he said. "She wrote about Jaron often."

"Did she?" It was impossible to sound as if I didn't care what my mother had really thought of me, and the curiosity burned my heart. I knew she loved me, because all mothers love their children. But she had stood with my father when they first sent me away, and I'd never quite gotten over that.

"Jaron had the reputation for being a difficult child," I said. "Did she ever forgive him for that?"

Conner smiled. "Interesting choice of words, Sage, to assume she thought there was anything about Jaron that needed forgiveness. She believed he was just like her. He may have been difficult, but she loved him all the more for it."

We had to move on quickly from that conversation. It was too close to me, too hard to think about.

Conner also provided me with a convenient story of how I escaped the pirates. According to him, I had seen their ship approaching and escaped in a rescue boat moored to the ship. I had hidden in Avenian orphanages in fear all this time, coming forward only when I heard rumors of the deaths of Eckbert and Erin.

I urged him to change the story a little. "Have me hiding at Mrs. Turbeldy's orphanage. That way, if any of them claim to know me, we can acknowledge it was me, but in disguise the entire time."

Conner's face brightened. "This is why you'll convince them tonight! You have a great gift for thinking fast when necessary."

So when Conner announced that I was finally ready, I was not prepared for what happened next. He invited Mott into the room, who was carrying rope in one hand and a length of fabric in the other. Mott's face was pale and he entered the room barely able to look at me.

"Are you ill?" Conner asked him.

"No, sir. I just . . . we can't do this." Then he glanced at Conner with moist eyes, and I understood. Mott shook his head. "If you knew . . . this boy —"

"Do it," I said, turning to Mott. It took all my strength to force the words out, knowing what was coming. "You're Conner's miserable dog, aren't you?"

Without warning, Conner grabbed me around the neck, where he held me while Mott tied my hands. I noticed he gave me a little slack on my wrists, but it didn't matter. Despite the churning inside me, I had to let Conner do what he was going to do. Then Conner released me, and Mott tied a gag in my mouth. He still refused to look at me, but I saw deep creases in the lines of his face. He wasn't any happier about what was going to happen than I was.

"Remember, Mott, don't leave any marks," Conner said.

Mott put a hand on my shoulder and for the first time looked into my eyes. He squeezed my shoulder gently, his attempt at an apology, then speared his fist into my gut.

I stumbled backward and fell onto the floor. It was difficult to draw in a breath, especially with the gag between my teeth, and I barely had time to recover before Mott yanked me to my feet again. He unfastened the top three buttons of my shirt, then walked behind me and hooked his arms through my elbows, pulling my bound hands tightly against me. I grunted from the pain in my shoulders and down my back, but he gave me no room for movement here.

Conner withdrew a knife from a sheath and walked up close to me. He put the tip of the blade against my chest and held it there. "I know it was Tobias who tried to kill you before," he said. "But he couldn't do it because he's weak. A leader needs to be strong, Sage. Do you believe that?"

I didn't move. All I could focus on was the point of the blade.

"Of course you do. You killed Veldergrath's man when he tried to attack Imogen. So you can be strong, and I admire that. But you must know when to be strong, and when to give up control. In a very short time, you will become the leader of Carthya. Before that happens, I need to make it very clear what the arrangement will be between you and me."

"No marks, Master Conner," Mott said.

Conner glared at Mott, clearly annoyed. But he lightened the pressure of his knife and said to me, "You will be king in any decision a king may make. However, from time to time, I will have suggestions for you. You will obey them without question or hesitation. If you do not, I will expose you as a traitor to the crown, and believe me when I say I can do it with no danger to myself. If you do not obey me when I give the command, then you will be publicly tortured and hanged in the town square for treason. Princess Amarinda, if she is your wife by then, will be expelled from Carthya, to forever live in humiliation, and if you have children, they will die of starvation and shame. Do you believe I can make this happen?"

I still did not move. Conner's face twisted in rage. He reared back and, with his free hand, punched me again in the gut. Mott still braced me from behind, so there was nothing I could do but bite down on the gag and groan in muted pain. He hit me two more times, once in the chest and once on my shoulder. Then he ripped me away from Mott and threw me on the floor. He knelt beside me and hissed into my ear, "You are nothing other than what I have made you into. I have followed through on my threats to other royals. Attempt to betray me and meet their fate. Do you understand?"

I nodded and he lifted me back into a sitting position. He said, "In your first act as king, you will remove Veldergrath as a regent. Tell the court you suspect Veldergrath may have something to do with your family's deaths and you refuse to have him as a sitting regent in the court. Your second act as king will be to install me as your prime regent. I don't care who you replace Veldergrath with, though as your prime regent, I am happy to recommend names if you are unfamiliar with them. Do you agree to this?"

I nodded again. With his knife, Conner cut the ropes binding my wrists, then sliced through the gag on my mouth. As soon as he did, I spat at him. He wiped the spit off his face, then slapped me hard across my cheek.

"This would be easier if you accepted that what I want is a

better situation for us both," he said. "You are the lowest form of life Carthya has to offer, yet I am making you a king. Stop fighting me, Sage, and let us be friends." He seemed disappointed that I gave him no response, then he stood and said to Mott, "Clean him up and get him dressed. I'll have Imogen bring something to eat very soon. Do not leave him alone until I return." Then he wiped his hands, straightened his jacket, and left the room.

# · FORTY~NINE ·

As soon as Conner left, Mott was by my side, helping me up off the floor and onto the bed. I rolled onto my back and groaned, holding my side.

"I think he cracked a rib," I said. "He punches a lot harder than you do."

"To be fair, Your Highness, I was holding back," Mott said.

I wanted to laugh, but over the past two weeks, I'd learned how much that could hurt. So I just closed my eyes while Mott unbuttoned the rest of my shirt and felt around for any injuries he might detect.

"Why didn't you let me tell him the truth?" Mott asked. "He's going to find out soon enough anyway, and you could have saved yourself all this pain."

"He'd never have believed it," I said. "He should know who I am better than anyone, but all he can see is the boy from the orphanage. That's all he'll ever see of me."

"Perhaps so," Mott said. "Other than a tiny cut on your chest, I can't see any damage."

"Trust me, there's damage. Couldn't you have stopped him?"

"Only you could have." He began sliding my shirt down my arms. I let him do all the work. "What were you thinking by spitting at him at the end? Begging for more?"

I answered with an "ow" as Mott pushed my left arm back too far. He apologized and moved more carefully.

"You are the biggest fool of a boy I've ever known," Mott said. Then his tone softened. "But you will serve Carthya well."

"I wish I felt ready to do this," I said. "The closer we come to the moment, the more I see every defect in my character that caused my parents to send me away in the first place."

"From all I'm told, the prince they sent away was selfish, mischievous, and destructive. The king who returns is courageous, noble, and strong."

"And a fool," I added.

Mott chuckled. "You are that too."

Getting dressed in the outfit Conner had planned for me took quite a while. It was fancier than the usual clothes we had at Farthenwood, and immediately reminded me of the one thing I'd never missed of castle life. The tunic was long and black with gold satin ribbon running from my chest to the bottom hem. Beneath it I wore a white, full-sleeved shirt that gathered at my wrists and was too tight on my neck. A dark purple cape hung from my shoulders, clasped with a gold chain that was heavier than it looked.

"Real gold?" I asked. Mott nodded and offered me a pair of new leather boots and a ridiculous hat that had a long white feather in it. I took the boots and ignored the hat.

I sat in front of a mirror as Mott combed my hair smooth and tied it back with a ribbon. "Your cheek is still red from where he slapped you," he said. "But it should fade before we reach the castle."

"I hope it stays. Let it remind Conner of how important he thinks he is to me." I caught Mott's eyes in the mirror. "Do I have your loyalty?"

Mott nodded. "You have my life, Prince Jaron." He finished by tucking down the collar of my jacket, then said, "What do you think of yourself now?"

"It's as good as I might expect to look."

There was a knock at our door. Mott opened it and Imogen walked in with a tray of food. Her eyes were red but dry. I wanted to ask Mott to leave so that I could speak with her, but I knew he had to obey Conner's order to stay. Besides, there was really nothing more I could say to Imogen than had already been said. She would be the greatest casualty in this plan, which was entirely my fault. If it was possible to apologize to her, I didn't know how.

She set the tray on the small table in the center of the room. Mott started to tell her to bring the tray over to me directly, but I held up my hand and said I'd come get the food. She must have noticed something different in the pained way I walked, because she furrowed her eyebrows and looked questioningly at me. I smiled in return, but I don't think she believed it.

"Do you want her to leave while you eat?" Mott asked.

Ignoring Mott, I asked her, "Have you eaten yet today?" She cast a sideways glance at Mott, but I said, "Imogen, it was my question, not his."

She slowly shook her head. I uncovered the lid to my tray and found a deep-dish meat pie and a thick slice of bread. "There's more than enough for both of us." She mouthed the word *no* to me, but I pretended not to see it and with my spoon dished her out a sizable portion, which I set on the plate where the bread had been. I handed it to her with the spoon and said I'd eat my half after she finished using the utensil.

"Have you eaten, Mott?" I asked.

"I'd better have, because that meal won't split a third time," Mott said.

Once Imogen began eating, she devoured the food as if it were the first she'd eaten in days. She finished her meat pie and then found the napkin and carefully wiped the spoon clean before handing it back to me.

"Do you want more?" I asked. "I'm not hungry."

She shook her head and stood, backing away from the table with a bowed head.

"She comes to the castle with us tonight," I told Mott.

"It's not Conner's plan —" Mott began.

"It's my plan, though. What have Tobias and Roden been doing all day?"

"Conner heard a rumor last night. He sent them into town to see if they can learn anything."

"What's the rumor?"

"That there are other princes, Your — other princes, Sage. It appears that Conner is not the only one with this plan."

"Yes, but Conner has an advantage the others don't, correct?" Mott returned my smile. Imogen noticed the exchange between us but of course said nothing.

Conner returned to the room just as I was finishing the meal. He ordered Imogen to return the tray, and Mott to wait outside, then he shut the door behind us. He carried two bundles in his arms.

"You look good," he said.

"Better than I feel," I responded coolly.

Conner looked at me without sympathy. "I trust your bruises will keep my words in your memory for a long time."

It was safe to say that I would never forget them. Bile rose in my throat every time I thought of his cursed words. I tilted my head at the bundles. "What's in them?"

He began unwrapping the first, smaller bundle. "You've seen this before," he said, revealing the emerald-encrusted box. "It belonged to Queen Erin. There is something about her that few people knew. Indeed, I did not know it myself until I took this box after her death and saw the contents." He slid a thin bronze key into the lock and opened the box. All I could see were a few folded papers.

"What are they?"

He handed them to me. "You will put these in your pocket. I think we have more than enough to earn your identity, but it's always wise to have a backup."

I unfolded the papers and an inadvertent gasp escaped me. I had known my mother was artistic but did not appreciate her abilities while I was a child. It was a simple sketch of me at about the age I would have been when she and my father first sent me away.

I became fixed on the way she drew my eyes. Not with the arrogance or defiance the castle artists inevitably gave me, but with the subtle details only a mother would notice, as if she saw things about her son that everyone else missed. Looking at the pictures, I saw myself the way she must have seen me, and as I gently brushed my thumb over the drawing, I felt her love for me.

Then I noticed Conner studying me as I looked at the drawing. I quickly folded it and shoved it in a pocket of my tunic.

Conner continued to watch me. "Prince Jaron?"

I scratched my face. "Guess I'll have to get used to people calling me that. Do you think I can eventually pick up Sage as a nickname?"

"No, you cannot." Conner smiled and his expression relaxed. "But I suppose I should begin calling you Jaron, to get you used to it." He hesitated. "For a moment there, I thought —"

"What's in the other package?" I asked.

It was a sufficient distraction. "Ah!" Conner set the box down and began unwrapping the other bundle. "This is the proof that will seal your identity. When the prince boarded the ship that day four years ago, he was wearing his crown. It has been lost all this time, assumed to be at the bottom of the sea. Indeed, even if a diver had found it with the intention of putting forward a false prince, the metals and jewels of the crown would have been damaged by the salty waters. But see it for yourself." He finished unwrapping the bundle and pulled out the crown I had last worn on that ship.

It was a circlet of gold, with rubies set at the base of every arch, and was trimmed in braided gold bands. The crown had been made for me to grow into, so I suspected it would fit better now than it used to. It was in perfect condition, other than a dent I'd created when I fell from a tree once while wearing it.

"The pirates rescued this from the ship before it sank," Conner said. "They presented it to me as proof of Jaron's death."

I'd left the crown behind before I snuck off the ship. I had intended it as a symbol of my having abandoned the royal family forever.

"Face the mirror," Conner said.

I obeyed, and watched as he set the crown on my head. The weight of it resurrected a flood of memories for me. As of that moment, I was the prince again. And soon the entire country would know it.

## · FIFTY ·

Conner's plan was for Cregan to drive him and me directly to the castle in time for the announcement. I argued that Tobias, Roden, and Imogen should come with us, but Conner expressly forbade it. So I nodded at Imogen, and then shook hands with Roden.

"It's not too late to back out." Roden's grip was powerful. "You never wanted this."

"No, I never did." We had no disagreement there. "But this is my future, not yours."

A flash of anger crossed Roden's face, but he backed off while I shook hands with Tobias.

"I think you're supposed to be the king," Tobias said, smiling. "The stars are shining for you tonight."

He must have felt the note I placed in his palm when we shook hands, and he hid it well when we pulled our hands apart.

The ride to the castle was very quiet between Conner and me. He had started our ride by trying to quiz me on any last-minute details. I assured him that I knew everything I had to know, and told him to let me have my silence.

I watched the castle rise into view as we approached. I hadn't been there in four years, and when I left, I had never expected to see it again. It was one of the younger castles in the surrounding region and, as such, had borrowed heavily from other countries' architecture. It was built of the large granite blocks from the mountains of Mendenwal and used the round, heavily decorated turrets of Bymar rather than the plain and square turrets common elsewhere. Like Gelyn's architecture, the heart of the castle was tall and layered, while its wings were long and square. And small ledges extended beneath the windows. To the people of Carthya, it was the center of their government, a symbol of the king's power, and a sign of the prosperity we had always enjoyed. To me, it was home.

However, it quickly became apparent that we were not the only ones trying to get through the gates. A dozen carriages were ahead of us in line. One by one, a castle guard spoke to someone in the carriage at the front of the line. A few got through, but most were turned away.

Conner leaned his head out the door and signaled to a carriage that had been refused entrance. "What's happening?" he asked the occupant.

"Can't say exactly. Whatever I said to the guard, though, he waved us away. Can you imagine such rude treatment? I happen to have the long-lost son of Carthya, Prince Jaron, with me!"

I started to lean forward to get a look at him myself, but Conner pressed me back into my seat.

"Do all these carriages hold the missing prince?" Conner asked.

"There are several frauds, I'm afraid. Several carriages contain nobles invited to the castle to greet whatever king is named tonight, and they are allowed through. But my boy, er, the prince, is with me, so they have chosen poorly."

"Let us hope the correct boy is crowned tonight," Conner said, and then wished him well as our carriage moved forward. When we were alone again, Conner added, "His boy looked nothing like Prince Jaron. The guards must be screening for possibilities here at the gate, letting only the most probable candidates through. Don't worry, Sage, your resemblance is close enough to get us through."

I wasn't worried.

But when we reached the gate, Conner learned the truth about the screenings.

The guard looked at me and arched an eyebrow. At least he was impressed. "Who is this?" he asked Conner.

"Prince Jaron of Carthya, as you can plainly see. He must be presented at court before a new king is named."

"I've seen many Prince Jarons tonight," the guard said. "Have you anything else to say?"

This was a request for a code word. It was an old tradition

amongst the royal family to have a code word in the event that an impostor ever tried to enter the castle, or if we had to enter the castle while in disguise. The guards at the gates of the castle were the only other ones who knew the code word even existed. If Conner had known the code, he would have asked if the queen planned to wear green at the dinner tonight, because it was the only color he had brought to match her dress. At least, that had been the code four years ago.

All Conner could do was shake his head.

"I'm sorry," the guard said. "You may not enter the castle tonight."

"But I'm Bevin Conner. One of the twenty regents."

"Then what I meant to say is that you may enter." The guard flashed a glare at me. "The boy with you may not."

"He is Prince Jaron."

"They all are."

Conner yelled at Cregan to turn our carriage around. "Fools!" Conner hissed, swatting at the carriage door with his hat. "Are we defeated so easily?"

I leaned back in my seat. "There's a secret way into the castle."

Conner stopped his swatting. "What? How do you know?"

"I've used it."

"You've been inside the castle? Why didn't you tell me?"

"You never asked. There's a river that flows beneath the kitchen. As food is prepared, the garbage is dumped into the water and the river carries it away. The river is gated, but there is a key so that the gate can occasionally be cleared of larger obstructions."

"And you have a key?"

I pulled a pin from my jacket. Imogen hadn't felt me take it from her hair the night before. "I can pick the lock."

Conner smiled, impressed with what he thought was my ingenuity. In fact, I'd suspected all along it might come to this. Thus, the pin.

Conner's face fell as he further considered my suggestion. "We shall be filthy if we go that route, unfit to enter the throne room."

"That guard just now said you could enter through the gate. I can enter through the kitchen."

Conner shook his head. "Absolutely not. We must stay together."

Which, unfortunately, I also suspected he would say. So I shrugged it off and said, "We'll be fine on this route. There's a dirt path to the side of the river, wide enough that we can easily walk there single file. It will lead us to a door into the kitchen. It's never guarded, but we'll need help to restrain the kitchen servants while you and I continue on into the castle."

"Mott, Tobias, and Roden." Conner's eyes narrowed. "Did you know this would happen? Is that why —"

"I brought them so you wouldn't kill them. There's one other condition. I don't want Cregan coming with us. Order him to stay back."

"But if he can help —"

"He doesn't come."

"Very well." Conner thought for a moment. "How do you know all this?"

"I ate from that kitchen a lot when I was younger."

Conner misinterpreted my answer and said, "For the first time, Sage, I'm glad to have chosen a thief and an orphan as my prince."

# · FIFTY~ONE ·

As my note had instructed, Mott, Tobias, Roden, and Imogen were already waiting at the river entrance into the castle when we arrived. Conner looked surprised to find them there but must have explained it away in his mind. He called to Cregan, "Take this carriage back to the inn and wait for us there. I don't want it here to arouse anyone's suspicions."

"Have Tobias take it," Cregan said. "He's not useful for anything."

"Then he's not useful for managing a carriage. Get going. We must hurry too because I fear we'll be late."

I led the way up the river. Imogen was behind me, then Conner, then Tobias, Roden, and Mott at the last. Almost immediately, a roof of dirt and rock rose over our heads as we entered a tunnel leading beneath castle grounds. The castle walls were not much farther ahead.

I had found this entrance myself at age eight. The kitchen staff all knew how often I used it to sneak in and out of the castle grounds, but they liked me and never told anyone. I was finally found out when I fell into the river once and returned to the castle smelling of rotten fruit and moldy meat.

"It smells horrible in here," Tobias said.

"Nobody promised it'd be pleasant," I called back to him.

As it grew darker, Imogen walked closer behind me. I noticed she kept one hand ready to grab my arm if she started to fall in.

We reached the gate, which was in desperate need of a cleaning. The gate was clogged with large, rotting chunks of food and debris. It dammed up the water to a higher level of reeking muck than usual.

"I'm going to be sick," Conner said, covering his nose with a handkerchief. "The smell!"

I hid my smile, but do admit I enjoyed the fact that he was having a difficult time. I used the pin to pick the lock within seconds. It was an old lock with soft tumblers. Once I was king, I'd have to order a better security system placed there.

We went through the gate, and after another few minutes of walking, I informed the group that we had passed beneath the castle walls. Now that we had come this far, we were provided a little light by occasional oil lamps. When servants came down there, they often had their hands full and needed a lit path. It wasn't much light, but we were grateful for it.

"How much farther?" Conner asked.

"Not far." Here, the path widened and we were able to walk several persons across. Conner caught up to Imogen and me, Tobias and Mott were behind us, and Roden lagged behind.

"Keep up, Roden," Conner scolded. "We are pushing against time."

Roden answered with a shout of surprise. We turned to see what the trouble was. Cregan held him by the neck with his knife.

"Cregan!" Conner yelled. "What are you doing?"

Our group widened into a circle. Mott had his hand on his sword, but he wouldn't draw it. Not unless Conner ordered it. And he'd wounded himself only two nights ago after I'd killed Veldergrath's man. He'd be a weakened opponent if he did have to fight.

"Change of plans," Cregan said, his mouth curved into a nasty sneer. "Your orphan boy won't be king after all."

I took a step forward and nodded at Roden. "But why threaten your own choice for king, Cregan?"

Cregan grinned evilly, then released Roden and handed him his sword. Roden didn't even have the courtesy to act surprised. He'd known all along that Cregan was following us.

"You are traitors!" Conner said. "Traitors to this plan, to Carthya, to me. Why, Cregan?"

"I'm making my fortune. Once Roden's on the throne, he will make me a noble, then I'll take your place as regent. Won't be long before I take everything you have."

Conner turned his glare to Roden. "After all I've done for you, this is your repayment?"

"You'd have left me at Farthenwood to die," Roden said stiffly. "I owe you nothing."

"Then I'll have no guilt in ordering your deaths," Conner said. "Mott, finish them."

Before Mott was able to withdraw his sword, Cregan advanced with his knife and said, "Mott can't kill both Roden and me before one of us gets to either you or your phony king. Roden is better with a sword than you might imagine. I trained him myself."

Roden arched his head. "And for that brief time I was your prince, you told me everything I'd need to know to convince the regents."

"Not everything," Conner said. "You won't succeed."

"Yes, I will," Roden said. "Only Cregan and I go on from here. Hand me the crown, Sage. If you cooperate, everyone leaves in peace."

Maybe Roden believed that, but I could tell from the expression on Cregan's face that he had no plans for any of us to leave here alive.

"Sir?" Mott asked. Other than Cregan and Roden, he was the only one carrying a weapon.

"I don't know." For the first time since we met, Conner sounded weak. "I didn't expect —"

"We're at a standoff," I said calmly. "Maybe you and Roden will get one of us. But even with your small brain, Cregan, you must know that Mott will get one of you, too. Whether it's you or Roden who falls, neither of you can win this way."

Cregan's face fell. He had not expected us to call his bluff.

"The stronger of us should be crowned," I continued. "Can

we all agree on that?" Roden nodded. Hesitantly, Cregan and Conner did as well. "Then Roden and I fight. The winner goes on to the castle. Do you accept the challenge, Roden?"

"Your back is still injured," Mott warned.

"Good point. If Roden wants to make it a fair fight, then how about if I'm the only one with a sword?" I grinned, but nobody else liked the joke.

Cregan licked his lips, savoring the idea of seeing me fall. "It was never going to be a fair fight, boy. Roden's too strong."

Roden looked back at Cregan, then to me. "Okay, the winner advances to the throne. Please give me the crown instead, Sage. I don't want to kill you."

"Lucky coincidence. I don't want to be killed."

That infuriated him. "Stop making a joke of this, as if I'm no threat! I'm better at the sword than you might expect, and I've seen you fight."

I removed the crown from my head and handed it to Mott. "Don't let it get dirty. Let me have your sword."

"It's heavier than the prince's was," Mott said.

I locked eyes with him. "Mott. Your sword." With an obedient nod, he handed it to me.

Roden attacked immediately, while I was still facing Mott. One of the advantages of being a left-handed person who had been forced to train with his right, I blocked his advance with my left hand, then rotated toward him and struck him hard at his weaker side.

Roden stumbled back with an expression of surprise at my

abilities, but he quickly advanced again and swung harder at me. He'd improved significantly since I last fought him, and those were only in practices. This time, his blows were intended to kill, and he watched for me to make even the tiniest mistake.

"You were faking before," he said, parrying my thrust. "You've been trained to fight."

"If you knew my father, you'd know that I was trained for show. He never intended for me to actually fight."

Roden smiled and cut toward me, aiming low. "I'm still better than you."

"Perhaps, but I'm handsomer, don't you think?"

That took Roden off guard, and I was able to swing around and kick him in the side. He fell to the ground, but kept his sword ready. I started toward him with my blade. All it would take was a quick slash and this match would be over. But I hesitated. Could I strike after promising to save his life if he wasn't chosen as prince? Did I still owe him that? I backed up to higher ground. This match would not end with his death.

"You could've killed me there," Roden said, leaping to his feet and advancing. "Why didn't you? Oh." Roden came to his own answer. He grinned as he engaged my sword again. "I should've known from when you stabbed Veldergrath's man. You don't have the stomach for killing. Unfortunately for you, I do." Then he brought his sword down from over his head. The force of his blade crashing against mine set me off balance and I stumbled down the bank.

In the limited space we had between the wall and the water, Roden continued edging me toward the river. I didn't like the idea of falling in. I'd lose the sword fight and possibly my life. Also, I'd end up smelling really bad.

Our blades moved faster and harder, but Roden's confidence was unshakable. If Cregan had chosen him for his natural ability, then he had chosen well. I wished Roden could be on my side after this, because he'd make an excellent captain of the guard.

Finally, my boot hit on a rock, throwing me off balance, and Mott's sword fell from my hand. I dove for it, but it slid into the river. Behind us, Cregan laughed, sensing victory. Roden lowered his sword and walked up to me, his blade near my throat. I arched my head and backed into a squatting position, but the blade followed me.

"Do you offer mercy?" I asked.

"If you accept that I win this challenge. If you concede that I win and give me that crown, then you and the others may go in peace. That is the mercy I offer. I am Prince Jaron."

"If you were Jaron, then you'd never fall for a simple trick like this." I flung my leg to the side and swept it beneath Roden's feet. He landed on his back with a hoarse groan. I grabbed the rounded edge of the blade and wrenched it from his grasp, then stood and aimed it at his throat.

Roden closed his eyes. "It's what you said you would do on your very first day," he mumbled. "Beg mercy and trick your opponent. I'd forgotten."

"No!" Cregan yelled. "Not him!" He ran at me with his knife outstretched. Mott stepped between us and grabbed his hand, twisting it behind his back. To regain his balance, Cregan clutched at the crown in Mott's other hand. Mott stabbed him in the back with the knife, and Cregan fell into the water, pulling the crown in with him as well. Blood seeped through the water as both the crown and Cregan's body were carried away downstream.

"I surrender," Roden said, lowering his head. "Do what you must."

I placed a hand on his shoulder and pulled my sword away. "I'd have brought you with me into the court, Roden. We could have been friends."

Roden shook his head. "I don't need friends. All I wanted was the throne. Please just kill me here."

My words had been sincere, and it was difficult to remove my hand. "Go away, then. Run and never find me again."

Roden looked up at me in an attempt to determine whether it was another trick. But I motioned with my head for him to leave and lowered the sword. Wordlessly, Roden scrambled to his feet and ran out of the tunnel. His footsteps echoed in the tunnel until he'd gotten too far for us to hear him anymore.

"The crown!" Conner said, standing near the edge of the dark water.

"There's a chance it'll get carried on Cregan's body back to the gate," Tobias said.

"It's probably sunk already," Conner said.

"Let me try to find it." Tobias turned to me. "Sage, when you are king, let me be one of your servants."

"Be my friend instead," I said. "Go find the crown." Tobias bowed and ran back down the river.

Above us, we could hear the faint tolling of bells. "The meeting's begun!" Conner shouted. "We have to hurry. There's only minutes to spare!"

I started forward, then gasped and stumbled to my knees. "You're hurt?" Mott cried, then called to Conner. "Wait!"

"I can help him." Imogen didn't flinch in the moment of Conner's and Mott's shock at hearing her speak, but continued, "You two secure the kitchen and stall the meeting. I can get Sage there."

Conner's strained voice revealed the panic he felt. "Sage?"

"Just get to that meeting." I looked directly at Mott. "Go now."

Mott nodded and took Conner's arm. "Sir, Prince Jaron will be there. Let's go."

"I will get there in time," I told Conner. "Have Mott secure the kitchen for us."

They ran ahead and Imogen knelt beside me, asking, "You knew about Roden and Cregan. How?"

"It was their last chance to make Roden the prince."

She reached for the hem of her skirt, intending to tear off strips for a bandage. "Where are you hurt?"

"Nowhere. Everything's fine. Really." I smiled and held out my arms to prove it to her. "I just needed a reason to get separated from Conner. Do you think Mott has secured the kitchen yet?"

"I don't know. I don't understand — you faked that injury?"

"I've got to go now. There's not much time left."

I stood to leave, but she grabbed my arm. "Your crown."

"I won't need it."

"Sage —"

"Will you make me one promise, Imogen?"

She pressed her lips together, then said, "What is it?"

This was harder to ask than I'd expected, but I forced the words out. "Next time we meet, things will be different. Will you try to forgive me?"

"Forgive you for what, becoming the prince? Because I understand now why you're doing it."

"No, you don't. But you will. If there is any reason to forgive me, will you try to do it?"

She nodded. There was so much trust in her eyes, so much innocence. She had no idea what she was agreeing to.

I kissed her cheek, then said, "Wait here until Tobias returns with the crown. With that, he'll be able to get you both through to the throne room. I wish I could take you with me, but this last part I have to do alone."

"Go, then, and may the devils give you clearance."

The devils wouldn't be a problem. It was the regents I needed on my side.

## FIFTY TWO

A meeting of the regents was in full progress when Conner breathlessly entered the throne room. He was the only one who had come in late, and his arrival caused an unwelcome disruption.

"If there were any occasion for you to arrive on time, Lord Conner, this would have been it." The man who spoke was Joth Kerwyn, high chamberlain to King Eckbert. He was almost as much a part of the castle as the bricks and mortar, having served the king for his entire life. He wasn't a large or powerfully built man. Quite the opposite, in fact, and yet he could command a room of a thousand with just the wave of his hand. There was no one who had been more loyal to King Eckbert and few who had ever loved Carthya so much. The lines on his aging face told the story of years of worry and the weight of counseling royalty on their most difficult decisions. Now he was facing the greatest task of his career: peaceably finding a new king for Carthya. Because if civil war broke out amongst the different factions vying for the throne, Carthya's enemies would use the opportunity to advance on the country and destroy it.

Conner gave a polite bow to Kerwyn. "My lord High Chamberlain, I had trouble getting here. Forgive me, please."

There were nineteen other regents in the room, seated according to their rank at a long rectangular table. Conner's place was near the end, but he hoped that by the close of the evening, he would replace Veldergrath at the head of the table. This was a vain and largely useless group, few who had ever worked a real day in their lives. Even if they knew of the risk and expense Conner had undergone to bring a prince to the throne, they would never appreciate the valiancy of his efforts. Conner had accepted that it was his role to save Carthya. But this collection of stiff-necked, silk-wrapped snobs would never understand that.

"You may take your seat," Kerwyn said. "I have already made the announcement formally declaring King Eckbert and his queen and son to be dead. In only moments, the death bell will toll, one round for each royal."

Almost immediately, the bells sounded throughout the castle. Their ring would carry beyond the outskirts of the capital city and would signal to the commoners that a royal had died. Three patterns of the bells would confirm the rumors were true. The entire royal family was gone.

When the bells fell silent, Kerwyn continued, "Lords Mead, Beckett, and Hentower, who traveled to Isel this past week, have confirmed for us that Prince Jaron must have died in the pirate attack four years ago. Therefore, we are left with no alternative, but to —"

"There is something more to that story." Conner's words were smug and tilted toward the self-righteous. This was a speech he had practiced so often in his head that he could repeat it in his sleep. "May I speak, Lord Kerwyn?"

Kerwyn nodded permission at him, and Conner stood. "With deference to my fellow regents who searched for proof of Jaron's death this past week, they are wrong. Prince Jaron survived the pirate attack four years ago. He still lives. He is the rightful heir to the throne and should be crowned this night the king of Carthya."

Veldergrath stood, pointing a long finger at Conner. "Then I was right! You did have him hidden at your home."

"Only for his protection, Lord Veldergrath, until now. Surely, you can see how his being alive may threaten anyone else who hoped to become king tonight."

"Is that an accusation?" Veldergrath began hurling obscenities at Conner. The two regents on either side of him held him back, and other regents around the table murmured loudly to one another.

Finally, Kerwyn stepped forward. "So where is this prince of yours, Lord Conner?"

"He's coming. As I said before, we had trouble getting here."

"Naturally, you did. I'm told there were several Prince Jarons who had trouble getting here."

Conner spoke above the chuckles of his peers. "They didn't let anyone through at the gate. No doubt the prince will punish the guards there for failing to recognize him."

"If he were the prince, he would have known how to get through. The royals always know how to get through."

"He must have forgotten." Conner's face paled, and he held on to the table for support. "But Prince Jaron will be here. Then you'll see."

Hearing footsteps in the hallway, he turned to the doors of the throne room expectantly. Almost as if on cue, someone did enter. But it was not who he hoped to see.

"Mott?" Conner said.

"Only regents are allowed in this meeting," Veldergrath said. "You may wait with the other guests and nobles in the great hall. That's where the new king will greet his people."

But Mott seemed to see only Conner in the room. "He isn't here? He came through the kitchen a long time ago."

"Perhaps your false prince is lost in the castle," another regent said, to laughter in the room.

"He grew up here. Of course he's not lost." It was an attempt at confidence, but desperation cut too clearly through Conner's words.

"I propose we continue this meeting." Veldergrath waited until all eyes were on him and then added, "We must not keep the people waiting. And I'm sure whoever is chosen as king will want to speak to Lord Conner on the subject of treason."

Then something must have happened in the adjoining room, the great hall where hundreds of citizens had gathered to wait for the announcement of the new king. What had been a steady hum of conversation suddenly fell completely silent.

Behind Mott, a castle servant burst through the doors. "Forgive me, regents," he said, forgetting the customary bow of his head. "But you should all come into the great hall. As quickly as possible."

Although they were twenty men and women of great status and power, well trained in decorum and manners, no one would have known it by the way they hurried from the throne room. The only one who did not push his way out was Kerwyn, who slid through a secret door between the throne room and the great hall. He was the first to see what had caused the entire crowd in the great hall to fall silent.

For Prince Jaron was standing at the head of the room.

# · FIFTY~THREE ·

I was in no hurry. All that mattered was the order in which I completed this plan. I stood on the dais at the head of the room, the platform reserved for royalty or the courtiers required near them in this formal setting. Behind me were the thrones of the king, queen, and Darius. Jaron's throne was no longer here. I wondered how long I'd been gone before it was carried away.

The room was filled with a few hundred people, none of whom I recognized. But they clearly recognized me. I had come through a door connecting directly from the private rooms of the royal family. There was no announcement of my arrival, but apparently it hadn't been necessary. Their wide eyes and total silence while staring at me confirmed that.

I saw Kerwyn come through the door from the throne room, where he and the other regents had been meeting. Him I recognized. He'd hardly changed over the past four years, still a powerful presence, and someone I'd always respected. From his expression, it was obvious he knew who I was supposed to be. But he seemed to be fighting his own eyes.

"Who are you?" Kerwyn asked, cautious as always.

The first order of business was to withdraw my sword — the real sword belonging to Prince Jaron. Before leaving the castle four years ago, I had hidden it beneath a loose floorboard in my old room, accessible only by crawling under the bed. My room had remained exactly as it was the night I left. My sword was still there as well, and other than a thin blanket of dust, it looked exactly as it had before.

I balanced the sword horizontally on both hands and knelt before Kerwyn as he approached me.

"You know me, Lord Kerwyn. I am that boy who burned the throne room, the boy who challenged the king of Mendenwal to a duel. I am the younger prince of Carthya. I am Jaron." A whisper passed through the room. Kerwyn seemed unimpressed, but he was still listening.

I stood, but pointed to a nick in the blade of the sword. "After I lost the duel to that king, I threw this sword in anger, and it hit a sharp corner of the castle wall. You later returned it to me privately and said that if I don't respect my sword, no one will respect me. Then you apologized because you had also heard what the king said about my mother, but you hadn't dared to challenge him."

Kerwyn faltered a moment, then recovered. "Someone could have overheard that."

"Perhaps so, but it was I you spoke to that day." Without taking my eyes off his, I reached into my pocket and pulled out a small golden rock. It was the last gift my father had ever given me, inside the satchel at the church. Since I stole it back from Conner, it had never been hidden especially well. Anyone who wished to venture high onto the ledges of Farthenwood would have found it. Later, I moved the rock to the bank of the stream on the outskirts of Conner's estate, where it hid in its careful place amongst a thousand other ordinary rocks. "This is for you." I pressed the stone into Kerwyn's hand.

Kerwyn turned it over in his hands, unimpressed. "Imitator's gold? It's worthless."

"No, it's real gold. I am real, Lord Kerwyn."

Tears filled Kerwyn's eyes. He pulled a creased and worn paper from his pocket and unfolded it. His hands shook increasingly as he read it. Then he turned to the audience and said, "This note was given to me by King Eckbert about a month after Prince Jaron's ship was attacked four years ago. I was instructed to keep it with me at all times and to read it only if someone ever came forward claiming to be the prince. This is what it says." He read aloud, "'Many may one day claim to be the lost prince of Carthya. They will be well rehearsed and some may even look the part. You will know Prince Jaron by one sign alone. He will give you the humblest of rocks and tell you it is gold.'" Kerwyn folded the paper again, and then said to the audience, "Lords and ladies of Carthya, I present to you the son of King Eckbert and Queen Erin. He is the lost royal of Carthya, who lives and stands before you. Hail, Prince Jaron."

Then he turned to me and fell to his knees. He took my

hand in his and pressed the note into my palm, then kissed the back of my hand.

In turn, everyone in the room sank to their knees and said, "Hail, Prince Jaron."

Kerwyn looked up at me, and a single tear fell onto his cheek. "Your pants are filthy, as if you rolled in the dirt before coming here. I would expect nothing less from the boy I remember."

I smiled. "I've come home. Do you know me now?"

"In a crowd of a thousand boys claiming to be the prince, there would be only one with the same look of trouble in his eye. I promise never to forget you again."

Suddenly, as well as I thought I had everything planned out, I was at a loss. Should I tell them to rise, or issue a command? They were all watching me, waiting for what I'd do next.

There was only one person in the room who had failed to kneel. Bevin Conner stood at the back of the room, frozen. I walked into the crowd, which stood and magically parted before me.

Conner found his words and spoke them slowly. "It cannot be. You — I suspected it once or twice, but . . . was I blind?"

"You saw who you wanted to see, Conner, nothing more."

"He sees nothing but a fraud, and so do I," Veldergrath said from behind me. "This is clearly an impostor."

I turned and smiled at him. "You are relieved of your duties as prime regent, Lord Veldergrath." Then to Conner I said, "See how I keep my promises? For now, you are my new prime regent."

Conner didn't return the smile. He was still more frozen than not.

"You cannot do this!" Veldergrath sneered. "Who are you, really? I heard Conner combed through the orphanages of Carthya. No doubt he found you there amongst the other fleas and vermin."

"He did. I lived in several orphanages at various times, and went by the name of Sage. Trace my records back as far as you can. You'll find the first entry about four years ago, shortly after Jaron disappeared."

Veldergrath laughed at that. "So you admit to being one of them? Now you expect *me* to bow before *you*?"

I grinned. "You're right. That is funny." Then I laughed with him, laughed so hard that I put a hand on his shoulder to better share the joke. He didn't appreciate that and slid my hand away, like brushing an earwig off his clothes.

With my other hand, I lifted a coin from his vest, and then rolled it away on my fingertips. His laughter ceased, and another chorus of whispers echoed through the room.

"You know me, don't you, Lord Veldergrath?" He rubbed his silver ring as the signs of anxiety washed over his face. I nodded at his ring. "I stole that from you once, right off your finger. You remember that, I'm sure. It was hours before you noticed. You told my mother I was incorrigible."

"Apparently, little has changed," Veldergrath muttered.

More loudly, I asked, "Do I have guards in here? Escort Lord Veldergrath out of this castle." I flipped his coin back at him. "Come up with any questions you may have to verify my identity. We'll meet again soon, and I promise that I will satisfy you."

Two guards appeared on either side of Veldergrath. One took his arm and began to pull him away, but he shrugged them off and said, "No, Your Highness. Now that I see you up close . . . there will be no questions." Then, like a scolded dog, he walked out ahead of the guards.

"I have questions," a voice said, again behind me. This voice I had also heard before. It was the one person I least wanted to see, though it was the most inevitable.

The betrothed princess Amarinda stood in the center of the aisle I had created by walking there. Her hair was much fancier than the last time we met, piled high on her head and full of curls and ribbon. She wore a square-necked, cream-colored dress intricately patterned in gold tones and trimmed to match the ribbon in her hair. She would have already heard the bells tolling for the deaths of the royal family. I could only imagine the pain she must have endured this evening, wondering who had been chosen as the new ruler of Carthya, and what he would do about her. No matter what her anticipations might have been for tonight, one thing was certain: She did not expect me.

I walked over to her and gave a polite bow. "Princess, it is good to see you again."

The hard expression on her face made it clear that she did not feel the same way.

Aware of the many eyes on us, I moved closer to her and whispered, "Can we talk?"

Her tone was icy. "Talk with whom? A brazen servant, a ragged orphan, or a prince?"

"With me."

"Here in public?" I hesitated and she added, "We'll make a scene if we're only talking. Dance with me."

I started to protest, but she was right. A dance might be the best shield for the conversation we had to have. So I nodded at the musicians in the corner to begin a song. With little attempt at concealing her disgust, she took my hand and moved with me to begin the steps.

"The cut on your cheek is still there, though much improved from what it was before," she finally said.

"It was never intended that you notice me that night," I explained.

"Then you should not have spoken to me the way you did."

"I sometimes lack the talent of knowing when to speak and when to keep quiet."

"That's not true," she snapped. Then she took a deep breath

and fell back into rhythm with the dance. "You had every opportunity to be honest with me about the one thing that mattered most! It was no lack of talent. You designed it that way."

"I never lied to you that night, not once."

"Even after I begged for it, you failed to tell me the truth. Only the devils know the difference between that and a lie. You have hurt and insulted me."

I had no answer to that and only said, "You will never find me dishonest with you again, Princess."

"I hope not. Neither to spare your feelings nor mine. How shall I address you now? You're no longer Sage."

The dance step called for me to lean to my right. If she noticed me wince from the ache in my ribs, she didn't acknowledge it. When I stood straight, I could speak again. "Call me Jaron."

"You dance like a royal, Jaron. Better than your brother did."

"Don't compare me to him."

She stiffened. "It was my attempt at a compliment."

"Darius and I are very different people. If you think of him when you think of me, I'll always be a failure to you."

Her eyes fluttered, blinking back tears, and we fell into silence. We both knew there was more to be said, much more, and yet we completed the rest of the dance without another word.

As the music ended, Amarinda pulled away from me. "What happens now, for me?"

"Whatever you want," I said.

"All I want is to be happy," she said softly. "But I fear that is too much to ask."

My smile at her was weak and apologetic. I hadn't caused my brother's death, but I was a consequence of it. "We'll talk later. In private."

She agreed, though the look of disgust had returned to her face. "May I have your permission to leave now? I'm upset and wish to be alone."

I nodded at her, and as Amarinda disappeared into the crowd, I was again alone in a sea of strangers.

Still at the head of the room, Kerwyn said, "Your Highness, there must be a ceremony to make your new title official. I regret that your old crown is long lost."

"I have it!" Tobias pushed forward through the crowd, holding something wrapped in a kitchen towel in his arms. He was wet and smelled horrible. I wondered how he'd made it this far into the castle. He stopped when he saw me and bowed. "So you were the prince all along. Why couldn't I see it?" Then his face paled. "Oh, the crimes I've committed against you."

"You committed them against an orphan named Sage. You've done nothing to Jaron."

Tobias nodded and unwrapped the towel. "Your crown, my prince."

Conner was suddenly there beside him. He grabbed the crown and said, "I am his prime regent. It is my duty to crown him in the ceremony."

As we walked forward together, Conner whispered, "If you forgive me here, I will serve you forever. On your terms . . . Jaron."

I said nothing. Although it did not go the way he had intended, Conner's plan was complete. Mine was not.

# · FIFTY-FOUR ·

The ceremony to crown me king went by very quickly. Kerwyn produced the Book of Faith, which Conner read from to administer the Blessing of the King. When it was finished, Kerwyn gave him a ring, which Conner placed on my finger. "This belonged to King Eckbert," Conner said. "It was your father's."

"The king's ring." It was heavier than I'd expected, made of gold and imprinted with my family crest. It was too large and looked funny on my hand, like something I'd stolen rather than inherited through birthright.

Then he lifted from a ruby red pillow my crown, still wet from having been washed. "This is a prince's crown. A new one will be commissioned for you immediately, but it will do for now." He placed it on my head, this time with much humbler and gentler hands than had crowned me at the inn.

Conner went to his knees again and said, "Hail, *King* Jaron."

"Hail, King Jaron!" the audience echoed.

"Be a better king than your father was," Conner said softly. "You come to the throne at a time of great upheaval."

"There is always upheaval," I said. "Only the reasons for the troubles change."

"You have the betrothed princess. She will support you."

"She hates me."

"So do I. And I just crowned you king."

Conner smiled as he said it, but it probably wasn't a joke.

"I kept my promise to you," I said, still keeping my voice quiet enough so that only he could hear us. "You have the position you wanted."

"You are the true king," Conner said. "You may place me anywhere you desire."

"So I shall." Then more loudly, I added, "I want the prime regent, Lord Bevin Conner, arrested for the attempted murder of Prince Jaron four years ago. Arrest him for the murder of an orphan boy named Latamer. And also for the murders of King Eckbert, Queen Erin, and Crown Prince Darius."

Whispers and hisses flew through the room. Conner turned to me with panic-stricken eyes. "No, I didn't —"

From a pocket of my jacket, I pulled out a small vial.

"This is oil pressed from the dervanis flower," I said. "It took me a long time to figure out what sort of poison might have killed my family. Entire nights searching through the books in your library. I'm not a great reader, that's true, but if the subject matter interests me, I can comb through books quite quickly.

Oddly enough, I found the answer in a book in your bedroom. Dervanis oil is tasteless and requires only a single drop to produce a lethal dose. But it doesn't kill immediately. A person will go to sleep feeling fine and never wake up again. Dervanis oil is hard to come by, yet this was in a strongbox in your office."

Conner shook his head, then his eyes darted left, and he thrust his hand inside his jacket. "As I always said, *Sage*, if I go down, so do you!" But he failed to find what he was looking for. He drew back and searched his jacket.

I released the cuff of my sleeve, and a knife he had hidden in his jacket fell into my hands. "If this is what you wanted, then I shall have to increase the charges against you."

Two guards appeared on either side of Conner and each took his arm. "I can't imagine the pleasure you must be taking in this moment," he said nastily.

My temper flared. "Pleasure? I'm staring at the man who killed my family. Whatever I feel now, trust that pleasure is the furthest from those feelings."

"You said you were my prince. Is this what that means to you?"

"I am your prince. But I am Carthya's king. You'll understand why, in the hierarchy of my titles, you must lose."

"Why didn't you tell me from the beginning? If you had told me who you were —"

"Then I couldn't have unmasked you. I'd have doomed my own rule, just as my family was doomed."

Behind me, Kerwyn sighed. Addressing Conner, he said, "What if Jaron had been only an orphan? Surely, you couldn't have expected him to fool the court for long."

"He didn't need much time," I said, keeping my eyes on Conner. "He needed a prince only long enough to get himself named prime regent. No matter what happened afterward, he would become the controlling power in Carthya."

"Well done," Conner said. "Jaron was always described as a clever boy, but I underestimated you." I started to wave my hand to dismiss him, but Conner quickly added, "You are guilty of crimes too, Your Majesty."

Facing him full on, I arched an eyebrow. "Oh?"

"Even when you said you didn't want the throne, you were all that time plotting to get it. You lied to me."

Anger surged through me, and I didn't disguise it well. I leaned close to him and hissed, "I did tell you lies, Master Conner, but none of consequence. I was telling the exact truth when I said I had no desire to be king! If there were anyone — *anyone* — I felt could take my place without the entire kingdom's collapse, I would gladly step aside. If I could return to be that boy you snatched from the orphanage, I'd leave now and never look back. If you knew what it meant to be king —" I sighed and shook my head. "Of all Carthyans, I am the least free."

"And what of my freedom?" Conner asked. "Shall I beg for mercy?"

"Beg mercy from the devils." I spoke more calmly now.

"You said you would sell your soul to them for this plan. Your plan worked, and the devils may have you."

"If the devils have me, then you are their king," Conner spat at me. "I will forever curse the day we met!"

"Take him to the prison," I told my guards. "He will be there for some time. Conner, it appears you will be unavailable to fulfill your duties as prime regent. Therefore, you are relieved of that position and stripped of your title as a noble."

Once Conner was dragged out of the room, I directed the musicians to play. Then, exhausted, I fell into my father's throne. No, my throne. I was king now. The reality of that was incomprehensible.

One by one, the various members of the audience came forward to greet me personally. I didn't know most of them, though I recognized several of their family names. They had been of little interest to me when I was ten, and weren't much more interesting now.

"You have come home to a country that mourned your loss these past four years," Kerwyn said, standing beside me. "See your people celebrate you. Will you join them?"

It wasn't that simple. "I still feel like the boy in the orphanage," I murmured. "I'm lost here."

"But this is your home."

I traced my finger along a carving in the armrest of the throne. "It was my home because my family was here. I'm alone now, and I don't know where to begin."

"You are still young, Jaron. Perhaps a steward would be appropriate —"

"I'm king now. No one else."

Kerwyn dipped his head in acknowledgment of that and stared with me across the audience. Quietly, he said, "Not everyone will welcome your return. The enemies at our borders will feel tricked. There will be anger."

"I know."

"War is coming, Jaron."

A fact I understood down to my very bones. Despite that, I looked up at him and cocked an eyebrow. "But surely their spies cannot travel so fast as to ruin this night. There is still a little time to laugh." He started to object, but I stood and said, "They must see me laugh, Kerwyn. At least for tonight."

With that I walked into the audience. Again, they parted for me. This time, I saw the person I'd been looking for all evening.

Imogen stood at the back of the room, looking very small and frightened. When I approached her, she lowered herself into a bow and remained that way.

"Please rise," I said. "It's still me."

She obeyed but shook her head. "No, I don't think it is."

"How much did you see?"

"All of it, Your Highness."

"Must you call me that?"

Her voice faltered. "I must."

"Do you forgive me? Can you?"

She lowered her eyes. "If you command it, then I will."

"What if I don't command it?"

"Please don't ask me that."

Kerwyn came up beside me. "And who is this, King Jaron?"

I took her hand and led her to the center of the group. "She is a lady in disguise, just as I was disguised as an orphan for four years. She is Imogen, and her family has debts to Master Conner. She has fully repaid those debts to me these past two weeks, in expert nursing care and compassion. Her father is dead, but using my power as king, I posthumously declare him a nobleman of Carthya. She is a nobleman's daughter and will be treated as such."

Imogen shook her head. "No, don't. I can't repay this."

I turned to her and lowered my voice. "Imogen, you owe me nothing. You are free, and I wish you well in life." I gave her hand to Kerwyn. "Will you see that she is given a comfortable room and dressed to fit her title? She may stay as long as she wishes, and at whatever point she asks it, see that she is provided a way home."

She smiled through her tears and bowed to me. "Thank you . . . King Jaron."

I smiled back at her. "Thank you, Imogen. I wouldn't have survived these past two weeks except for you."

Kerwyn led her away, but when he looked back at me, I

could almost see a new weight fall upon his shoulders. Difficult times were ahead, for Carthya and for me. But even pending war should never ruin a good party. With a smile on my face, I turned to the group and said, "Carthyans, tonight I am home again. Let it be a celebration. Tonight we dance!"

# · ACKNOWLEDGMENTS ·

*Jeff, you are my best friend and true companion.*
*I thank you for sharing each day of your life with me.*
*My thanks also to Ron Peters. Without your encourage-*
*ment, friendship, and sharp critiquing eye, I might have*
*given up a long time ago. And to the late Tom Horner,*
*who saw details others overlooked. I miss our association.*
*Finally, I wish to thank Ammi-Joan Paquette and Lisa*
*Sandell, for your invaluable roles in bringing* The False
Prince *to life. It is an honor to be associated with each*
*of you, and I look forward to many great years ahead.*

# · ABOUT THE AUTHOR ·

JENNIFER A. NIELSEN collects old books, loves good theater, and thinks that a quiet afternoon in the mountains is a nearly perfect moment.

A major influence for this story came from the music of Eddie Vedder and one of his greatest songs, "Guaranteed." From his line "I knew all the rules, but the rules did not know me," Sage was born. Sage's personality is his own, but Jennifer did borrow two of his traits from a couple of students she once taught in a high school debate class. One of them was popular, brilliant, and relentlessly mischievous. He could steal the watch off a person's wrist without their knowing and would return it to them later, usually to their embarrassment. The other student had a broad spectrum of impressive talents, not the least of which was his ability to roll a coin over his knuckles. If he had wanted to, he'd have made a fine pick-pocket. As it was, he went on to become a lawyer. Go figure.

Jennifer lives in northern Utah with her husband, their three children, and a perpetually muddy dog.